D0173261

Lightfinder
Aaron Paquette

Lightfinder© Aaron Paquette, 2014
4TH EDITION

PUBLISHED BY KEGEDONCE PRESS
11 Park Road
Neyaashiinigmiing, Ontario N0H 2T0
www.kegedonce.com
Administration Office/Book Orders
RR7 Owen Sound, ON N4K 6V5

Printed in Canada by Gilmore Printing
Design: Red Willow Designs
Author photo: Nadya Kwandibans, Redworks.ca

Library and Archives Canada Cataloguing in Publication

Paquette, Aaron, 1974-, author
     Lightfinder / written and illustrated by Aaron Paquette.

ISBN 978-0-9868740-7-9 (pbk.)

     I. Title.

PS8631..A6757L53 2014   C813.6   C2014-902685-4

Sales and Distribution - http://www.lpg.ca/LitDistco:
For Customer Service/Orders
Tel 1-800-591-6250 Fax 1-800-591-6251
100 Armstrong Ave. Georgetown, ON L7G 5S4
Email orders@litdistco.ca

We acknowledge the support of the Canada Council for the Arts which last year invested
$20.1 million in writing and publishing throughout Canada.

 Canada Council **Conseil des Arts**
for the Arts **du Canada**

We would like to acknowledge funding support from the Ontario Arts Council, an agency
of the Government of Ontario.

50 YEARS OF ONTARIO GOVERNMENT SUPPORT OF THE ARTS

Dedication

For my children
Thank you for being the light in our lives
And may you always find that light in your very own hearts

Chapter 1 - Aisling

– Save me.

The words were barely a whisper, but full of sadness. There was an urgency to them that scared her.

A giant, glowing orb floated past her in a flash of brilliant light that would have blinded her if her eyes had been open.

Open?

I'm dreaming, Aisling realized.

– Save me!

It was a distant scream.

– Save me!

She awoke with a small cry and sat up, covered in a film of sweat. Her phone was playing its wake-up tone. Aisling brushed the snooze button and lay back down, waiting for her breathing to slow.

She'd had this dream before. At first she thought it might have been the effect of eating too much pizza and Diet Coke, but no: she knew this was no ordinary nightmare. It was far worse than any bad dream she'd ever had. It was too real, too serious. Behind the pleading was a warning.

Who am I supposed to be saving? Why am I so on edge?

Her Kokum would have been able to figure it out, or her mother, but both of them were out of her life. She tried to ignore that old feeling of loneliness that washed over her and shake it off. She had to be at school in an hour and she couldn't afford to miss the bus again. Pulling her long black hair into a ponytail, she put on a pair of black leggings and a flowing grey knit top. She grabbed her bag and her jacket and a banana for breakfast.

Her long legs felt awkward as she half-walked, half-ran to the bus stop. It was a grey, chilly morning, and the glass buildings of the city reflected low, scudding clouds. She had moved to the city to get into a better high school and now these dreams were making her late. She didn't want to be kicked out after only the first couple of weeks.

Aisling's Dad worked as a safety inspector for the oil patch in Fort McMurray, a remote, northern oil town bursting with mud and money. She had moved into his two-bedroom apartment after nervously asking if she could stay during the school year. She had been delighted when he had said it would be okay, but when he was away she had to be responsible for herself.

"You're almost sixteen, and you've always tried to do the right thing. I think I can trust you to keep things together and get yourself to school. That is, if you don't zone out on me and sleepwalk to the mall every day. Must. Go. Shopping!" He laughed.

She rolled her eyes. Then laughed, too. Even though her Dad was a total nerd, she loved him and loved that he always tried to make her laugh. She used to sleepwalk all the time and he never stopped teasing her about it. When she was younger she would give her mother terrible frights, walking out of the house in the middle of the night.

One of those nights, when she was five years old, she woke to her mother's wide eyes staring into her own. Her Mom was shaking her, fingers digging deep into her tiny shoulders. The shock of waking up outside, shivering in the dark, scared her so much she started screaming and screaming and couldn't stop.

Then her Dad was driving. She didn't know how she got in the car. Through the darkness and the low-lying fog they finally rolled to a stop in front of her Kokum's house, the stones in the driveway crunching under the tires. She loved her grandmother and always felt safe with her. Dad lifted her effortlessly and carried her inside and they must have called ahead because Kokum was already awake, drinking some tea and cooking up some frybread.

"Sit down, sit down," Kokum said, waving them toward the kitchen chairs. They were the old padded vinyl kind with aluminum frames. Aisling liked the earthy orange and green colours of them.

Kokum pulled out the bannock and set it on some paper towels to cool. The sweet smell filled the room. She wiped her hands on her apron and turned around, her cheerful wrinkled face unusually serious.

"Now my girl, what is the matter?"

Aisling tried to speak but her throat squeezed tight in fear.

"Ah, I see." Kokum nodded and bent her head for a moment. When she raised it she was singing. Very quietly and very soft. So soft Aisling couldn't quite catch the melody. As her Kokum sang, a gentle calm started to spread over her and she sat very still in her father's arms, head bent slightly, listening to that beautiful old voice. It felt like being wrapped in a comfy old blanket, safe and warm by a cheery little fire. Aisling was at peace.

"Thanks, Mom," her father said, and Aisling felt his juddering sigh of relief, felt his arms loosen. She realized he must have been scared too. But why?

"It's nothing," Kokum smiled and gave them each a piece of bannock, partially wrapped in a paper towel so they wouldn't burn their fingers. They bit into the soft, warm breads, pleasure registering on both their faces.

"Now, my little dreamer, what is the matter?"

Aisling remembered that moment so clearly. Was it really ten years ago?

Almost to the day.

She let her mind wander back to that cold night and the reason she had been so frightened. It wasn't really the dark, or even her mother shaking her awake. It was what she had seen.

And she had never told a soul.

Chapter 2 - Eric

Eric sat at the kitchen window, ignoring the notebook of sketches spread open on the table in front of him. He was watching his mother. She was sleeping in a lawn chair, her head back, her legs sprawled out and her arms hanging down off the edge of the chair. He examined her face. It looked different when she was asleep. The lines were softer, the scowling lines between her eyes disappeared, and she even seemed to be smiling. She looked younger. She looked beautiful.

He liked to imagine that she would wake up with that serene, beautiful face, excited to see him. She would laugh and they would play games. She would ask him about his day and he would tell her. She would gasp in surprise at his adventures, or get outraged at his humiliations. They would eat dinner together and at night when it was time for bed she would tuck him in, his blankets warm and his pajamas soft. He knew it was what a little kid wanted, and at 12, he wasn't a little kid anymore. But it was still his favourite daydream.

The clouds were getting darker. The rain began, spit by spit. He went outside and shook his mother's shoulder.

"Mom, you have to wake up. It's raining."

She didn't move. The bottle of whatever she had been drinking fell from her lap.

"Mom, come on!"

She grunted.

The rain had really started now and frantically he looked around until he saw a blue plastic tarp tucked in beside the wood box. He ran over to his Mom and wrapped it around her. That would keep her body dry against the rain. He hopped into the house and up on the closet shelf was her sunhat. He wrapped it in a plastic grocery bag. The rain was a downpour by the time he got it on her head and he was chased back inside by the violent thunder.

On his stool at the kitchen window he watched her, fear in his eyes.

He picked up a pencil and began absently sketching in his notebook. Leaning his head on his hand, he pulled up, wincing in pain. He had gotten a black eye at school earlier that day but had forgotten about it until now.

He hated junior high. He felt small and it hadn't been very long before the older boys had started picking on him. Today he had tried to get to the bus faster, but they caught him. He was so scared that he couldn't respond to their taunts, he just stood there in silence.

"Tough guy, huh?" Tommy said, giving him a shove. Tommy was the biggest of them and the meanest.

"What's the matter, baby can't talk?"

The other two boys started sucking their thumbs, laughing.

"Or did mommy forget to teach you how to talk because she was too busy begging for another drink?"

The other two then pretended they were drinking, stumbling around.

Eric's face reddened in shame. His Mom had started drinking again a few weeks ago. Yesterday she had taken to Main Street, asking everyone who passed by if they would spare her a few dollars for "medicine."

It only lasted until one of her friends saw her and got her off the street, but it had been the talk of the kids at school all day. He knew his Mom had a problem, but she had been sober for years. He didn't know why she suddenly started drinking again, but he felt like the bottom of the world had just dropped out from under him. The last time she had been drinking he barely remembered, but he knew it had been the last straw for his father. They got divorced and he moved away - not that Eric ever saw much of his Dad before that. He worked out of town but he always sent them money, always sent cards and letters. Aisling told Eric he would understand one day, but what did she know? She left him too this summer and now he was all alone.

"Oh look, baby's gonna cry!"

And that's when he dropped his bag and took a step forward. He didn't know what he was going to do. He was small, skinny and uncoordinated. It didn't matter, anyway. Next thing he knew he was on the ground covering his punched eye, listening to the cruel laughter as it drifted away, the bullies finally leaving him alone.

He missed the bus and walked the two hours home, crying sometimes, but trying to be strong. When he finally got home he found his mother out back.

It was still raining and evening was setting in. He turned on the porch light, got a slice of cold pizza from the fridge and sat back at the window.

Watching.

Chapter 3 - Aisling

"Aisling Cardinal?"

"Um, yeah, that's me," she said feeling like everyone in class was staring at her. She didn't know anyone, hadn't grown up with any of them, and had never felt more strangely than she did now, walking into the music room only to find that it was set up in a semi-circle, pretty much ensuring that she would be the focus of attention as soon as she slipped in.

So much for no one noticing I'm late.

"Nice of you to join us."

"I missed my bus."

"I'm sure."

The music teacher was a woman in her fifties, a little overweight. Though she was trying to look serious there was a sparkle in her eyes.

Aisling stood at the door, not sure what to do.

"Well, come on you willowy thing, grab a seat. Soprano, I take it?"

"I - I don't know. I've never sung in a choir before. They said I had to take an option and I didn't know what to choose for the first two weeks and - "

"And so you picked the one you thought would be easiest to catch up on, that you could just ... float through?"

The class laughed a little, enjoying the show.

Aisling's face reddened in embarrassment. *Oh god, please don't let me start sweating!*

"Well, actually, I um, I used to sing a little with my ko- uh… my grandmother when I was younger, and, well…" she trailed off, feeling like a stupid little neechee girl from the rez. *How could I have thought I could fit in here? They probably all think I sniff glue or don't shower or something.*

"Fine, fine, it's okay. Just sing a little for us and we'll put you in the right section. I'm Mrs. Larson, by the way."

Already near tears Aisling couldn't quite believe what she had just heard. "You want me to sing? Now? In front of everyone?"

"This is Choral, dear. Is there a problem?"

Aisling thought about her little brother, Eric, and how he refused to say goodbye to her when she was leaving, how bad she had felt going. She couldn't allow moving to the city to end with her running from this room in tears and shame over - what? A song?

So what if they think I'm a backward girl from the reservation. Maybe they all think my family is begging on the streets somewhere or living on welfare.

They weren't, they worked hard. Sure, there were a few things she wouldn't want anyone to know, but she had made a promise to herself - and in her heart to Eric - that the reason she was leaving home was to build a good life they could all share in. She wanted to be an example for him.

I guess it starts here. Even if they laugh at me.

She knew everyone was waiting, so she walked to the centre of the room. It was shaped like a small amphitheater so all her new classmates were having a good look. She wasn't sure what to sing. Something from the radio? Nothing came to her.

Then she imagined her Kokum standing there with her, and she knew what song to sing. It was one they had made up together. It was a simple little thing but she had always loved it. It made her feel happy and free and like she could do anything. It seemed right to sing it now, if only to give herself some courage.

She opened her mouth but her throat was too tight and tense. Her voice squeaked and cracked. She stopped immediately, clapping her hands to her mouth. The room erupted in laughter, but she could see one boy not laughing but simply staring at her. His blonde hair was almost covering his eyes and she couldn't really tell, but she thought he was nodding to her, encouraging her. He held up two fingers in a peace sign and pursed his lips like he was taking a selfie. She almost laughed despite her predicament.
Encouraged by this little joke, she cleared her throat and began again. This time she knew she started well. The room still hadn't settled down and a few girls were still whispering to each other. Aisling kept singing anyway, the words and the music starting to fill her with that happy confidence she used to have when she was little.

You are where you are, little one
There's nowhere else to be
Open your arms to the wind, little one
Let your heart come fly with me

Over the land and waters
Through the stars and sky
Let the earth's light guide us
And love us by and by

As she sang her voice grew stronger, but not louder. They always sang it softly together as if it were a special secret. As the last words faded into a whisper Aisling opened her eyes. They were all staring at her. She should have known better. She must have sounded terrible.

Mrs. Larson made a small noise in her throat. "Soprano, I think, though you do have a bit of a range there. Please be seated." She indicated a few empty chairs to her left.

As she passed, Mrs. Larson handed her some sheet music and Aisling went to her seat, relieved to be out from under all those eyes. In fact, there weren't any eyes on her at all. They had all stopped looking at her completely.

I must have really stunk.

She looked at her music, seeing that it was more complicated than she thought it would be, little dots running along lines stretching across the page in rows. She had never had to read music before. She didn't even know that was what she was going to be doing here. *I really should have watched more Glee.*

That's when she noticed the boy from earlier. His head was bent and his eyes hidden under those ridiculous bangs, but she could see through the wisps of his hair that he was staring right at her. *He might be a little weird, but at least he helped me.*
She chanced a smile and gave a little wave. He waved back and then turned his attention back to Mrs. Larson. She had just tapped on her music stand to get the class' attention.

"Okay everyone, let's try it again and this time watch your breathing."

She raised her hands above her head, her conducting wand held at the ready.

As her arms came down to begin the music Aisling felt a sharp pain in her heart as though someone had just stabbed a knife into it. She screamed and collapsed to the floor.

Chapter Four - Eric

Getting on the bus the next morning wasn't easy. Eric had tried to hide the bruising around his left eye with his mother's make-up, but he really didn't know what he was doing and in the end gave up, washed his face and walked down the road to his stop. He could hear the murmurs as he made his way down the aisle to grab a seat. He saw the sidelong glances and smirks as he passed by the other kids. He wished he was going to school on the Rez, but Aisling had pressed his mother to sign him up in the nearby town.

"It's not the city, Eric, but you'll get there soon enough. Then you can decide if you're coming back to the Rez or choosing your own path. Most of the kids you know won't ever realize they have that choice, but you will."

He loved his sister, he really did, but when she started getting all motivational he had to stop himself from rolling his eyes at her.

And so here he was on the bus. Surrounded by people. Alone.

He sat back and watched the woods bounce by as the bus navigated the rutted road that led to the highway.

"Nice shiner!"

Eric looked up. There was a boy standing over him, dark hair, dark eyes, half a smile. "You mind shoving over?"

Eric shoved over.

"So, what's your name and how long have you been in the UFC?"

Eric looked at the boy in surprise. Was he making fun of him or was he actually talking to him? The kid must have been in Ninth Grade and he was wearing name brands all over, right down to his slim Puma shoes.

"Uh, Eric?"

"Are you asking me? Well okay, 'Uhhhhric', my name's Cor. Pleased to meetcha." He stuck out his hand. "Well, are you going to shake or what?"

Eric took Cor's hand in his and gave a sort of awkward, limp pump.

"Man, oh man, we're gonna have to toughen you up a bit, huh? So, like I said, Uhhrric, where'd you get the beauty mark there?"

Eric was surprised by the fact that there was suddenly someone who not only took the time to joke around with him but who actually seemed to feel like he was worth talking to. He decided to tell the truth.

"I tried to fight these kids who were giving me a bad time and I got clobbered."

Cor turned serious. His eyes darkened and there was a glint of light that seemed to shine out from them. His dark hair fell in a spread across his face like a bird's open wing. "That sucks. Tell me what happened."

Eric told the whole story, the way he seemed to have been singled out from the beginning of the year, how he was pushed into lockers and made fun of, and how it was all Tommy's fault.

"I don't even get it! What did I ever do to him? You know what he is?" asked Eric, feeling angrier and angrier by the second.

"What?" asked Cor, prompting him with a slight smile.

"He's a douchebag!"

"Well, the world's not all like that, Uhhr-man. There are a few good ones."

"Prove it."

"Okay. You like my iPhone?"

To be honest, Eric had been watching Cor flick the icons on the screen of the device the whole time they were talking. He had his own mp3 player, but it was a WalMart special for $30. His parents weren't poor, his mother does work - *did work*, he thought sadly - and his father does send money, but they had the idea that he was too young for anything as expensive as an iPod, much less his own phone.

"Well, yeah, it's awesome. Good for you." Eric felt a little jealous and a little ashamed of the stupid music player clipped to his jacket.

"Well, then, it's yours. You look like you could use it more than me, and besides," Cor paused, locking eyes with Eric, "I like you."

He tossed the phone carelessly in Eric's direction. Eric scrambled for it and it dropped out of his hands and onto the floor of the bus. The bouncing of the bus caused it to start to slide under the seat in front of them, and Eric snatched it up quickly. *Why am I always such a klutz?* he thought, as he nervously checked the phone for any damage.

He looked to see if Cor was laughing at him, but the older boy was looking out the opposite window.

"Are you - are you serious?"

"Sure thing, buddy. I like that you tried to stand up for yourself and who cares about a phone anyway? I'll just get my Dad to buy me a new one."

"You must be rich."

"Nope. But my Dad is!" Cor flashed a quick grin that lit up the whole bus. It almost seemed as if the noise of the other conversations got a little quieter, and the bus ran smoother, just for that moment.

"Thanks, man." Eric put the phone in his pocket, making sure to zip it up. Cor might not care about an iPhone but Eric sure did.

For the first time in weeks, Eric smiled.

"Ooof!"

"What a loser!" Tommy laughed as Eric gasped for air. He couldn't breathe and now he knew why they called it getting the wind knocked out of you.

Eric had looked for Cor at lunch. He didn't want to act desperate for a friend but he was desperate. He walked around the hallways, checked the cafeteria and finally resorted to walking the outside grounds. Big mistake.

Just my luck, Eric groaned as Tommy and the gang walked around the corner. And so here he was, trying to pull a breath into his body and looking at the iPhone lying on the ground in front of him.

Oh no! I thought I zipped up that pocket!

But there it was and Eric couldn't even reach out for it.

"Whoa! What's this? A present?" Tommy asked in feigned excitement and surprise. "For me?"

He leaned down to pick up the phone and as he did he whispered into Eric's ear, "You tell anyone about this, you little worm, and you're dead. That's what you get for telling people you think I'm the dumbest kid in school. Who's dumb now, you stupid loser?"

He spat in Eric's face. Eric watched their shoes as the boys walked away, leaving him alone and in breathless pain.

Eric burned with rage and hatred. Tears flowed down his face. After what felt like forever his gut unlocked and he gasped for air. What was Tommy talking about? Eric couldn't recall saying anything about him, much less have anyone to say it to.

So this is what it's all about? A stupid misunderstanding? Where'd he even hear that from?

"Not your best week, huh, kid?"

"Cor?"

"The one and only. Can you get up?"

"I think so." Eric rolled to his chest and slowly pushed himself up until he was on his knees. "I lost your iPhone."

"It was yours, and no you didn't. Why do you think I came looking for you? I heard Tommy and his buddies laughing about it in the washroom."

"You didn't tell anyone?" Eric was surprised. He thought Cor was on his side.

"No, numbnuts, you want a big production on your hands? You get the adults to deal with your problems and you'll never hear the end of it. No offense, buddy, but you need to start fighting your own battles. And win them once in a while." He looked pointedly at Eric's bruised face.

No one had ever said anything like that to Eric. He knew why. It was because he was the baby of the family and that's how everyone always treated him. Like a baby. That is, if they even noticed him. Aisling hadn't called in at least a week and Mom, well, she just gave orders and you didn't question. Being the baby for him had always meant *shut up and do what you're told.* No one ever took him seriously. But it seemed that Cor did.

"How? How do I win?"

"Come here," Cor indicated a spot beside him on the steps where he sat, leaning back, relaxed. Cool. "I want to give you something. Geez, look at you. Getting presents all day."

Eric limped over to the stairs and sat down.

Cor reached into his school bag and pulled out a stone. He handed it over and Eric turned it around in his hands, examining it. The stone was about the size of an egg and was a uniform speckled gray. Just like any old river rock he'd seen a hundred times.

"A rock?"

"Sure, why not? A friend of your very own. Haven't you ever had a Pet Rock?"

Eric laughed.

"No. I don't get it. What does it do?"

"What doesn't it do, Uhhr-culees? It listens, it cares and it's great for holding down papers. It makes a great doorstop!"

Eric gave a half-smile and looked slightly confused. If this was supposed to cheer him up, it was stupid. And it was working.

"Kid, listen." Cor's own smile disappeared. "You need to learn how to be steady and hard like this rock here. You need to stop looking so hurt and vulnerable all the time and get yourself a shell. A thick one. You think you'll amount to anything lying in the dirt covered in your own snot and tears, waiting for someone to come save you? Not gonna happen. You're alone in this world and the sooner you figure it out the better off you'll be. Sorry to burst your bubble, but you got potential. Start using it."

Eric listened, but there was something off with what he was hearing.

"You're only a couple years older than me. What do you know?"

"What do I know? A crapload more than you and that's for sure," Cor said, frowning and standing up. Eric suddenly realized that he'd just pushed away someone who might be his friend, someone who might help him.

"Wait, Cor, I'm sorry."

"Geez, kid! Settle down and stop apologizing. You're right. If I want to help you to stand up, I shouldn't knock you down. So stand up. That's right. Pick up your rock and get to class. I'll catch you later."

"Okay, okay, but honestly, what am I supposed to do with this stupid rock?"

"Hold on to it. When the time comes, you'll know what to do with it." And with that, Cor chuckled and walked back into the school, the heavy metal door clicking shut behind him.

Eric stood up, still a little tender in the stomach and made his way to the washroom to clean himself up.

Making an excuse to get out of math class early, Eric put his books away in his locker and headed outside. If possible, he'd be the first kid on the bus before anyone else even got out of school. He wasn't sure running and hiding was the right thing to do after Cor's pep talk, but he honestly didn't think a little lecture was going to suddenly make everything better.

He heard the main doors to the school open and glanced back. There was Tommy alone, earbuds plugged in and browsing through the iPhone in his hands. Eric looked around for somewhere to hide but, of course, it was all open space. The road, the field, the bit of woods at the north boundary.

Eric started walking, making for the woods. If he could only reach the woods he could hide and wait for everyone to leave.

He got ten steps in before he heard the shout.

"Hey, loser, where you think you're going?"

Eric glanced over his shoulder and saw Tommy jogging toward him. Eric broke into a run, heading for the trees. Tommy sped up to catch him.

Fear coursed through Eric, making his legs rubbery and slow, his breath ragged. He took a wild-eyed look behind him and could see Tommy gaining ground quickly. If he could just reach the trees. There was no one else but the two of them and Eric was terrified of what would happen when he was caught. The first bushes passed and he made it. He was about to leap deeper into the cover of the woods when he felt a hard shove and he was sent sprawling to the ground, his palms scraping against the rocky soil, tearing off skin and embedding little pebbles and grit into his flesh. It stung sharply but soon paled in comparison to the crack of his skull against the trunk of a birch tree. Eric bit down on his tongue and blood flowed into his mouth, stars dancing across his vision.

He scrabbled around, pushing himself up against the tree, struggling to stand. Tommy was facing him, panting and sweaty.

"You're dead."

Eric pulled himself up, wiping off his bloody hands on his hoodie, his breath coming out as hot steam in the chilly autumn air.

His left hand brushed against the stone in his pocket and he reached in, fingers curling around the smooth, cool surface.

"Got another present for me, do you?" Tommy asked, advancing slowly, watching Eric's hand. "You know what to do with it. Give it here."

Eric felt a coldness descend on him. It was much more clear than any anger he had ever felt, much more distant. He felt strong, like the rock in his hand.

"No."

Tommy stopped and looked confused.

"What did you just say to me?"

"I said no. I'm not giving you anything else. And you're going to leave me alone. Listen Tommy, I never said anything about you to anyone, so just drop it and walk away. Right now."

Tommy's face went purple. "You. You are gonna get it!" and he rushed toward Eric with fists clenched and raised.

For Eric, it all happened so slowly. As Tommy moved forward, Eric pulled his hand from his pocket and swung the rock with all his might. He felt the sudden, jarring shock as it connected with Tommy's face, sending the older boy sideways as he collapsed to the ground and lay still amid the bramble and leaves.

Blood dripped from Eric's hand and he felt a heat in it. It was like his hand was on fire and then the heat slipped out of him and into the cool, bloody stone. He shivered with the sensation, like he was getting colder and stronger at the same time. He felt powerful. He looked at Tommy on the ground and felt the thrill of victory sweeping through him. Rummaging through the bully's pockets Eric found the iPhone. He shoved it into his own bag.

He turned his back and walked away, leaving the boy among the trees.

He'll wake up later and he'll be sorry he ever messed with me.

A crow landed in the trees above him as he left the woods.

It would soon be joined by others.

Chapter Five - Aisling

Light flashed in front of her eyes. *Am I dreaming again?*

No, she was awake. Sounds came to her now. Voices.

"Is she taking any drugs? Does she have any medical conditions? Who are her parents or guardians?"

The questions came urgently and she could feel a breeze passing over her face.

"Aisling? Wake up! Get up!"

There was intense pressure on her sternum.

She gasped and opened her eyes. She was in a hallway, faces looking down at her with concern, everyone moving quickly. She was on a bed wheeling past patients, nurses, doctors. A man with graying hair and light blue eyes was pressing his thumb hard against her chest.

"Ow! What are you doing? Where am I?"

"You're in the hospital. I have to ask you some questions."

"Oka-a-ay-" She was confused and feeling scared.

"What drugs are you on? Have you been drinking? Huffing?"

"What! No, of course not!"

The doctor looked skeptical.

"Why would you ask me that?"

"Because, young lady, that would make our job of figuring out why you fainted in the middle of school a little easier."

"Well, the answer is no so you can take your doubtful look somewhere else. What? I'm Native so I drink?"

The doctor looked shocked and then his face became very serious.

"Don't be offended, Aisling. Asking is my job. I believe you, but you have to understand how many teenagers I get in here due to overdosing."

"Oh."

She was embarrassed for jumping to the conclusion she did. Her bed slid to a stop inside a room separated into two sections by a blue curtain. The room was cold and bright, like a cheerless, antiseptic version of heaven. She watched the nurse as she started up different machines and set out implements on the counter against the wall. Mrs. Larson was also there, along with the boy from her music class.

"What happened? What am I doing here?"

Mrs. Larson approached the side of the bed, looking down with worry on her face.

"We don't know, dear. You just yelled out and fainted. Jake ran to call 911 and here we are. I have to go fill out some paperwork and call the school but I'll be back shortly. Just try to relax."

She smiled softly and left the room, leaving Aisling alone with the nurse and … Jake? Was that what Mrs. Larson had said?

The nurse pulled up a stool. "I have to take a blood sample, Aisling. Just lay your arm flat and I'll tie this around up here. There we go. A nice fat vein. I hate it when they're hard to find and I have to go digging around for them. Ready? Here's a pinch … got it."

Aisling watched uncomfortably as her blood filled up the vial. It was dark and thick and pumped into the small container quite quickly.

"There we go. We'll just get that tested to make sure you're okay. Oh, and I'm supposed to ask for the number to your parents or guardians?"

Aisling gave her father's work number and her mother's home number. The nurse walked out with the information and the blood. And that left Aisling and the boy alone together. He was staring at her.

"Hi?" she ventured, feeling awkward in the silence.

"Hey. I'm Jake. Are you okay?"

She raised an eyebrow. "Jake … want to try that question again?"

He lowered his head a little. "I just meant, are you feeling better?"

Great people skills, Ais, she said to herself.

"Right. Hey, thanks for calling the ambulance. I'm not sure what happened, but to be honest I feel fine now."

"You scared the heck out of everyone. It was all panic and some of the girls were crying. You, uh … you know how to make an interesting first impression, anyway." He said and waggled his eyebrows.

She smiled. "Yeah, sorry about that. I guess it was as good a way as any to escape the humiliation of my stupid audition."

"Stupid audition? What are you talking about? You were awesome!"

"Yeah, right. Is that why everyone avoided looking at me like I was some kind of freak?"

"Well, yeah. But you're a freak because that song was so, I don't know, beautiful. I've never heard anything like that and I bet no one else has either. We were in awe. I felt like I was on some kind of cliff looking out over the ocean or … yeah, whatever…." He trailed off awkwardly.

Aisling was surprised. Apparently, she'd read the whole situation quite wrong. She felt a little better about her audition - aside from the whole falling down unconscious part. But what Jake had said about the music - she had a sense of what he was saying.

"Like you could just fly forever and everything would be all right? That's how it was for me when my Kokum would sing it."

"Well, something like that. Seriously, it was the first time that saying made sense to me. You know, the one about music taming the wild beast?"

"Rowrr!" she growled, scrunching up her face.

This time he laughed.

They heard clicking heels approaching from the hallway and looked over expectantly. Mrs. Larson came through the door, her face set in an expression of shock and confusion.

"Mrs. Larson, are you okay?" Aisling asked.

Their eyes met and Aisling could see tears in the older woman's eyes.

"Oh, Aisling, I'm so sorry to have to tell you this but an hour ago, your father..."

Aisling felt the pain that had stabbed her heart before. It consumed her and filled her but this time she remained conscious and she was sure of the thought before Mrs. Larson could continue.

"He's dead."

Chapter Six - Eric

The long, brown grasses swayed in the slight autumn breeze, whispering to each other in the long afternoon sun. Leaves scuttled across the bare patches of ground, their dry, papery voices eager to be heard as their fragile remains chipped and crumbled away. Eric walked up the long driveway to the house, his shadow stretching out before him. The adrenaline from the fight after school had left him, but the cold anger and strength remained.

He opened the creaking front door and entered the house. His mother was sitting at the kitchen table, head in her hands.

Another hangover, no doubt, he thought with disgust. He was a little surprised. He'd never thought about his mother that way before.

He went to the fridge and poured himself a glass of milk, then sat down.

"How are you?" he asked, gentler than his thoughts.

She made no reply, only seeming to sink further into her herself.

"Mom?"

"When you leave, Eric, just be careful."

"What? What are you talking about?"

"It's all happening. I thought I could stop it if I could just stop dreaming, but nothing works. It all just keeps happening."

"Mom, you're talking crazy."

She raised her head then and looked at him. Her eyes were clear. Sober. Red and puffy with tears. She looked at him for a long moment and then smiled. A weary smile full of sorrow and rue.

"You're right, son. I am crazy. And it's all my fault. Your Kokum tried to help me but I pushed her away. I pushed away your father, too. It's all my fault."

Eric could feel a tension growing in the air, but he didn't know where it was coming from. His breath started coming faster, and he could feel a panic coming over him. His hand went to his pocket and fumbled with the stone lying there, cool and firm. Some of his fear began to subside. Instead, he started to get angry.

"Stop it! Stop sitting there feeling sorry for yourself! Stop drinking away our money and pull yourself together."

"Eric, I didn't drink today, I promise," she said, shocked into defending herself. "I have to tell you something, please sit down."

He hadn't even noticed that in his anger he had stood as if preparing for a fight.

He took the seat across from her and waited. She started crying again.

"I'm not going to sit around all day waiting for you to stop whining."

"Eric! I… Your father…."

"What does he want? To say sorry he won't be here for my birthday again?"

His mother straightened, her face transforming from pathetic and weak to a firm set of jaw, fire in her eyes.

"Your father's dead!"

Eric was stunned into silence.

"He's dead and I didn't stop it!"

"You're insane. I just talked to him a few days ago."

"It happened this morning, Eric. There was an explosion. He's dead."

Eric's anger started to melt away and a sob escaped him, coming from deep inside his chest. It hurt. His entire world was collapsing in on him.

"Can we call someone to find out? Maybe it was just a mistake. Maybe we can do something."

She looked at him with such compassion in her eyes that it hurt even worse.

No. I don't want this. I have to be strong like Cor said.

He tightened his grasp on the stone, to remind himself. As he did so he found himself annoyed with his mother's pitying look. He was no baby. And besides, what did she just say? It was her fault, she didn't stop it? I pushed him away, she said. And he knew it was true. He knew that everything was her fault. He didn't have a father to teach him to fight so he was pushed around. He didn't have a sister to help him because she would rather move away than stay around the crazy woman they called mother. She was responsible for everything bad in his life. His rage boiled up and out of him.

"You killed him! If you were better he wouldn't have left! He'd be alive! You killed him!!"

She stood up and came to his side of the table. She tried putting her arms around him. He jerked back out her embrace and shoved her away.

"Don't touch me! Don't ever touch me again. Go have another drink, you murderer!"

There was such pain in her eyes but he just saw it as more proof of her weakness. He realized he had to leave. He could never trust her again. He sneered and turned away, ignoring her sobs and tears. He grabbed his stuff and left the house.

He would never return.

Chapter Seven - Aisling

The highway flew past in a blur of grey, working its way past hills and valleys, over rivers and under bridges. The monotonous flick flick flick of fenceposts lulled her into a daydreaming haze, stretched barbed wire undulated across her vision, keeping time with the rise and fall of her breath. They were driving back to the Rez to help her mother prepare the wake and funeral for her father. Her mother had sounded so strange on the phone. Not sad as Aisling had expected, but robotic. Numb. She couldn't decide if that was going to be a good thing or not. The one piece of good news was that Kokum would be there to help.

How many years had it been? Three or four, at least. They got postcards from time to time as her grandmother jumped from place to place. When they had seen her off at the airport, Kokum had jokingly said she was off to her real job now: traveling! They all laughed, but Eric and Aisling were also a little sad to say goodbye. A few years might seem like nothing to someone so old, but to them it was going to be forever.

It wasn't, but it did feel like a lifetime ago. Her Kokum was back and her father was dead. Aisling realized she was going to have to move back to the Rez, go to school there. It wasn't so bad, really, but there was no consistency at the school. Teachers came and went and there just wasn't the budget for everything she wanted to learn. Not in science, anyway, and there weren't any music programs. She shook her head. She knew she was being selfish, but she just couldn't bring herself to believe that her father had actually died. It was like she was living in a dream.

> *Don't think about dreams!*

She shook her head again and sat up, stretching.

She looked over at Jake and he glanced over at her. She noticed he didn't take his eyes off the road much when he was driving. When he had found out she was going to be taking the Greyhound home he volunteered to drive. She appreciated it but didn't want to be a burden, especially on someone she had just met. But he was so insistent and so kind that in the end she just couldn't say no.

The truth was she needed a friend right now.

"You awake, then?"

"Yeah, thanks for letting me sleep. I meant to keep you company."

"Don't worry about it. You needed to relax. I'm just glad you were able to rest, you looked exhausted."

"Oh, thanks. So in other words, gross?"

He gave a half-hearted, sheepish grin. "That's not what I meant."

"I know," she said, swatting him softly on the arm. "I'm just joking around. I need to joke or it feels like I'll fall apart."

He looked serious for a moment, then he smiled.

"Okay, I've got one for you. Pull my finger!"

She looked at him, unbelieving, then burst into laughter.

"You're disgusting," she said when she caught her breath. "I don't even know why I laughed!"

He winked with a satisfied grin and turned back to the road.

She leaned against the window of the truck, the glass cool against her forehead, and she smiled to herself. Up in the sky, a large eagle soared. They passed through a small town in the broad river valley and began climbing the slope that lead to the reservation. She didn't feel so heavy anymore. In fact, the thought of Eric and her Mom - and Kokum! - was making her happier by the second. She took a deep breath and watched with growing anticipation as the landmarks of home started passing by on the sides of the highway.

Soon, everything will be all right.

Chapter 8 - Eric

The sun was setting and it was getting cold. He was still warm from walking all afternoon but he was getting a little worried. He'd been in such a rush to get out of the house that he didn't think. He could have brought a tent, a blanket, a change of clothes, but he was so angry there seemed to be no time to waste. He just had to leave.

That anger was fading, but he had made up his mind and he kept onward, one foot in front of the other. As the sun began to slip behind the thinning branches of the autumn trees, Eric made a choice to head for the highway. There was a chance he would be stopped by someone who knew his family but there was no way he was going to spend the night in the bush with no shelter. He felt like he should have been born just knowing instinctively how to survive in the woods, but he had to admit he didn't have the first clue. Things were a lot different when there was no adult around to make the fire or set up camp.

He cut cross country, passing through stands of small woods, farmer's fields and low brush, taking stock of what he did have stashed in his backpack: a Swiss Army knife, a bottle of water, a few apples and granola bars, hat and gloves. He had a small LED flashlight and a sketchbook and some pencils for when he felt like drawing. He pulled out a granola bar for his supper and kept on walking.

It was twilight when the deer came out.

He stopped, still in the cover of the trees, watching as they slipped from the shadows into the wide field to his right and started eating the grains left behind by the plows and threshers. From old to young, they gingerly stepped between the furrows of the soil, ears constantly flicking around listening for the slightest sounds. Eric held his breath.

A young deer, older than a fawn as the spotting was gone from his coat, was walking closer and closer, seemingly unaware of the boy. Eric barely exhaled and the young buck looked up quickly. Its large, liquid eyes gazed into Eric's in softness and wonder and Eric felt a softening inside himself, as if a clenched fist around his heart were relaxing.

"Hey there," he said, still mostly hidden in the trees. He held out the granola bar he had been eating. "You want some?"

The deer stepped a little closer still, its neck was stretching out far as it was able, and sniffed the bar in Eric's hands.

Suddenly the quiet animal dropped heavily to the ground and a split second later Eric heard the sharp crack of a rifle in the distance.

The young deer had a hole in its side and was breathing in short spasms, arching his head back and forward, the velvet on his small antlers scratching against the stones piled at the edge of the field. With one last shudder, it lay still, its final breath coming out in a small puff of steam.

Eric heard the shouts of the hunters in the distance and slipped deeper into the woods, away from the dead animal. He knew the hunters likely hadn't been able to see him and he didn't want them to. He was shaking with cold and with sorrow, tears streaming down his face for the trusting deer, for his dead father, and for himself, alone in this dangerous world.

He felt that cold hand wrapping itself around his heart again, blocking out the pain. He welcomed it, willed it to shield him from his hurt. He wiped his eyes, clearing the blurry vision and then saw the last hint of the purple sunset drop under the edge of the world. The small pinpoints of the stars came into existence one light at a time like cold distant fires igniting to ward off the darkness. He emerged from the woods to see the highway stretched out across his path. There was a glow coming from over the rise and he made his way toward it.

It turned out to be a small gas station with a mini-mart. Eric breathed a sigh of relief and hurried his pace, hoping for a little warmth and a moment in which to plan his next move.

Inside the store, Eric nodded to the clerk behind the desk who glanced up from his Sudoku to appraise the boy. The furrows of the old man's eyebrows stretched over the rim of his glasses and kept on climbing up his balding forehead.

"Hot chocolate?" asked Eric, hoping to stop the man's questioning look before something drastic happened to the wrinkled old face.

"In the back, in the back," the old man muttered, turning back to his puzzles.

Eric found the automatic machine and pulled a cup out of the dispenser, placed it under the hot chocolate nozzle and pressed the red button. His cup filled with the steamy liquid.

As he fitted the lid over the cup, the door opened again and Eric was surprised to see Cor walking through. Cor smiled and walked over.

"You drink coffee?" he said. "Pretty cool."

Eric was about to explain but then stopped. He liked that Cor thought he was cool.

"Yeah, well, one for the road, right?" he said instead.

"What's that mean?"

"I'm leaving. Taking off. I can't take it here anymore. It was nice knowing you, though," Eric stuck out his hand, trying to look more confident than he felt.

"Not so fast. We just met I'm not letting you take off just like that."

Eric felt betrayed. Cor was going to rat him out

"You can't do anything about it, Cor, so don't even try. You have the good life so don't even."

"The good life? Is that what you think? What? Because I have fancy stuff? Get real. If you had any idea what my family was like…."

And he fell suddenly silent. Unreadable emotion played across Cor's face. He took a deep breath.

"Come on," he said, "I've got your drink."

Dropping a bill on the counter, he picked up a bag of chips.

"Keep the change, man," he told the clerk as he walked out into the night with Eric.

"So, Eric, where are you going then?" he asked once they were a few feet away from the door.

"I dunno. I was just … walking."

Cor gave a short bark of laughter.

"Sounds like a good plan. Can I have a try?"

Eric shrugged.

"Okay, get behind this building and wait there. I'll be back in less than an hour and then we're heading out. Let's get out of this place together."

Eric was speechless. He could feel his spirits rising. Instead of feeling sorry for himself he started to feel excited, like he and Cor were about to head out on some adventure. He had so many questions but decided to keep them to himself. He didn't want to jinx it.

"All right. I'll wait."

Eric went behind the store and hunched down, his back against the wall. After a few minutes, he pulled out his notebook and a pencil and began to sketch in it, both to pass the time and to find a little comfort.

A motion at the edge of his vision caused him to stop sketching. He looked up. About ten meters away, on the gravel between the asphalt and the line of dark green trees behind the gas station, he saw a beautiful little red fox. It had just emerged from the trees, and it locked eyes with Eric. They both froze for a moment, the fox's eyes dark, shining pinpoints against its shock of orangish fur.

Eric was entranced. But at the same time, he felt almost as if someone had held a mirror up to himself, and he felt strangely ashamed.

And as quickly as it had appeared, the little fox was gone, the flash of white fur at the tip of its tail disappearing into the thick brush beneath the trees.

Eric started thinking again, about the deer, and of his mother's tears. There was still a chance to go back home, to crawl into his own bed and pretend everything was alright. He felt very small and very lost, and a sort of ill feeling that made him homesick and queasy. He didn't want to make Cor angry, but now that he took the time to think about it running away seemed a little extreme. Besides, what was his mother going to do without him? What would he do without her?

He made up his mind. He stood up and brushed the dry grass off his clothes. He was just going to have to apologize and hope Mom wasn't too mad at him. He walked to the front of the store, fumbling with the change in his pocket.

I'll just give her a call.

"Hey buddy! Miss me?"

"Cor! That was fast!"

"Well, like I told you, I wasn't too far. Check it out."

Cor pulled Eric back behind the building and proudly laid out his loot. A tent, sleeping bags, matches, a fishing rod and tackle, fire starters, a lightweight cook set with dishes and utensils, a hatchet, clothes...everything they would need. He stuffed it all back into his backpack and did up the belt around his hips.

He flashed his smile, teeth almost glowing in the dark.

"Okay, Eric, my man. Let's hit the road."

Chapter 9 - Aisling

The driveway was overflowing with vehicles as Jake's old truck creaked to a stop. Jake and Aisling hopped out, the gravel drive crunching under their feet.

She felt nervous. What if things were different with her grandmother? How was Eric holding up? She had so many questions and wasn't sure if she wanted the answers. How did life get so complicated?

The front door opened and Auntie Martha stepped outside, arms held out almost as wide as her smile.

"There she is, finally! *Astum!*" Martha always peppered a bit of Cree in what she said. Aisling liked it. Like adding spice. She happily obeyed the command and went directly over to her Auntie who rewarded her with a deep hug and a kiss on the cheek.

"Hi, Auntie. How are you?"

"Oh, I'm just fine. I'm saving my tears for the wake so don't you worry about me. We have a lot of work to do if we're going to send my brother off right. And who is this handsome *moniyaw*?"

"Oh hi! I'm Jake," he said, stepping forward, taking Martha's hand and giving it a firm shake.

"Hmmm. Hello, Jake. Are you worried about being the only cowboy surrounded by us Indians?"

Jake laughed nervously.

"Don't worry. We only scalp you once you've turned eighteen. It's the law now."

"Auntie ...." Aisling said reproachfully.

Martha threw her head back and laughed, her ample body shaking in mirth.

"Yes, yes, well come on in. All the aunties will want to see if this boy looks like a good candidate for a second husband."

She led them inside the packed house where women of all ages were moving around everywhere, jamming themselves in the kitchen, preparing food, making plans, drinking coffee and tea, writing lists. They were all chatting and laughing and gossiping with amazed and expectant faces at every new tidbit of information about their neighbours.

"Where's Kokum Georgia?"

"She's coming, she called a few minutes ago. Why don't you go get settled? Jake here can sleep in Eric's room."

"Okay. Thanks, Auntie."

They grabbed their bags and Aisling showed Jake to Eric's room and then walked a little further down the hallway to her old room. Shutting the door behind her she gave a soft sigh and lay down in her old bed. She'd only been gone a month and a half but it felt like forever. Everything seemed so young and girly. Her boyband posters were still up and the glow-in-the-dark stars her father put up for her when she was seven were still there too.

She closed her eyes and immediately the dream took her.

– Save me!

She'd been through this so many times now, and this time, instead of just watching, helpless, she did something she hadn't yet thought to try: she asked a question.

Who are you? What do you need?

The light seemed to hold still for a moment, then that soft, whispery, watery voice asked its own question.

– You can hear me?

Yes! And to be perfectly honest you've been scaring me half to death. Who are you?

– I am Mother.

My mother? I don't think so. What's going on here?

– You can hear me! You have power! Why are you letting him destroy me? Save me!

The sheer power of the demand shocked Aisling into silence once more. She felt overwhelmed by the sorrow of the plea. How could this being need the help of a 15-year-old girl?

Why me?

– How can you ask that? You have power. Will you do nothing? Will I die, too, and all my sweet children?

It was difficult to keep her thoughts straight. It wasn't like being awake where life just went along logically, if a little chaotically. This dream place was always changing, as soon as she had one thought it would drift away into another. Dreaming was like navigating across steep sand dunes where the footing was always shifting. Just keeping track of the conversation was taking all her effort. This was the strangest dream yet and the intensity of this … Mother … was too much to take. She felt herself spiralling into a panic.

I don't know what you're talking about! She yelled into the light. *I don't know what to do*!

The light got brighter and a flood of images started pouring into Aisling's mind, too many for her to understand but with a familiarity that coursed through her like a shot of adrenaline.

I … remember ….

This was her dream, it had always been her dream, and now she knew why she used to scream.

Her eyes opened. There was a soft knock at her door and she heard Jake's voice whispering her name.

She stood up, a little shaky, and opened the door a crack.

"Aisling, I thought you'd want to know that your Grandma's here. At least I think it's her. I saw her go upstairs and people were calling her Georgia. Are you going to be long? I'm starting to feel a bit like a fish out of water here."

She's here!

Aisling said a quick thanks and left Jake alone as she took the stairs two at a time.

Her mother's door was slightly ajar, leading into a room dimmed by closed curtains. She hadn't even thought of coming up to see her Mom when she got home - Auntie Martha had so deftly directed her to settle down and catch her breath first. Just one more sign of her Auntie's old skill at keeping everyone feeling happy.

But now Aisling stepped into her mother's room, trailing wisps of her dream along behind her. Her mother was in bed and her Kokum sat in the rocking chair next to it. As a little girl Aisling had spent many days sitting in that bed talking to her mother as Eric was soothed back to sleep by the gentle rocking.

They looked up at her when she entered and Kokum beckoned her over and they embraced for a long time, letting the years apart fill and entwine with love until things felt right again. She leaned over and kissed her mother on the cheek, frightened by how thin and pale she was.

"How are you Mom?"

Her mother didn't even smile. She just closed her eyes and silently wept.

Aisling looked at her Kokum with deep concern. Kokum Georgia rubbed Aisling's hand in hers and smiled softly.

"My sweet girl, I've been gone too long. I promise I won't leave you again. Too long…I've lost my beautiful boy - my son." she had to stop talking for a moment until her throat cleared.

"You're here now, Kokum. Please don't cry or I'll start and I feel like I won't ever stop."

Aisling's mother opened her eyes and there was fear in them.

"Has he come back yet?"

Aisling misunderstood her mother's shock and confusion.

"Mom, Dad's not - "

"Not your father, Aisling. Eric. Is he back?"

"I didn't see him." She looked to her grandmother.

"No, me neither."

Kokum Georgia closed her eyes, breathing deeply. After a moment they opened and she looked intently at Aisling's mother.

"He's not here. Caroline, where is Eric?"

"I - I don't know! We had a fight and he left last night. I called all his friends, all our relatives. No one has seen him."

Aisling grew increasingly alarmed. What was going on? Had Eric run away?

"Caroline, sleep now, don't worry. Aisling and I will go look for him, but for now, do as I say for once - and sleep."

She started humming, arranging the sheets around Aisling's mother and settling her down into the pillows. As she did, Caroline's eyes closed once more and her breathing slowed. The muscles in her face softened, letting the temporary peace of sleep enfold her.

Aisling felt her heart slow to a normal beat as well and although she was confused and scared, she felt a little more able to deal with things. Then, for the first time in her life, she put two and two together. She was surprised she'd never noticed it before.

"Kokum, how do you do that? How do you make us feel so safe?"

"So you figured it out. I suppose I shouldn't have hoped that we'd have more time. I'm sorry, my girl, but things have just gotten a little more complicated."

"You're not making any sense, Kokum, and I don't think I can take it. I feel like I'm going nuts."

Kokum was silent for a few moments, letting Aisling know she had been heard. Then she spoke.

"Your mother and father always wanted you and your brother to have normal lives. I didn't agree with what they thought was normal, but I respected them. I always thought there was so much more time, but I was wrong. I know you're confused, my sweet girl but this isn't a good place to explain anything right now. We *must* find your brother. I'll be in the back yard. Come!"

She left the room, the dimness, the sleeping Caroline, and Aisling with her mouth hanging open in utter bewilderment.

After a moment, Aisling gently shut the door and went outside.

Chapter 10 - Eric

Cor taught Eric a lot about surviving in the outdoors, things he had never paid attention to before when he'd gone camping with adults. Eric started the fires at night by himself, gathering kindling from the dry underbrush and pulling old, hanging moss off the pine trees to create a bed for the flames. Then he carefully added twigs and long strips he hacked from hunks of wood with the hatchet. After that it was just a matter of keeping the flame going with larger pieces of wood.

It made him feel competent and capable.

On the third night of running they sat by their fire, eating the last of the food Cor brought.

"Well, I have money enough to buy groceries, but last I looked there didn't seem to be much in the way of stores around here," Cor grinned.

"What are we going to do?" Eric asked. He wasn't too worried yet. After all, his stomach was full and the fire was warm and cheery, but he did wonder what tomorrow would be like.

"We'll have to fish or hunt. I know how to lay snares, but that's kind of hit or miss. You?"

Eric shook his head. All he was thinking of was the deer.

They were silent for a time, the crack of the fire punctuating their thoughts. Eric watched the sparks fly up into the air, imagining that the little embers of light just kept on floating upward to become stars in the endless sky. He wished he could fly too, away from the guilt he was feeling.

He had missed his father's wake. They'd be finishing up the funeral about now. He tried to block out images of his mother, so sad and alone, and of Aisling who would have come back from the city. His aunties, cousins, uncles…. He was having trouble remembering why he had run away in the first place and a wave of sadness hit him. He was mortified when a sniffle escaped him. He hoped Cor hadn't heard.

"Think of something else."

Cor's words were whispered, understanding.

"How? I just don't know what to think right now."

"Eric, I don't blame you for Tommy. He was a bully. You did the right thing, but do you think anyone else will understand?

"Tommy? What does he have to do with anything?"

"Wait a minute, are you saying that's not why you were running? You don't know?"

"Know what?"

"Tommy's in the hospital. It was on the news. He's in a coma. Geez, I thought that's why you were taking off!"

"The hospital?"

"Yup. Hanging by a thread. Unless it snapped in the past couple days."

Unless it snapped.

"What did I do?"

Cor sat up and brushed his hair back with a quizzical look.

"You stopped getting pushed around. I saw you lying in the dirt. If you hadn't stopped him it might be you in the hospital now. But knowing you've got such a great left hook makes me feel way safer out here."

Eric couldn't help feeling a glow of pride at Cor's compliment, even though he wasn't sure he *wanted* to feel that way. But Cor had a way of making things better, of taking away Eric's fear and making him feel strong.

He slipped his hand into his pocket, feeling the cool stone there. Strong, like the stone. As he traced its surface he found his homesickness drifting away and a cold sureness replacing his doubts.

"Thanks, Cor," he said. "For everything."

"What are friends for? Now we better get some sleep. Tomorrow, we hunt."

Chapter 11 - Aisling

She always knew something was strange about her family but now that she had noticed just one thing - the power of her Kokum's song - Aisling saw so many different pieces start to tumble into place that she was not only confused, she was angry. By the time she reached the back door she was absolutely fuming and she emerged onto the porch with a slam.

To call the land behind the house a backyard would be a bit of an understatement. The house opened out into a field of several acres ringed by trees and brush.

Standing a few yards from the house in the long grass was her Kokum, a mauve, puffy winter jacket covering her body down to her knees, the hem of her floral print skirt billowing in the slight breeze. Aisling saw her grandmother was wearing long underwear and the oddity of it managed to break her anger a little. That and the tall, young black man standing beside the old woman.

Kokum looked back at the sound of the door and beckoned to her granddaughter.

Aisling walked down the steps into the field full of medicine. In younger, warmer days she and Eric scampered around at Kokum's direction finding the different plants she described and waiting beside them until their grandmother would come and inspect the flowers or leafy things to see if it was indeed what she wanted. When they got it right, she would give them a piece of candy and Kokum would kneel down to cut off what she needed, or dig out the root. Then she would sprinkle a little tobacco and say a small prayer of thanks.

As Aisling approached she studied the young man. He was older than her, about 18 or 19 she guessed, and he looked uncomfortable, pulling the collar of his jacket up and hunching his shoulders against the breeze. Lazy, loose curls fluttered about his head, seemingly pulled in all directions.

"This is Matari, Aisling. He came back with me from Australia. I know you have questions and truly, you need the answers more than you know. Matari and I will attempt to answer them all. Matari, my Aisling."

If she was surprised at the strange visitor, Aisling was doubly surprised when he spoke. She'd expected a deep voice. What she heard instead was a friendly tenor, laced heavily with an Australian accent.

"G'day, Aisling. I've heard a lot about you." He took her hand and gave it a quick shake, amused at her astonished look. "Don't worry, I don't bite, except when I'm starved. Speaking of which, now that I've come back from running your errands, Gran, can we get fed? Or else I really might start having a go at whatever's handy!"

Aisling didn't know what to say, and she stood there feeling for all the world like she'd just slipped into another dream.

"Sweet love, will you go grab this beanpole some bannock? We can't find any trace of Eric back here so we'll walk down to the front road. There's my girl."

Numb, Aisling walked back into the house. In the raucous kitchen she sidestepped her cousin who was carrying an unusually large bowl of gravy.

"Hey, Ais. So sorry about Uncle Dan."

"Thanks, Lee. How did you get sucked into all this?"

"What, a guy can't work in the kitchen? Besides," he said in a loud voice so everyone could hear him, "you know I'm the best cook in here!"

There was laughter and mocking jeers and he slipped away with a smile. "Catch you later, cousin, I've got to take this gravy out to my car before these ladies try to cover me in it. I'm tasty enough as it is!"

More laughter followed after him, including Aisling's own.

She grabbed a few pieces of bannock and tossed them in a paper bag. Then she went to collect Jake. She suspected he would be hiding out in Eric's room but when she got there it was empty. Puzzled, she was about to go search the house when she heard a sound at the end of the hallway, coming from her own room. She hurried to the door and found Jake with an incredulous look on his face.

"Bieber? You have posters of Justin Bieber? That's rich."

"Shut up. I was twelve when I put those up!"

Jake laughed again and she pulled him by the arm, forcibly removing him from the bedroom. She kept getting turned around with so many different emotions since she'd arrived here. She could feel the stress of all her conflicting thoughts and feelings stretching her patience tight.

"Jake, there are some seriously messed up things happening here and I'm sorry, but I think you should go home."

His smile faded abruptly.

"Go home? What's wrong? Did I offend someone?"

"No, nothing like that, it's family stuff."

"Is there anything I can do to help? Maybe we can just fix this up. I'm sorry I laughed at your posters."

Aisling looked at the sincerity written on Jake's face, his eyes full of concern. This is why she had come to trust him so quickly, she realized. He had a good heart.

"Maybe. Let's go and ask my Kokum."

She grabbed his hand and pulled him along behind her. They only paused to put on their jackets and shoes and then went to rejoin the two waiting figures down by the road.

"Frybread!" cried Matari as Aisling handed around the bannock. He took a bite and closed his eyes in utter contentment. "Mmm, good – but Gran, yours is better," he said around a mouthful.

Kokum just smiled. She looked Jake up and down, content to wait.

Aisling hurriedly made the introductions. She felt a pang of jealousy that Matari seemed to have such a good relationship with her Kokum. It was as if her grandmother had found the time for everyone else besides her or Eric.

"So you want to help us look for Aisling's brother, Jake?"

"If I can be of any help, ma'am."

"Very well. We can can use any help we can get," she said. "Are you ready?" this time to her tall, skinny companion.

"Yes, please stand back a bit. There's been so much traffic I'm not sure if I'll uncover anything but I'll give it my best."

They did as he instructed and he walked down a little further to the dusty, crumbling asphalt of the old road, brushing his hands on his pant legs. Aisling watched in curiosity as Matari slowly began to walk in wide circles. He didn't kneel down and examine blades of grass as she assumed he would, rather he kept his eyes open, almost casually glancing here and there as he made his slow, arcing progress, drawing up his knees and planting his long legs in slow, birdlike steps. Kokum whispered to Aisling that this was a very rare and very old Anangu tracking technique. Anangu was the name of Matari's people, she added in response to the girl's quizzical look.

Aisling held her breath, willing this strange boy to find something, anything. But he kept on and they continued to watch. After 10 minutes, she began to suspect that it was a waste of time and she turned to go back inside.

Matari's brow furrowed but his face quickly became calm again, a slight smile touching the corners of his mouth. He gave a slight nod, then stopped his search and waved them over.

"I believe I've discovered his direction, but to follow this path means literally hours of searching."

Kokum sighed. "I was afraid of that. Every moment that passes is precious. We'll have to let everyone know we're going. We just can't wait."

There was something bothering Aisling and she finally put her finger on it.

"Kokum! Why aren't we calling the police? Isn't there some all-points bulletin or Amber Alert or something they can put out?"

"They'll take him away if they find him, Aisling, and we can't let that happen."

"Can't let that happen? What if he dies! Isn't it more important to just get him back safe? Anything could be -"

Kokum started humming to herself.

"Stop that! Stop trying to control me! I'm going to call the police right now."

She turned and marched away.

43

She grabbed her purse from the living room, ignoring the extended family, ignoring their questions and greetings, their offers of condolences.

She went to her room and started dialing on her mobile phone.

"Put it down."

She jumped in surprise. Auntie Martha was sitting in the chair at her old study desk.

Guiltily, she did as she was told.

"Don't try any tricks on me, Auntie. I'm on to all of you."

"Hmmph."

Martha at least had the grace not to deny anything; she simply sat back with an assessing look on her face. Aisling broke the silence first.

"Well?"

"Well, what? You're on to us, right? We must be really nasty people."

"You know that's not what I meant."

"Oh really?"

"Yes, really. Come on, Auntie, give me a break. I'm sorry. I'm just so worried and heartbroken and …."

Aisling couldn't help herself. The tears started and she couldn't hold them back anymore. She was shaking with the pain and her head was pounding. She cried, her voice small, quiet, empty. She had fallen into a nightmare and didn't know how to get out. These kinds of things shouldn't be happening, not to her, not to Eric, not to anybody.

Her Auntie sat beside her on the bed, arms wrapping around her. Aisling didn't resist, she leaned into that warm, soft bulk and let herself be loved. Comforted. She cried for a long time, her grief playing itself out.

"I'm okay," she said, after her tears had stopped and she was left quiet and exhausted. In a small voice she asked, "I don't understand what's happening."

"Hmmm. My dear, what have you been told so far about what's going on."

Aisling wiped her eyes with a tissue from the box on her bedside table.

"Nothing, Auntie. I feel like I tripped and fell down a rabbit hole but I haven't even hit the ground yet."

"And you never will. Not ever again. Aisling, we got too complacent and let ourselves believe we had more time than we did, that much is obvious now."

"Kokum said the same thing. What's happening?" she felt her emotions rising again and did her best to quell them before they got out of control. One cry was enough.

"My dear girl, the signs are here. It's started."

"What? I don't understand."

Her Auntie looked away then took her hand and looked deep into her eyes.

"The end of the world."

Chapter 12 - Eric

Fishing was a bust, so Cor suggested they move on to snares. Neither of them could fathom why the fish refused to bite but refuse they did. It was tantalising - and incredibly frustrating - to see the silvery glint of the sun on the swimmers' scales, the lure dangling in front of their disinterested fishy faces.

The boys were getting hungry, so Eric stripped to his boxers and jumped into the deep stream to see if he could throw a couple of the whitefish to shore. All he got for his efforts was a soaking and a chill. Lucky for him, the sun was warm. He got dressed and eventually stopped shivering.

"It's not that I don't appreciate your enthusiasm, Aquaman, but try not to kill yourself in the process," Cor said, giving Eric's back a pat.

"So it's snares, then?"

"Snares it is. Once you're dry I'll show you what I've set up."

A little later, clothes only slightly damp, Eric knelt beside Cor to examine the thin lines of wire set in loops along what they guessed might be game trails. One ambitious snare involved a young, flexible sapling bent down with a bit of rope. Tied to the end of the rope was a small length of wood notched at the end like a severe underbite. It connected to another bit of wood with an accompanying overbite. This overbite piece was hammered firmly into the ground, the pressure of the sapling keeping the two joined together. The idea was that the snare was hooked up to the underbite piece. If an animal were to get caught its struggles would unhook the wooden clasp and the sapling would spring straight again, bringing the animal with it. This served two purposes, Cor explained. The first was obvious: the animal wouldn't be able to run to free itself. The second was that it would keep other predators from chancing onto their catch.

Eric admired the ingenuity of Cor's trap and was pleased to learn how to set it up. He felt positive their empty stomachs would soon be fed. But at the very thought of food, his stomach grumbled in complaint.

They returned to their camp to rest, build their fire, and wait.

Eric was using his Swiss Army knife to carve a block of wood he had taken a liking to.

"Whatcha doin', Michelangelo?"

"I dunno. I just picked this up the other day and I kind of see something inside it that wants to come out."

"Didn't know you were such an artist."

"Well, I'm not really. I like to sketch a little, but I've never carved anything before. Thought I'd give it a try since we have some time to kill."

"Pretty cool. Is that what you've been up to? Drawing? I thought you were keeping a diary or something."

"Uh, no! Diaries are for girls!"

"That's what I thought! *Dear Diary, today those stupid fish wouldn't even get caught. They're so stuck up, I bet they think they're too good for anyone. I did kind of think the big cute one was checking me out, though.*"

They both laughed.

"For reals, Eric. Can I see your sketches?"

"They're kind of personal. I don't think they're any good."

"What, at 12, you're friggin' Van Gogh? You're not up for a scholarship; I'm just curious is all. But hey, if you don't want me to see, that's cool."

"Well … I guess it would be okay. Just don't make fun of me or anything."

Eric pulled out his sketchbook from his bag as Cor came over to look.

There was a drawing of a sleeping woman, her face at peace and very pretty. A couple of trucks, spaceships, then a young deer. It was dead, with a hole in its heart. A fox, a few ravens and crows, and then Cor looked up sharply.

"You drew a picture of me?"

"I-I hope you don't mind, Cor. I was just doodling."

"Mind? This rocks, man. You really do have talent. Seriously." Cor paused then, "I don't have anything to say, Eric. Just crazy."

Eric glowed under the praise.

"Let's go check the snares," he said.

"Race you!"

They clambered to their feet, shoving each other back, each trying to get the lead. They laughed so hard they couldn't even run, just stumble and shove in the general direction they wanted to go.

On one of their game trails, two squirrels were caught in the wire, strangled to death.

"Wahooo!"

Cor looked pretty pleased with himself and with Eric's shouts of happiness. They disentangled their catch and hurried back to the fire.

"Do you know how to cook these?"

"Yeah, buddy, but I have to warn you, it's pretty gross."

Eric found his appetite had increased out in the wild. The fresh air and the long days of activity served to put a sharper edge on his normal hunger pangs. His mother had told him he was growing and she wasn't surprised by how much more he had been eating.

He didn't want to think about her. He just wanted a new life, a simpler life.

"I don't care, I'm so hungry I could eat them raw right now."

So Cor showed Eric how to gut and skin the little animals. They drove the carcasses onto sharpened sticks and started roasting them over the fire. The smell was amazing and Eric's mouth just kept watering in anticipation of the feast. He was bothered by the eerie resemblance of their skinned squirrels to little, headless people but he tried to keep his mind off it. The fat melted, sizzling the meat and giving off a maddening aroma.

At last the meal was ready and they raised their food to each other in salute. Then they got down to eating.

The taste was gamey and the flesh sinewy and tough. But to the starving boys it was manna from heaven, better than any cheeseburger or fries. By the time they were down to the small bones, they felt satisfied and happy. They sat back, enjoying the feel of food in their stomachs.

It was at that moment they heard a sound in the direction of their sapling snare and flying overhead, soaring farther than they thought possible, was a rabbit that looked as shocked as they were by its sudden trajectory.

It was a few seconds before either of them spoke.

"I don't think he's coming back."

They roared with laughter, holding their bellies and wiping their eyes. At last they calmed down, exhausted and in good spirits.

"Geez, you're smart, Cor. I'd hate to be in one of your traps."

Eric was sure Cor hadn't heard him as the older boy made no reply. Instead, he just stood up and walked away.

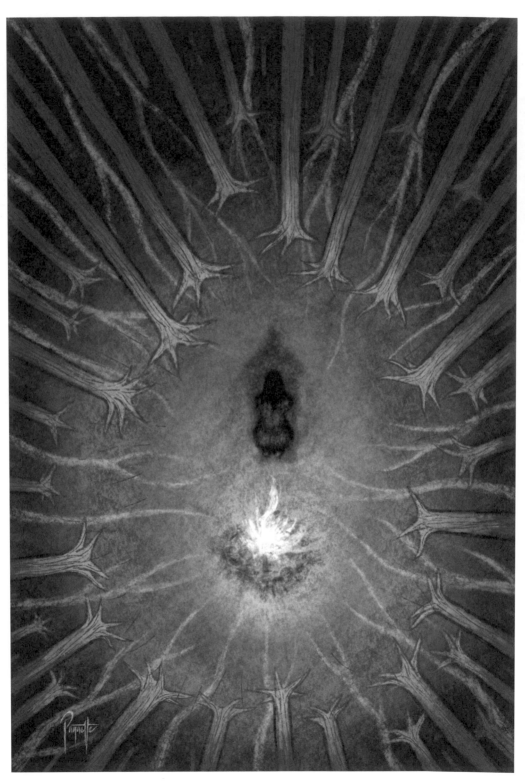

Chapter 13 - Aisling

They had been on Eric's track for a couple hours when Matari motioned for them all to stop. They were approaching a field and he reached the tree line then sat down on his knees. His eyes were closed.

"There was a death here."

Aisling's heart fell into her stomach and she looked worriedly over at her Kokum and Auntie. Jake touched her softly on the arm. We're too late! Something terrible had happened and they hadn't done nearly enough to stop it.

And Aisling still hadn't gotten a full explanation. After her Auntie's prediction of doom, Kokum had come into the bedroom and sat with them. She asked them to come with her, for Eric's sake, and Aisling had too many years of obedience and respect for her Elders ingrained into her to refuse. She felt trapped between tradition and necessity, and tradition had won. For now.

Matari opened his eyes to the silence and saw the sadness on the faces of the group behind him.

"Oh no, no, no! Not Eric! I've never encountered this creature before but I'm guessing it was a deer or elk."

Aisling sighed. Then was angry at Matari's lack of consideration. She stormed up to where he knelt and looked at the ground. She saw nothing that would let her know anything had passed by, much less died here. It was frustrating - depending on someone she didn't even know to lead them on what was probably a wild goose chase.

She wanted to yell at him for freaking her out but instead she said, "Well, don't just sit there, let's go."

He nodded and stood, casting around in those stupid wide circles of his. She had her doubts about his tracking technique. From everything she'd heard, you got down and looked for clues, you didn't just wander around and then suddenly know where to head.

But after a second or two, he was back on the supposed trail and the group of them were off again, deeper into the woods.

After another hour they were at the gas station.

"The store?" Jake said, "After all that he came to the store?"

Kokum went inside, Aisling followed as Matari walked off. *To prance around in circles or something.* She knew she was scared and shouldn't be angry at Matari, but she pushed the feeling down, tossed her hair over her shoulders, and stepped inside the store. She needed to be angry at *something.*

The old man behind the counter was talking to Kokum.

"Too many kids, I don't know. All the same to me."

"It was only last night."

"I said, I don't know. Take care of your own children!"

"He likes hot chocolate," Aisling said quietly. Eric never did like pop. Anytime they stopped on road trips he'd get hot chocolate. She always thought it was weird.

The clerk glanced over at her.

"Hmmm. Funny. Yes, he was here last night. Big spender. That's all I know. You got a poster or something?"

Aisling shook her head.

Kokum thanked him and they went to rejoin the others.

Jake was waiting and motioned for them to come around the back of the station. Auntie was talking to Matari and they looked confused. She looked up as they rounded the corner.

"Georgia, you better hear this."

"Eric was here last night," Kokum told them.

"Yes, he was," said Matari. "But now I'm a bit gobsmacked."

"What's the matter?"

"I can't figure it. It's like he met up with someone but I can't find the other trail."

"Are you sure there was someone with him?"

Matari frowned and stared at the ground.

"Yes. It's for sure. But it's nothing I've ever seen."

"Can you follow?"

"I see Eric plain as day, but this other person.... Gran, I have no idea what's going on, but, yeah, I can follow."

"Well, let's keep going, maybe we can figure it out on the way. Martha, how are you holding up?"

"As well as you, my mother. But the sooner we find Eric the better. It's been a long time since I walked so far."

Aisling hadn't even thought about the old women and how tired they must be already. She didn't know what to say but decided she would keep an eye on them. Again, Matari led and they all followed, like little ducklings in a row. They passed back into the bush tracing a little meandering stream. Redwing blackbirds flew up and around them as they passed hidden nests in the tall grass. Aisling smiled at their protectiveness.

She bumped into Martha before she realized the line had stopped. There was a little clearing and Aisling could see the remains of a fire.

"They stopped here for the night. Good stuff. I'll take a look around, see what I can see. Why don't you ladies have a rest?"

Kokum didn't say anything, nor did Martha as they helped each other to sit down on the trunk of a fallen tree. Aisling brought them her water bottle and they accepted it gratefully, taking turns drinking. Jake went to see if he could help Matari, though he seemed intimidated by the few years age difference.

The old women started looking a little better after a few minutes. From not far off they heard a shout of pain.

Aisling ran towards the cry. "Stay here! I'll be right back!" she called over her shoulder.

The trees opened up a bit and a small bank led down to where the stream had widened. Matari was sprawled on the ground and Jake was standing over him.

"Jake! What's going on! What did you do?"

Jake looked over with a look of complete surprise.

"Nothing! He just fell down. He told me to stand back."

"Matari, are you okay?"

"No worries. But I need you to help me up, mate."

They got themselves under his arms and half-dragged him back to the waiting women.

He sat down heavily and Martha put her hands on either side of his head. She closed her eyes and whispered something Aisling couldn't quite catch and then Matari straightened, placing his own dark hands over Martha's old, weathered ones.

She chuckled and patted his cheek.

Kokum had been looking down, deep in thought. She raised her eyes, "Is it that bad?"

"Worse. I was kind of expecting it, prepared. But it still hurt like mad and it was a narrow escape on my part."

"What was it?" Jake asked, "Some kind of trap or something?"

"You might say that, mate."

Kokum spoke again.

"How far ahead are they?"

"I'd say less than a day, but at our pace that could well stretch out if we give them enough time."

"Then there's no going back, we have to stay with them. If our mystery person didn't know they were being followed, they'll have to suspect it now. Hopefully you were quick enough."

"I think I was, but we should assume I wasn't, just to be safe."

Kokum met Aisling's uncomprehending eyes and sighed deeply.

"Then we will stay the night here. We can't just go rushing blindly along this trail. We need to take some of this precious time to explain a few things. I'd rather keep on, but Aisling needs some preparation before we continue. Aisling, it's time you got some answers. Jake, thank you for your help but you need to go back from here. Your family will miss you."

"Not really. My parents are on a dig in Mexico. I can stay another day or two."

"We couldn't ask that of you, and there are some … family matters to discuss."

"You mean like magic or something? I - I - don't want to be rude but I do pay attention, I've seen a few strange things, so if it's that stuff, don't worry. I won't tell anyone."

Aisling felt kind of stupid. Jake had figured out in a few hours what had taken her 15 years to see.

"And to be honest, you couldn't drag me away from this now. If it's okay, and if you could use the help, I'd really like to stay." He looked at Aisling and gave a quick, shy smile.

Everyone was looking at him in stunned silence.

Martha whispered to her mother and Kokum closed her eyes. Then Kokum regarded Jake as if trying to see something hidden, some hint of his character that she might have missed. She looked hesitant but said, "Very well. Go with Matari back to the house and get us supplies and let everyone know we are okay."

"I can call Lee and he can help them find everything, "Aisling volunteered, hoping to smooth over the suddenly awkward moment. She had one bar on her phone but that should be enough to reach her cousin. It dawned on her that she hadn't checked Facebook the whole day. That was a first for her. Right now it seemed like the last thing she wanted to do. "And Kokum, if we don't find Eric today, can Lee call the police?"

Kokum nodded reluctantly.

She walked over to Matari and Aisling could see her gesture toward Jake. Matari shook his head but finally seemed to agree with whatever her Kokum was saying.

I guess I shouldn't be surprised Kokum doesn't trust Jake. I just wish she could see how nice he's been to me.

They made the arrangements, and when the boys had gone Kokum pulled a shell from an inside pocket and she and Martha began preparing a smudge. As they made their preparations Aisling gathered wood and twigs for a fire. The area was stripped of easy kindling so she had to walk a little farther to gather fuel.

"Not too far!" Martha called out and Aisling obeyed, thinking about Matari.

A cheery fire was soon crackling away in a ring of stones. Kokum lit the special dried plants and with the rising smoke came that old familiar, comforting smell of the smudge. Aisling especially liked the smell of the sage. She watched the weathered hands of Kokum Georgia as they gathered the sacred smoke and brought it to her face, her heart, over her head and down her body. They all took a turn, silently and in prayer. For the first time since she got news of her father's death, Aisling felt calm and at peace on a deep, true level. Her anxiety had melted away and she knew it was time to learn the secrets her Kokum had guarded so well.

They sat in a small circle around the fire. It was small enough that they could be close and it gave off a comforting warmth against the coming night.

As they sat in silence, Aisling could feel their energy combining, the way it always did when people sat together. She'd seen people in the city try it but they always had an agenda so she never got the same feeling. Here, it was simple. Just sit. She knew this practice. Eventually what needed to be said would be said and what needed to be known would be known.

"I'm going to try something," Kokum said finally. "I want you to close your eyes and listen to my voice."

Aisling did as she was instructed.

"What do you see?"

"Nothing." Silence. "Wait, I can see the fire against my eyelids."

"Turn away from the fire, into the forest,"

Aisling turned around.

"What do you see?"

"This time I really do see nothi - " Aisling paused. "Did you bring some fire around here?"

"What do you see?" she could hear the slight anticipation in her grandmother's voice.

"Well, the flickering of the fire...."

As Aisling watched with her eyes closed she saw that it wasn't the same red glow of the fire, but more gold and silver. It wasn't flickering so much as....

"Pulsing!" she cried.

"Yes..." And the next words came on a softly exhaled breath. "Look deeper."

Aisling didn't know how to look deeper. But she tried. She shut her eyes tighter, squinting into the darkness, but the light faded away. Her Auntie spoke up.

"Don't squish it out, child. Relax."

She relaxed and slowly the pulsing light returned. She slowed her breathing, allowing it to become deep and regular. As she did so the light became less and less blurry, more distinct. She was reminded of the first time she went on a plane. It was a foggy night and she watched out the window as the lights of the city dropped below them, faded by the dark, dewy air.

This was different, though, less orderly. As she watched, she saw that the light coursed along pathways, like a river system. It was faint and it brought to mind being in the hospital, the nurse tying a tube around her arm.

"Veins!" she said with sudden realization.

The two older women nodded to each other.

"Turn around again, my love," her Kokum said. "You have done well."

"What is it?" Aisling asked in wonder.

"It is the blood of our Mother. The blood of the earth."

Chapter 14 - Eric

Eric leapt to the side, avoiding the arrows of the Archer. He ran forward, two hands on his Great Maul and brought the massive weapon down on his enemy. The Archer fell on the spot, his valuables falling around him which Eric gleefully gathered up. He had gotten very good at killing. At first the blood bothered him, but he didn't even notice it anymore. He looked forward every night to the chance he'd get to slay new foes and increase his experience points. He was already level 35 and it had only been a week.

He usually only played once Cor had gone to sleep, preferring to give the game his entire focus. The phone didn't get any bars or internet so no calls or email or anything, but he was concerned about the battery life on the device. It was quickly reaching empty. He was concerned since it was the only thing to do besides walking for hours every day to a new campsite and scrabbling to get enough to eat.

It had been over a week since they'd struck out on their own, and already things were changing. He was surprised how much time was spent just thinking about or trying to get food.

They'd gotten pretty good at snaring small game and Cor had worked on his Catapult (as they'd come to call his special trap) until rabbits weren't flung halfway across the world anymore. It busted them up each time it happened, but it was so much better - when the snare was set off and they finally found the rabbit hanging among the thin branches. Cor cut the wire and held the animal up proudly, then swung it around his head in triumph. He passed it on to Eric and he had done the same until he lost his grip and the carcass went rolling off into the bush, raising dust along the way. They looked at each other and laughed.

But it was when he turned off the game and was lying alone in the night that Eric thought back on it and felt sad. He felt cruel and that didn't sit well with him. Maybe it was part of growing up, he reasoned. Maybe boys just get mean and that's how they turn into men. Maybe. But it didn't stop him from feeling like he was losing something. He decided he wasn't going to think about it anymore. It just made him homesick and he didn't want that. The problem was, he didn't know *what* he wanted.

They couldn't roam around the backwoods forever. Neither of them had talked about it yet but Eric wanted to know what they were going to do. The longer they stayed out here, the more lost he felt. He didn't like feeling out of control. Eventually his thoughts slowed and he closed his eyes and fell asleep.

The next day as they were packing up their gear he mentioned his concerns to Cor.

"Well, where you wanna go then, Uhhrks?"

"I dunno. Just … somewhere."

"Always with the master plans, huh? Oh hey, don't look so hurt, I'm only pulling your chain. Let's figure this out, okay?"

"Well, I bet they've called the cops by now to find us, right?"

"Right-O. So no main highways or towns. What else?"

Encouraged, Eric went on.

"I bet it's like in the movies, where if we get into another jurisdiction they won't keep looking for us, or the people in the new place won't know to look for us, anyway."

"Bingo." Cor snapped his fingers and pointed at Eric in approval. "Where do you suggest we go?"

"Well, since we were kind of heading west like you said, maybe we should keep on going but a little faster, right?"

"You asking or telling?"

"Neither."

"Well, make a choice."

Eric was getting used to this. Cor was always giving him chances to decide things, and it made Eric feel good. Confident.

"I'm telling, I guess."

Cor rolled his eyes and then caught Eric's grin.

"Nice," he laughed. "So then, in what direction do we head a little faster, sensei?"

"I didn't think that far. What do you think?"

"Well, since you're asking, I think we head through the mountains, but more south where they're less likely to look for us. Ever been to Banff?"

Eric shook his head but his eyes got wider with excitement.

"Banff? Oh man, that would be so awesome! Do you really think we could do it?"

"Sure. Might take us a week or two. I mean, I'm only guessing, but it sounds about right to me. And from there...poof! off to freedom." He slid a flat hand through the air like a bird banking off into the wind.

"Freedom. Okay, I'm ready. Let's get going."

"You're the boss."

They stood in silence, their backpacks hoisted and belted on.

"Umm ... which way?"

"No idea."

"We'd better find a map."

Cor tapped his finger to his temple, a large smile on his face.

"That means we need a store, and that means we need a road."

"We passed that one yesterday about thirty minutes back."

So they hiked back to the road and once there followed it south. It was a sunny day, as it usually was in Alberta, but the advancing chill of winter was getting stronger and harder for the daylight to burn away. Nevertheless, they built up a sweat as they slowly chewed up the distance with every step. The trees were almost completely bare now and Cor mentioned that he thought they wouldn't have much squirrel left when the cold really started and the little creatures settled down and hid from the cold. Eric just grunted in reply, his pack feeling as heavy as a dead horse on his back.

At last they came to an intersection and a small ancient gas station. Settling their packs down outside the door, they drank from their water bottles and went inside. A middle-aged woman with red hair sat behind the counter watching a tiny television. She looked over at them.

"Hello, boys. What'll it be today?"

"Can I use your bathroom?" Eric asked. It had been on his mind for hours. He hadn't used a real bathroom in forever and he was surprised how excited he was over something so ridiculous.

"It's for paying customers only, honey. You buying anything?"

"Yes! A map and some water and stuff!"

"All right, then," she smiled and nodded toward the back.

Eric rushed by an amused Cor and opened the door to porcelain paradise. When he emerged, still damp around the face and ears from washing up, they got all the supplies they needed as well as a few extras that they'd wished they'd had before. The station also sold some fishing and hunting gear and they debated what would be useful and what would just add more weight to their packs. There was only so much two boys could carry and so there were a few things for that reason alone that they had left behind after the first couple days of hiking.

They made their purchases with Cor's money and once outside they reorganized their packs and were back on the road. They walked on about ten minutes when Eric looked over his shoulder and felt a cold pit of fear in his stomach. A car pulled up beside them marked with the letters RCMP. The Royal Canadian Mounted Police. Eric glanced inside the car and the officer pointed directly at the boy and motioned for him to stop.

"Oh crap," Cor muttered. "Busted."

Chapter 15 - Aisling

"Blood?"

"Yes, Aisling. The Earth is not just a ball of rock and water. She is alive. That's what you are seeing."

Aisling swallowed. The pulsing continued and she watched as the little rivers of light stretched off into the distance. She turned her head slightly and saw a more rich and brilliant stream in the distance. She gasped in surprise.

"It's so bright over there, Kokum! How can I be seeing this?"

Her Kokum chuckled in the glow of the campfire.

"You were born with a second set of eyes, my sweet girl. As was your father, your mother ... well most of the family, really."

"And you?"

"Yes, me too. But none of us have eyes as strong as you. Ever since you were a little girl, you could see."

"Can everyone see?"

Martha spoke up. "Yes and no."

Aisling snorted.

"Well, that makes things much clearer, thanks."

"Cheeky girl," Martha said, turning her eyes heavenward. "You unveil the wonders of the world and she laughs at you. Open your eyes, Ais, and turn around. It will be easier than talking to your back."

Aisling took in the beautiful view one last time then turned around, slowly opening her eyes to the fire and to her Auntie.

"To answer you, yes. All of us can sense this after a fashion, but it's easier for you." She held up her hand in mock impatience as Aisling was about to ask another question, "Just try to be quiet for two minutes, please, my little talker! Okay? Now, I was saying, it is easier for you in the same way some people are better at singing, or better at sports."

"That's just genetics, Auntie."

"And that's called a niece who thinks she knows everything. Fine then, if you have all the answers ...." She pulled out the water bottle and took a long swig.

Aisling got the message.

"Okay. Time for Aisling to shut up and listen, I get it. I'll try."

"Do or do not," her Kokum chimed in with a mischievous smile. "There is no try."

Aisling groaned but kept her mouth shut. There was quiet as the three of them looked at each other, suppressing the urge to laugh, each one trying to remain calm but secretly willing the others to break the silence. Martha sighed and gave in first.

"I shall continue," she said with some dignity. Aisling was glad for the humour. The humour of their family and of their community always helped them to get through the hard times. And goodness knew they had seen hard times. The words "Residential School" flashed through her mind and she shuddered. From her own experience, good, honest laughter really was the best medicine and at this moment she appreciated it even more.

"So ... *genetically*," and here Martha paused to give Aisling a look that said, *Any comments?* Aisling stayed as silent as a stone which seemed to satisfy the older woman. Martha continued, "...You have an ability to see these things easier and more clearly, and that's no big surprise. The stronger the gift, the more ... difficult it is to find someone who understands. So when you do find that other person, it's only natural that attachments form. And of course, marriage and then children, some of whom have your gift but stronger. Genetics."

Aisling nodded, it made a certain sense to her. The best she could come up with as an analogy was movie stars who dated each other because they were both used to the celebrity. But in this case, it sounded more like sharing a curse.

She wondered if that's why her Auntie had never married.

"Usually the talent doesn't show up until you're in puberty, but with you it came on much earlier. So early, we should have taken more notice. Should have, but didn't."

"That's my fault," said Kokum. "I was so distracted by my plans that I didn't see how close events were getting."

"You can't take all the blame, Mother. When history is stretching across centuries it's hard to stop and suddenly think in terms of mere years."

"I should have," Kokum said quietly and all their thoughts turned to Eric.

Aisling ventured a question.

"I get it so far, and for some reason I'm not even freaked out or anything. It just seems to make a certain sense. But what does seeing pretty lights have to do with the end of the world?"

"Not everyone's gifts are the same, Aisling. For example, I can't see earthlight."

She was surprised at her Auntie's comment. She'd just assumed the pulsing light was all there was to it. She suddenly felt sad for the kind woman. After seeing it herself, Aisling wished she could share that beauty with everyone.

"Your gift is you calm people, make them feel safe."

"Something like that."

"And so do you, Kokum, with your song."

Kokum nodded. "And your mother," she said, "dreams what will be, but she has no control. I have never been able tell if she is talking about a week from now or ten years."

"Why didn't she ever say anything about it to me?"

"Because she was angry about it, dear. It scared her very much. She would try to stop the bad things she saw from happening but never could. After a while she began to worry that she was causing the bad things to happen by dreaming about them. She got so wrapped up in the thought that she stopped remembering the sweet things she dreamt as well. That's why she stopped sharing her visions and started drinking. And that's why we kept all this a secret from you until today."

Martha nodded. "Danny asked that we allow you and Eric to live as uncomplicated lives as possible. We thought if we never said anything until you asked, you wouldn't have to worry about what was ahead."

Aisling knew that she should be shouting at them, denying everything they were saying, furious with their lies but she was completely calm. She looked up suddenly at Martha who gave a crooked smile and a wink.

"That's right, little bird, I'm helping you along. Do you mind?"

"No. Thanks, actually. It's like I should be freaking out right now, I guess. I don't know. Anyway, I'm glad to have any help I can to keep cool."

"Everything that's going on...." Martha closed her eyes and took a deep breath. "We believe Eric may be just as strong as you, Aisling. The two of you were to be our warriors once you were grown adults and now...."

"And now," Kokum interrupted, "all the plans, the shifting of the pieces – the war has begun and we thought we had another generation to go."

"The war? You mean like World War Three?"

Kokum's eyebrows went up.

"Exactly like that, you wonderful girl. That's exactly what it is. Here I am starting to feel sorry for myself and you just filled me with hope. We're not alone. This is a world war, not against nations and countries, but truly, against the worst kind of darkness."

She didn't want to know who their enemy was because knowing would make all of this much more serious to her, much more real. Yet Aisling had to ask the question.

"Who are we fighting, Kokum?"

The darkness of the night seemed to deepen. The forest trees shivered and then stilled themselves. Even the breeze slowed. Lit by the light of the dancing fire, her grandmother's face seemed more ancient than Aisling had ever seen it. There was weariness written in every line, and worry. But beyond that was something more. A strength of will and a calmness.

"We are in a war, my love. But you are not fighting anything or anyone, do you understand? You are protecting. You are preserving. You are nurturing the Earth and everything on it and there is one who is trying to take it all away, every last bit of it."

"Mother, don't – " Martha interjected.

"Oh, don't worry, I won't say his real name. But Aisling should have some name to call him by, even if it is just in English. He is a thief, a scavenger, and he carries darkness and lies with him wherever he goes."

"Who?" Aisling demanded.

"If we don't stop him he will take every good thing from this world and leave it a lifeless husk. He's done it before and he'll do it again. The Earth once had a sister, Aisling, and a child. They are both dead. The creature who did it we call Raven."

Kokum stood up as the headlights of a vehicle washed over them out of the darkness.

"And he has your brother in his claws."

Chapter 16 - Eric

His heart raced. Instead of running, his first thought was to kill the policeman.

He glanced over at Cor and saw the same seriousness in the older boy's eyes.

Sweating, Eric reached for the one weapon he had, the stone in his pocket. His Pet Rock.

The Mountie got out of the car. The lights on the top of the car flashed red and blue, and the officer's boots crunched on the gravel and the leather of his belt squeaked as he walked toward Eric.

Eric took a step backward. He wanted to take off his backpack. He undid the belt and let the shoulder straps slide down his arms until he was free. He felt light as a feather.

"Eric Cardinal?"

"That's me. What do you want?"

"Your family's worried about you, son. They want you to come home."

"What if I don't want to go home?"

"Well, that's not really a choice you have right now. You're a minor."

Eric saw Cor slowly moving around the police cruiser, so he kept talking, trying to sound tough.

"Well, it looks like I already made the choice, didn't I?"

"Yeah, son, it sure does. And now you've got another choice." The cop put his hands on his belt. A gun was holstered there and handcuffs dangled, glinting and reflecting the low autumn sun, "You come easy, or I will have to arrest you and force you to come along. Either way, you're going home."

Eric couldn't see Cor at all now.

Where is he?

He turned his attention back to the Mountie. He was a cop, sure, but he didn't seem like such a bad guy. Eric knew the man was just trying to do his job, but for some reason he kept up the punk kid routine. He put his hands in his pockets and the constable stiffened.

"Hands where I can see them, please. Don't make me use force, okay?" The cop glanced hurriedly around. "Hey! Where's your friend?"

The man seemed genuinely shocked that he somehow had failed to keep track of Cor, and he spun around.

Eric took his chance.

He removed his hands from his hoodie pockets, hefting the stone. It seemed much heavier than before. He raised his arm and brought the rock down hard on the back of the officer's head. Harder than he thought he was capable of. The cop didn't even make a sound. He just crumpled in a heap, legs bent awkwardly underneath him. He was dazed and just lay there looking confused.

Cor came out from behind the car. His eyes were wide and he looked at Eric with confusion.

"Holy crap! What did you do?"

"I had to, you know it!"

"Yeah, I know, I was kind of thinking the same, but this is heavy, man. This is a freaking cop!"

Eric looked at the man. He was still just looking up at them. Like a squirrel caught in one of their snares. Eric's hands were gripping his stone and he wanted to throw it away. Instead he watched, transfixed, as the blood from the impact soaked into the pores of the rock and disappeared. The blood on his hands disappeared into it as well. As it did, he felt that familiar surge of confidence and cold anger fill him and he relaxed. When he spoke it was as if a stranger was speaking.

"So what do we do now? Finish him off?"

Cor said nothing. Instead he went to the car and came back with a taser.

"Ever use one of these?" he asked. Eric turned his cold eyes over to his friend and shook his head, but he stretched out his hand and took the device.

"It looks simple enough. I guess I just point it…" which he did, "…and pull the trigger."

He did that too, and two electrodes shot out, hitting the cop in the arm, a powerful surge of electricity travelled along the trailing wires and the dumb look of shock turned into a rictus of pain as the man's body stiffened and then slumped into unconsciousness.

"Let's drag him off the side of the road into those bushes," Eric said, tossing the taser aside. Cor did as Eric instructed and they each took an arm. It was difficult work for the two boys. They were only able to move him a few feet at a time. Eventually, though, they had the man deep in the brush. He was pale, but he was still breathing. Eric was grateful for that.

"Now what?"

Eric considered. The gun might come in handy but they might also shoot themselves in the foot or something. Better to just leave it. He looked at the car. They could probably get a few miles with it, but for sure it had a GPS tracking device installed. He walked over and looked inside the driver's side, finding the latch for the hood. He popped it open.

He went to the engine compartment and pulled off the battery wires. He didn't know if that would shut off the GPS but it was worth a try.

"Cor, help me with this."

He went back to the open driver side door and started pushing, using his right hand to steer the car off the road. There was a break in the trees and if they could get it rolling the car would be hidden from view from anyone driving by on the road. Cor shoved from the rear and soon the vehicle was moving and Eric jumped behind the wheel, steering it between the trees and out of sight.

The cruiser rolled to a stop and Eric stayed in the seat, breathing hard.

Had all that really just happened? It all seemed like a dream, and he closed his eyes, willing himself to wake up. *Just wake up!*

But nothing happened. His eyes opened and he was still sitting in a police car in the middle of nowhere, running for the British Columbia border. He'd assaulted a police officer. He'd put a kid in the hospital. He knew he could never go back home. If he were ever caught, they'd put him in a juvenile centre or maybe even jail.

He suddenly just wished he could be left alone. He wanted time to think, to try to figure a way out of the mess he'd so quickly made of his life. He grabbed his rock and stuffed it back in his pocket. If he was going to make it, he'd need the confidence the stupid thing gave him. He had a flashback of the blood being sucked into the stone as if it were a sponge or something. He pushed the vision out of his mind. He gave the rock a squeeze, just to make sure it was solid.

He leaned back against the seat of the car, trying to sort through the confusion in his head.

I didn't make this mess, he thought, *everyone else did. Was I the one who left the family? Was I the one who went drinking and sleeping for days? Was I the one with any choice about what happened in my life?*

Eric's anger grew and filled him, erasing his doubts. No, he had done the right thing in leaving. He wanted to be free to make his own decisions. He didn't want to have his life thrown into chaos every time someone older than him did something that he had no control over.

Now he was in control. Maybe he'd made of mess of things, but at least he was still free.

And he was going to stay that way.

He got out of the car and went back to the road. Cor was sitting on the backpacks, chewing on an apple. He looked up as he heard Eric approach.

"You okay there, chief?"

Eric nodded and picked up his bag, hoisting it back on his shoulders, feeling the weight.

"Let's go," he said.

Cor followed.

Chapter 17 - Aisling

Jake's truck bounced to a stop next to the campsite, and he and Matari got out, looking mightily pleased with themselves. Aisling helped Kokum to her feet and they walked over to greet the young men.

"Not bad for an old truck, eh?" Jake smiled, thumping the fender proudly. "I never took her off-road before but she did pretty good. Matari saw that you weren't too far from one of these farmer's tracks so we were able to get back here before you all starved to death."

"I am *totally* starving!" Aisling said, her stomach rumbling at the reminder of its emptiness.

"Well, everyone at the house said to bring this to you all." He reached into the cab and pulled a large metal stew pot out from behind the front seat.

"Neckbones!"

Martha and Kokum were delighted, and Martha deftly relieved Jake of the pot as Matari, smiling, carried a brown bag of groceries over to the campfire. Working with Kokum, they began to prepare dinner.

"And for you…" Jake said to Aisling as he pulled a chocolate bar out from his jacket pocket.

"You smart, smart boy," she said and gave him a quick kiss on the cheek as she snatched the candy from his hand and went to help out her Auntie. Jake touched his cheek in surprise, and followed after.

"My pleasure," he mumbled.

Working together under the truck's headlights they had a meal prepared in short order. They sat and ate, making small talk and small jokes. Aisling didn't ask anything about the Raven or the War she was supposed to be fighting even though she was dying to know more. It just seemed right to take the time to eat and laugh. From the sound of it, she didn't know how much laughter was going to be left once things got started.

I guess it's already begun, she thought.

They finished eating and again worked together to clean up as Martha put a pot of water on the fire for tea.

Matari and Jake had packed everything they'd possibly need into the box of the truck, reasoning that they might as well be comfortable if they were going to start off into the wilderness for who knew how many days. The boys went off a short distance and set up the tents they would be using and put down mats and sleeping bags for everyone. Fortunately they had even remembered flashlights and, even more wondrous, toilet paper!

When things were settled and the teabags had steeped, they all sat down around the fire, warm mugs in their hands. Aisling had decided on hot chocolate to help her feel closer to Eric, hoping her warm thoughts would reach him wherever he was.

We're coming to save you, brother. I promise.

With blankets across their shoulders, they were all settled and cozy. Since it got dark early this time of year there were only a few hours before it was time to sleep and the night was quite cold.

As the conversation slowed to a quiet murmur, Martha got up with a small grunt and threw a few more of the logs onto the fire. Kokum opened the pouch she carried and sprinkled some tobacco over the flames and sat back down.

"What's going on?" Jake asked, leaning away from the smoke.

"I'm going to tell you a story," Kokum replied, "but it is an old story that only a few people know, and even I only know a part of it. You must promise to keep the story between us and tell it to no one else."

"Is it a secret?"

"No, not really. Versions of it are everywhere, but the reason we don't talk about it too much is simply out of respect. Can you agree to this?"

"Yes, of course. Whatever you say. Ma'am"

"Hm."

Kokum then turned.

"Matari, I know you have been taught much of this in your own way, so there will be things in my telling that are different than what you have come to know."

"Right," he nodded in his usual cheery way. Then he turned serious. "But let's remember I'm learning, too, so it'll likely be new for me. I don't even speak my own language so all I know is the English versions. I can feel that something gets lost in the translation."

"As it will here. I'll do my best to illustrate it for all of you."

Aisling saw that she had something in common with Matari. She didn't speak her family's language either. She knew some Cree words here and there, and could understand a few things, but all she had was English, too.

Kokum motioned for them to stand.

"There are some stories about the Raven, the Sun and the Moon. This one is about Father Sky, Mother Earth, Sister Mars and the Moon. Over time, stories blend and change. Everyone has their truth, this is just one of those truths."

She paused.

"Long ago, a dream came. It was a dream of the beginning of all things and it has been passed down for thousands of years. We keep it alive by telling it, and I will tell it to you now. Listen and honour it."

Kokum took a sip of her tea and let the warm liquid run down her throat, soothing and preparing.

Then she began to sing.

And in the song, somehow she began to speak, so there was both music and a story running together, interweaving and transporting their imaginations like nothing they had ever experienced. They left the fire, the night and the woods, and they found themselves floating in a void, the quiet melody shuffling in and out of their hearing like the whisper of wind through new leaves.

"Everything was already here, it was all waiting. Who knows for how long? It was waiting until it decided it was ready. And so there was darkness. One day Everything wanted to see Itself and so out of darkness came light!"

The void split, fragmented into billions of pieces. Everything spread out from them in a rush of stars and galaxies, and then they were rushing too, falling out toward the edge of a lonely spiral of stars until they were looking at a single light in the blackness, spheres of fire circling the yellow star.

"In all of the cold and the fire, new things were forming, coming into being. Mother homes that we call Planets. Father Sky was there in the spaces above and in between. And they were alive. In this spreading out of everything, our place was being made. Our home."

A new sound wove into the music, a slow steady heartbeat, vast and strong, and then another.

"There were two sister planets here and they were born of the Sun. One of them, the eldest that we call Mars, had been fortunate enough to gather two small children to her and they circled her. They were her little moons and they danced, around and around. From her joy, the Eldest Sister produced a womb, land, water, air - a place for life to grow upon her face, and it was the first life."

They watched as the fiery planet slowed and cooled, and there were blue oceans and green forests that contrasted sharply with the red, rusty soil.

"The younger planet was happy for her sister but wished that she had a companion for herself. Father Sky was there and saw her loneliness and also her beauty. He couldn't help but fall in love. He loved her and she was happy. Then one day, in the midst of their affection, Father Sky brought a large rock, a meteor we would call it, from far away. The younger sister took hold of it as well, and together they pulled it into her heart. It struck so hard that a large part of her was torn away. It was something she gave freely. Over time it grew and formed into a beautiful silver ball and they were happy. They had created their very own child and they called it Moon."

They heard a third heartbeat join the other two, smaller, quicker and it made them all smile.

"The younger sister, who now could be called Mother Earth, was happy, and so was Father Sky and they all danced in the slow, steady rhythm of life. Their little Moon was so active and so bright that green things began to grow! There were animals and water and it was so beautiful!"

They group watched in wonder as Kokum showed them the amazing view of a green Moon. It seemed to be all plant life, but they could sense in Kokum's song the undercurrents of hidden streams of water, vast oceans beneath the surface and little creatures pulsing with activity.

"And then came a shadow from out of the big empty darkness between stars," Kokum sang. "He was cold, and maybe it was that cold darkness that birthed him. We will never know. But he was dark and clever and so we call him Raven. And Raven was hungry.

He was drawn to our little corner of the universe by the sound of joy, by the good song of life, and he hungered. He had never had anything, no food, no warmth, no family or friendship. Only cold dead space, and he was filled with that emptiness.

He saw the Moon, small and fragile and filled with the light of life, and he had never been more hungry! Just looking at all the happiness, all the light and life, it made him crazy with desire. But he saw also how strong Father Sky was, how powerfully Mother Earth was spinning around the Sun.

So he made a plan.

"'What a beautiful child you have,' he said to Father Sky, 'so healthy and strong.'

Father Sky was pleased by the words of the stranger.

"'Might I come closer and admire your Moon?'

Mother Earth and Father Sky thought that would be fine, and bursting with pride they watched as the Raven approached.

When Raven drew near he saw that the light from that little Moon was even more beautiful than he had imagined. It almost blinded him the way it shone so bright. And he hungered.

Carefully, he reached out with his claws. Slowly, he dug deeper and deeper. Stealthily, he began to feast. He ate, and he ate, stealing the inner light of the Moon, gorging on the glow of the sweet, defenseless, beloved child. He was filling himself with all the promise of what might have been. He stole and he stole until there was not one glimmer of life that stirred anywhere in the poor, dead little Moon.

And still, he hungered.

Aisling could feel tears on her face. She heard the quick, happy heartbeat fade and then stop completely. She wanted to help, but there was nothing she could do. She was watching ancient history. Instead, she let herself be taken again by the song and words of the story.

The elder sister, she cried out in sorrow, 'What has happened? Where is the Life Song of my sister's child?'

The Raven, wrapped in blackness and with pity in his voice, came to her in reply and said, 'Father Sky did it! He said he was hungry and I saw him eat!'

That is how cunning that Raven was.

Elder Sister was easily angered and she struck out at Father Sky and they fought, and the disharmony destroyed the music they all shared. Mother Earth looked at her lifeless child and wept in despair.

Raven watched all the chaos he'd caused and his evil heart was happy. This was also part of his plan. You see, the Elder Sister was so bright and much too strong for him. He watched the terrible fighting and saw how the battle was causing the red planet to lose strength. And yet her light remained beautiful and tempting. At last, Father Sky ran away from the fight. When he returned to Mother Earth he learned that his sweet little Moon was dead.

Elder Sister was tired from the fight. She longed to rest and to sleep but worried for the life she had grown. The fighting had ripped up her land and boiled her water. It was all chaos and she was so weak.

Raven came again and he whispered in her ear, 'Sleep, lovely Mother, sleep. I will watch over you and the life you've made. I will protect you from Father Sky. See how I close your wounds with my hands?

Raven dug into her with his talons, stopping up the damage. And Elder Sister believed, and was tricked into sleep.

Carefully, Raven grasped tighter to her wounds with his claws. Slowly, he dug deeper, opened wider and made deeper passages inside her. Stealthily, he began to have his feast. He ate and he ate and it was the sweetest thing he'd ever had, even better than the Moon. Nothing had ever tasted so good. This light was so much brighter, so golden, it filled him with fire, and on he ate and deeper Elder Sister slept. Raven gorged himself and still he went on, following the pathways of the light, pulling out every strand until he knew Elder Sister would never wake up again.

And still he hungered.

But something started to happen. The ancient fire of Elder Sister still burned, but now it burned inside Raven. He grew hotter and fiercer and soon he was on fire and screaming in anger and rage. He flew away from the feast, a flame streaking across the blackness back out into the cold emptiness beyond.

Looking up from their mourning, Mother Earth and Father Sky tried to wake Elder Sister but she would not rise. She slept and slept, and still she sleeps to this very day, a Red Star circled by her sad and lonely moons. The colour of blood and war.

Father Sky and Mother Earth were lonely. So they sang about their love and their loneliness, of their hopes and of their loss and Mother Earth made her own womb and carefully raised new life within it, close to her heart so she could always protect it. Father Sky built a barrier around her and filled it with clouds and rings of glowing, dancing light, green and purple, filling the skies at night.

The Earth was changing as they watched. It went from a dull brown and grey to a vast blue ocean surrounding a huge mass of land. It was amazing to watch as the land split apart, starting to look more like the continents with which they were familiar.

Then one terrible day, a meteor from the cold void streaked across the sky. Defying all chance, it broke through Father Sky's shield and hit Mother Earth, spreading flame all around her.

So many died, and there were very few that survived. Only the smallest creatures, the tiniest specks of light, made it through the fire. But they spread out and got stronger and one day they started singing!

It was a miracle - for the first time in ages new songs appeared. New songs and new singers. Their hearts were the drumbeat and their lives were the song. It was us, it was The People. The music was so strong and the light grew so bright that something that had been sleeping was disturbed. From out of the fireball that hit the Earth and almost killed everything on it awoke a Stranger.

That old Raven had returned. And he hungered."

Kokum's story faded out quietly on the wind and she looked up to the stars. Aisling followed her gaze and she knew that she would never look at the night sky in the same way again.

Chapter 18 - Eric

He was crying.

He hated crying. He hated the empty, weak feeling that filled him and spilled from him, spreading out and surrounding him in its lake of sadness. It was in these moments, when anger and coldness abandoned him that he questioned what he was doing. He kept seeing the policeman's eyes, dull and uncomprehending, gazing out at him like a trapped, wounded animal. And he had just left him there. To die from exposure, to be torn apart by scavengers.

At the time it seemed like the logical thing to do, the sensible course of action. Now, in the dark cold of the night, huddled in his sleeping bag, he felt the weight of it pressing against his chest making it impossible to breathe. He wanted to die, to escape from his own actions. He knew what some of the kids on the Rez did when it got to be too hard, when the abuse was just too much to take. He'd seen them do it. He'd tried it himself. He dug in his pocket where he'd hidden the Super Glue they'd bought at their last stop. It was supposed to be handy for fixing things that ripped or broke but tonight he was going to use it to keep himself together.

He opened the lid and put a couple drops of glue in a paper bag and breathed in the fumes. It hit him instantly, a dizzy, achy feeling that knocked the thoughts out of his head like a sledgehammer. He would have thrown up if he had the ability to move but he was knocked flat.

He stared up into the cold stars, seeking the blackness between the points of light that drove into his eyes like shards of glass. Only in the darkness could he find any kind of peace. The tears dried on his face and his breath steamed out of him like an escaping spirit. His right hand was clenched but now it relaxed. The stone he held remained cradled in his fingers. He had held onto that rock almost constantly since striking the policeman with it.

His thoughts spread out around him, replacing his sad lake with crystals of memory, shattered and disjointed. He was back on the school grounds, the first day of school. The sun was bright and the weather too warm for the jacket he was wearing. Classes were ending and kids were everywhere, waiting to get picked up either by parents or the bus. Those that lived in town were making plans to stop by the convenience store on their way home, or talking about joining track club, or chess club or ditching any extra school at all so they could get home and play video games.

Eric's dreaming eye split and he rose up in the air, above himself. He saw how awkward he looked, so skinny and nervous. He was shorter than most of the girls. Not that it mattered. He was too afraid to talk to any of them anyway. His dreaming eye looked around, seeing everything in perfect, crystalline detail. There was Tommy and his buddies, and just the sight of them gave Eric a jolt of fear and then a moment of satisfaction as he pictured Tommy lying face down in the leaves, himself standing tall above him.

There was a strange shadow around Tommy, and as Eric's dreaming eye zoomed in he saw the shadow was a bird, a raven, and it was as tall as a person. It said something to Tommy and Tommy stopped, looked around and said something back. This confused Eric and he concentrated harder. This must be a dream, nothing more, but it seemed so real. He concentrated harder and for a moment the raven swirled like smoke blown about by a soft breeze. Underneath the shadow was a person. The person was whispering in Tommy's ear and pointing at the skinny, gangly, lonely kid sitting in the trampled grass by the road, alone and silent.

Eric knew that face in the shadow and the shock of it knocked him out of his dream and back into the cold night. The buzz had worn off and his face was icy cold. His head was pounding with pain and his nose was bleeding. He crawled out of his sleeping bag, shivering in the night. The sky was now overcast and the first flakes of snow were falling silently from the black clouds.

He made his way to the backpacks, pulled out his sketchpad and flicked through it until he reached his drawings of Cor. He almost screamed when he looked at the pages. Instead of the boy who he thought was his friend were renderings of a large black raven, eyes glinting, even off the page and in the night's darkness. Eric dropped the book, eyes wide with fright and betrayal. He looked at the tent where the boy was sleeping. Eric had wanted to sleep under the stars tonight, instead of safe and warm beside Cor. He had wanted to make sense of the evil things he had been doing, to see if there was a way to go back home.

He was shivering with cold and fear. He knew he would never go home again, just as he knew he wasn't safe anymore and never would be.

He approached the shelter and carefully, so carefully, reached out to pull down the zipper. A tooth at a time so as not to awaken the sleeper within, he pulled the tab down inch by inch until he had space to look inside. He brought his eye to the opening, to spy out his companion.

He gasped.

The tent was empty.

Eric whirled around, stone held above his head to strike whoever was behind him. There was no one there.

He heard a rustle in the air above him. He looked up and saw a great raven nestled among the branches of the tree they'd camped beside. Eric scrambled back, falling on the damp, cold earth. He pushed himself backward, never taking his eyes of the terrifying creature sitting so still and silent in the shadows.

The bird rose up and spread its wings, easily wider than ten feet. It flew straight toward Eric, claws extended, craw widening, wings throwing brack and bramble and grains of earth and sand into Eric's face in the backdraft of its landing. Eric watched as great chunks of dirt were thrown up by the raven's claws as it dug in for grip and balance. The bird straightened and wrapped its wings around itself like a heavy cloak, shaking off the small debris caught in its feathers.

In a shimmering of mist it disappeared, and Cor stood in its place, his face unsmiling, his eyes locked onto Eric's.

"So now you know. Took you long enough."

Eric stared in shock, his mouth opening and closing, unable to say a word, his face smeared from his bloody nose, bits of dirt stuck to the cooling mess. He was crying again. Weak again, and utterly alone.

He began wailing. Crying like the lost child he was, crying for a future that was lost to him as well. In that moment he saw that he would never have a normal happiness again. He would never have the warmth and comfort of a family, would never meet a girl, or go to school or do any of the things a normal person did.

"I don't know what my father was talking about," said Cor. "For a while there, after the cop, I thought you might be strong but look at you, weak as a baby and crying like one, too."

Eric's cries settled into gasps of air, each one painful and wrenching, but he could talk.

"How? Why? Cor, I thought we were friends."

Cor looked ashamed for a moment, but then the disgust returned to his face.

"Kid, I can't be anyone's friend. I have to do what my father tells me, I don't have a choice."

"Who - what are you?"

"Dammit, kid. Stop worrying about me. You know what I'm supposed to do if you don't work out? I'm supposed to kill you. Rip out your guts and leave you in the woods."

"They'd know. People have seen you with me."

"No one's seen me, at least that they'll remember. I'm a shadow, kid. And now I have to kill you."

He spread his arms out and in the smoke that spread out from him, grew the raven again, stepping out of the shadow, pointed beak glinting in the pale wintry light. He pulled his neck back and up, one eye locked onto Eric, ready for the downward strike. It came like lightning and would have punched through Eric's stomach had it hit.

Eric saw the beak coming toward him. Just like the day he stood up to Tommy, everything in his vision slowed. He gripped the stone in his hand and raised it in front of him. He dug into the cold, wet ground, made soft by the falling snow until he touched something warm. He didn't know what it was but somehow he knew it would be there. It felt softer than water and as soon as he touched it, it began flowing up his arm, through his chest and into the stone. As soon as it touched the stone, however, it shrank back and tried to retreat, to flow back the way it came but Eric held on to it, forced it back into the rock in his hand, tearing it up from the ground by force.

The flow changed from a warm, cool white to deep, purplish red, glowing like pain. It filled the stone and mixed with the blood that had seeped in from Tommy, the police officer, from Eric himself. It mixed and grew brighter.

The beak drew closer and Eric lifted the stone to meet it. He watched as they made contact. A shockwave and explosion of light threw Eric down flat on the ground and the luminance blinded him, as if he'd looked into the sun.

He caught his breath and stood up, feeling for the trunk of a tree to support him. Everything was still in blackness and his eyes were filled with the aftereffects of the incredible and sudden glare. He heard a harsh, laboured breathing and knew it wasn't his own. He stood still, waiting for his vision to return to normal. He tried to make sense of what happened but it was all just a terrible nightmare that he couldn't seem to shake.

Finally, he could make out light and shadow, and he saw a black mound a few feet in front of him. He went over and using his foot, turned the heap over. He was hoping it wasn't the bird but Cor he would see, but almost changed his mind when the older boy was revealed. There was a wide gash across his face, stretching from his chin up across his eye and past his forehead, into the black, matted hair. It wasn't bleeding, but it looked raw. Eric could see that the boy's eye was completely destroyed.

The other eye, however, was not, and It was looking directly up at Eric.

"Finish it," Cor croaked.

Eric had to admit that when the light struck Cor, a part of him wanted to kill the boy. He had been so completely full of power that he felt it was the only right thing to do, to destroy his betrayer. That whispering anger and that feeling of power stayed with him. He didn't feel like crying anymore. Not now, not ever. In the brief moments of this night he glimpsed something bigger than he had imagined, much bigger than a self-pitying child's whining about having a normal life.

Something ancient and old had whispered to him from the stone, that showed him the joy of being able to protect himself, of being able to take what he wanted without fear. Eric had been about to die and something had awoken inside of him, some ability to steal strength from the earth and make it his own. Now that he knew about this ability he had, not only was there no going back, he never wanted to go back.

"I could," he said to Cor. "Now that I know how, I could crush you to a pulp, but I'm not going to."

"Why?"

"I'm going to use you. We're still going on our little trip. But you're going to tell me everything."

"What makes you think I'll do that? You're a kid, a snot-nosed kid with a toy. As long as you have that rock you have some power, but the instant you put it down you're nothing. Get out of here, go back home. Just kill me now. If you don't, my father will, anyway."

And with that Cor shut his eyes and turned his head, ready to die.

Eric stood over him, considering what he'd said. Anytime a little doubt worked its way into him, he killed it with the red light that still flowed inside him.

He dropped the rock and Cor opened his eyes at the sound.

"What are you doing?"

"Shut up," Eric said, and he knelt down. He dug into the soil again until he felt that flow. This one wasn't as strong but he hoped it would do. He had an idea of how this could work but without the stone he didn't know if it would.

He closed his eyes and tore the struggling light up from its roots, building it up inside his chest, then he opened his eyes and reached out to Cor's wound. As he touched it with the tip of his finger he let the light trickle down his arm and into the cut, picturing it healed. He traced upward and the light faltered as Eric saw the gash closing up under his touch. He refocused and continued the work. It wasn't the same without the stone. He didn't feel the same power and it was like something was being pulled out of him.

The job was finished and Eric slumped over, completely exhausted. He wanted to sleep and he was starving, with an incredible, empty hunger.

Cor's face was still a mess, but at least it wasn't hanging open. There was an evil scar where the wound had been and Eric hadn't been able to fix the eye. It was an empty place, a sunken pocket of scar tissue.

"The pain is gone, what did you - " Cor raised his hand to his face. His fingers felt along the newly closed scar, gingerly touching the empty socket.

"What makes you think I'm not still going to kill -" Cor never finished his threat. Eric had knocked him unconscious.

Eric pushed himself back and sat against a tree trunk. He was empty, tired, and ravenous. He rested for a while then got up to grab some food and a blanket.

He had a lot to think about and it was going to be a long night.

He ate and drank as much as he could handle.

And still he hungered.

Chapter 19 - Aisling

Spent by the day's exertions and the effort of her singing, Kokum had quickly retired to her tent for the night, and Martha grunted as she stooped down and crawled through the narrow tent door to join her. But Aisling was too excited by all she had seen and heard to sleep. She sat by the fire, shivering with the combined cold and excitement, and Jake sidled up beside her and put an arm around her shoulder.

He was pleased that she accepted the gesture and didn't try to pull back or brush him away.

Aisling was preoccupied. She looked across the fire at Matari, who also sat awake. She saw the dance of orange light and shadow play across his features, his heavy brow encircled with curls.

"Matari," she said, breaking the silence. Matari's red-rimmed eyes looked up from the fire to hers. She could see the warmth and kindness reflected in them, and for the first time her antagonism for this seeming interloper eased.

"How did you meet my grandmother?"

Matari gave a small, gentle smile as he considered the question.

"The Dreamtime," he said.

"You mean you met in your dreams, like when you were asleep?" Jake asked, incredulous.

"Close enough," Matari replied, "It's a place we go. It goes on from there, but that's a start. We only learn the truth of things in our Dreaming."

"You mean, like, in your sleep?" Jake repeated.

Matari smiled and nodded. "Sometimes that, too."

Jake let out a breath of exasperation. "Do you have to be so mysterious?"

"Yes."

"Why?"

"It makes me more attractive to women. Right, Ais?" He flashed a big grin.

"You should just answer the questions," Aisling said, smiling but earnest. "I really want to know why you are here."

Jake gave Matari a dirty look but said nothing.

Matari sighed and turned serious.

"Well," he began, "my family has something like the same gift as yours. Every year, our family and many others gather in the outback near Ayer's Rock - or Uluru, that's the real name - for the Dreamtime, and we share songs a lot like the one your Gran just sang for you. Our family always has the strongest dreams. The forms, the animals are different - the Raven is a Vulture or a Shadow in our telling - but the tales, the visions are near the same. After all, the danger's the same for all of us, unna?

"So about a year-and-a-half ago, my family is camped out for the Dreaming, and in the heat and the dust, we see this old woman coming near. She came with a big, floppy hat and sunglasses and a bag and a canteen and she was covered in dust, and when she took her hat off, we could see she wasn't one of us, but she wasn't one of the white ones neither. It was your Kokum.

"We invited her to sit with us and rest and eat, and she began to tell us her reasons for being there. Her dreams, she said, had told her to seek out others with the gift who could help her reveal the Raven and stop him. She said she had been travelling the world for years, following her dreams, and that they had led her to us. And we knew she spoke the truth."

Matari pulled up a piece of dry grass at his feet and began turning it in his hands as he thought back to the past. The fire crackled and snapped, and he spoke again.

"So your Gran, she stayed with us for about two weeks, took part in the Dreamtime," Matari said. "And we took a special interest in each other and spent a lot of time talking, and I helped look after her while she was there. She was actually quite tired from all her travelling. It was a long journey, she said, that had brought her to me."

"To you?" Jake said.

"Yeah, mate. Since I was small, my dreams have always been strong. I had this ability to see and know things that were hidden to others. It's hard to explain but it's kind of like sensing wind currents…change." He shrugged and smiled. "Well, one day, Gran says she wants me to go with her, that she needs me to come with her.

"And I believed in her and have been with her every day since."

Aisling listened to Matari's tale with rapt attention. Kokum had mentioned that Matari was going to help her understand all this and now she knew it was for her dreams. But suddenly Auntie Martha's voice boomed out from her tent. She must have been listening the whole time.

"Stop all of your talking and get to sleep, all of you," she called out. "We'll want to start early tomorrow."

Matari grinned and left the dim circle of firelight.

Aisling and Jake sat quietly together, staring into the dying fire, and Aisling suddenly became aware of the weight of his arm around her shoulder, his closeness to her. She felt herself blush in the darkness.

"So," she whispered, breaking a silence that had suddenly become awkward. "What do you think of my family so far?"

"You're all nuts," Jake said. "I love it. Here we are looking for your brother and I get to eat neckbones, see some cool magic and hear some kind of top secret story. Can't wait for tomorrow!"

She pushed him away playfully, wished him a good night, and followed her Auntie and Kokum to bed.

Once she settled into her sleeping bag, she lie awake for a while, listening to the soft snoring of the older women. She thought about Eric and hoped he was sleeping safe. The far away feeling she got at the campfire was still with her and everything was quiet save for the rush of wind through empty tree branches high above. Before she knew it, she was asleep.

- Save me.

That's the plan, but honestly, you've got to come up with a better opening line.

- You hear me.

I do. And I know your story. I'm so sorry about the Moon, about your child.

- Do not grieve. All things pass.

Aisling thought about that for a moment.

You mean everything will die?

- That is one way to see it. All things change. Everything will transform, my daughter.

Surrounded by the warm, soft light, Aisling found it difficult to think about anything ending. To her, death was a never ending darkness.

The light began to move, to shrink. She spoke out

What's wrong?

- Worry not. I am coming closer. Now that I have found you there is no need to cast out so far.

The light got smaller, more intimate and Aisling was delighted by what she saw. There, swimming in soft, dim, glowing currents was a giant turtle made completely of light. The turtle - Mother Earth - swam toward her, eyes full of ancient love and wisdom, yet young and full of exuberance.

You're beautiful!

- As are you my daughter. Come, swim with me.

I can't. I don't know how.

- It's simple, just follow me.

And the giant turtle turned and began weaving her way through the surrounding currents, gliding gracefully and effortlessly.

Aisling tried to jump into the flow but rolled head over heels, disoriented and thrashing her limbs.

- Softly.

She heard the call in the growing distance.

- Softly, and follow me.

She relaxed and closed her eyes, picturing herself in a pool, swimming through clear waters. When she opened her eyes again she was flowing along in the wake of the Turtle. She tried catching up and shot forward like a bird in flight.

Wow! This is amazing.

- I wanted to share this with you. How do you feel?

I feel so … awesome. Sorry, I don't know how else to describe it.

She felt almost overpowered by the feeling of love and amusement directed toward her.

- It is … awesome, isn't it? This place is where all songs join together. This is all the Life we share.

You mean, I'm swimming through people?

- You are traveling along their music, along the threads of their song. All Life is here, all growing things. Even the rocks, the dust, the water, and fire.

Why can't I hear it?

- Still your thoughts and you will feel it. You do not have your ears in this place, only your heart.

Aisling tried to listen with her heart and thought she caught an echo of something, but whatever she was supposed to be feeling escaped her. Instead she swam lazily around the avatar of Mother Earth.

I really can't feel it like that. I wish I could.

- In time …. In time …. If we have the time.

Aisling was silent at that. Then she asked:

What am I supposed to do to help?

- Stop the ending of the songs. He is abroad upon the land. He walks

across my face, my body. He digs and poisons. He is ending life, ending the songs. He must be stopped before we are all silenced in order to feed his empty soul. He can never be filled and yet he tries. He weakens me. He weakens me.

What do I do? Where do I go?

- You will know. Now that you have traced these currents with me, you will know. I am so happy to have you, my strong and lovely daughter. Go now and rest. I must leave, but I leave you my blessing.

The turtle reached out and touched Aisling's hair, pure energy flowing into her.

And she passed out of dream and into deep, restful sleep.

She awoke before dawn. The camp was still and silent. She got up and stoked the embers of the fire Matari had carefully banked, reigniting the little flame with some kindling and soft puffs of air from her pursed lips. She set water to boil and went about preparing breakfast.

Curious, she closed her eyes and tried to trace the veins she saw last night and there they were, pulsing with a steady, slow beat. It was almost disappointing, how easy it was once she knew how to look. She imagined it was something that should have taken her years of hard work and intense concentration but there it was, right in front of her.

Not everything has to be some kind of struggle, I guess.

She was cheered by the thought. As if in answer, the sky began to brighten with a rosy glow, like the flushed cheeks she got in winter when the cold wind blew. Small bird song slowly filled the air, ignited by the promise of the rising sun. She heard rustling in the tents and so she dished out scrambled eggs and bacon. Fruit slices on the side with the toast she had tried not to burn but burnt it certainly was.

Hey, not everything can be perfect.

"What is that delicious smell?" Matari's voice carried through the thin fabric.

"A hero's breakfast. Up and at 'em, all you sleepyheads. Everything's ready and there's coffee and tea."

"Wow, talk about going bush. Not exactly a feral breaky but I'll eat it."

It didn't take long after that for bodies to start pouring out of warm tents into the cold morning air, frosty grass instantly soaking pant hems.

"Mmm, smells so goo-"

There was an abrupt silence. Matari stopped in his tracks, staring at Aisling. Self-conscious, she wondered if she had something on her face.

"Aisling, what happened?"

"Nothing happened. What's wrong?"

She heard a gasp and turned around.

"Mother, look," Martha said, standing aside so Kokum could get a clear view of Aisling. Kokum stepped closer, as if unsure of what she was seeing.

"What? What is it?" Aisling asked.

Kokum smiled broadly, her eyes full of tears.

"You are truly blessed child, come with me."

She led Aisling to Jake's truck and turned the side mirror toward her granddaughter.

"Ho-lay!"

Aisling's hair was no longer just her natural jet black. From both her temples - glowing in the predawn light like soft, warm currents of energy - flowed pure white hair.

Chapter 20 - Eric

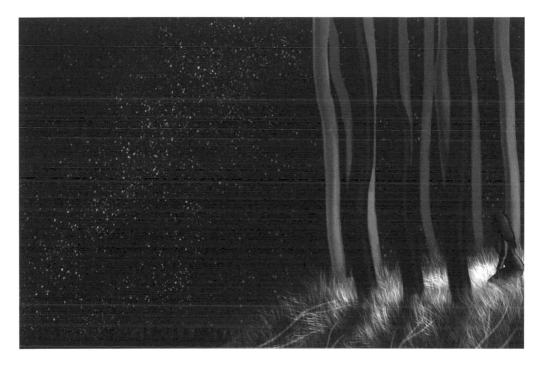

The stone needed blood. That's the first thing he learned. It didn't matter whose blood it was so he fed it rabbit, and when there was no rabbit, his own.

"Don't you think you should let up a little? You're pale as a ghost as it is. Plus it's pretty disgusting to watch you poke holes in yourself every night."

Eric glanced up at Cor who was skinning their latest catch.

"Save some of that for me then."

Cor shook his head, "Whatever, buddy. It's all yours," he tossed the body over and stood up.

"Don't go too far," Eric warned.

Cor just shot him a nasty look and stalked away into the bush. It didn't matter. Eric knew where he was. Ever since he'd healed Cor's face he could feel the older boy. It came in handy the morning after their fight. Eric had fallen asleep despite his intention to keep watch and Cor had snuck away while he dozed. He hadn't gone far so Eric raced after him, catching up about ten minutes into the chase.

"Going somewhere … friend?"

Cor nearly jumped out of his skin. That would've been a trick Eric wouldn't have minded seeing if it meant a giant raven came tearing out of it.

On second thought, maybe not.

"Geez, kid! Don't you know it's not nice to sneak up on someone? How'd you get to me so fast?"

"That's my business. You weren't planning to leave a defenseless little kid alone in the woods were you?"

"Defenseless, my butt. I don't know what it was that happened last night, but I do know I've got brains enough to get as far away from it as possible. You're dangerous, Uhhr. Too dangerous."

Eric didn't feel dangerous. With everything that had happened he was scared out of his wits himself. He could scarcely believe it, until he looked at Cor's face, which now only had one eye and was half-consumed by a red, angry, puckered scar.

"I healed you didn't I?" Eric said, as much to reassure himself as Cor that he wasn't a monster.

"Yeah, thanks. Great job, by the way. I always wanted to have a shot at being the Phantom of the Opera."

"You don't have to be sarcastic about it."

Cor looked up into the sky, as if entreating the heavens.

"You're the one who screwed up my face to begin with, remember?"

"Me? I was just protecting myself. You're the one who was going to pull my guts out."

Cor scratched the back of his head, squinting into the distance.

"Yeah, well, there is that."

They both stood still with the trees, neither of them sure what to say next.

"Well, anyway, you can't go. You need to take me to your father like you planned."

"I don't *need* to do anything. I'm out. I'm running, Uhhr, and if you were smart you'd do the same. On one hand I've got Boy Wonder here who can apparently blast fire, on the other, well, let's just say I'm a lot more scared of my Dad than I am of you and when he finds out what's happened I'm toast."

"Won't you be in bigger trouble if you don't bring me back to him?"

Cor scowled.

"I was supposed to bring you as my friend, a piece of silly putty, trusting and corrupted. Not … this. And why would you want to go anyway? The idea was to use you for something, some big plans or whatever. You're getting a free pass here, kid. Be smart. Take it."

"Somehow I don't think you've got my best interests in mind. I know you're the one who put Tommy on me. You were messing with me from the start, Cor, I see it all now. And you know what? I'm tired of people making decisions for me and hurting me, controlling me. I'm not weak anymore. Now I'm making the decisions."

Cor began a slow, lazy clap.

"Nice speech! Did it take you all morning to work that out? Do what you want, Eric. I'm gone."

Cor turned away from Eric and continued down the muddy game trail.

"Stop! Come back!"

A hand wave and Cor was out of sight, the trail dipping down into a shallow valley.

Eric closed his eyes and felt for Cor with his mind. It was easy. All he had to do was find the ribbons of light he'd discovered. He pictured Cor and in his mind's eye he was racing down the path until he saw the shadow of the boy. He glided up behind him, examining the shadow. There was a small streamer of light dangling from the head, the place where Eric had injured him and then healed the damage. Carefully he pinched the little glowing string between his thumb and forefinger, giving it a sharp tug.

"Oww!!" he heard from the distance.

A half-smile on his lips, Eric held his concentration. He kept pulling and he saw to his satisfaction the shadow forced to turn around, following the pain in his head. Soon enough, Cor was climbing the gentle rise and when Eric opened his eyes he saw his companion coming toward him, his face contorted in rage.

"You asshole! That hurts! How did you DO that?"

"Heap big medicine," Eric intoned.

"What the hell?"

"Take me to your leader."

Cor said something nasty under his breath.

"Whatever, man, you win. Don't say I never gave you a chance to avoid your own funeral."

"Thanks, Cor. You're a real pal."

"Now who's getting sarcastic? Come on, kid. Let's go get our stuff and then we'll hop right back onto the old yellow brick road."

"Wait. I want to know what these plans are. Why me?"

"'Why me?' Really? Not the most original question, is it? Why anything? You think I know the answers? I just do what I'm told, man. Life's easier that way."

They went back, struck camp and travelled on for one, two, three more days, the tension growing steadily between them each day. Cor had tried to escape twice more and twice more Eric had eventually found him and dragged him back. It was last night that he had shadowed himself into a raven. It was hours before

Eric figured it out. At first he despaired of finding the fugitive. He had been searching the bright rivers in his mind's eye, but he hadn't bothered to check the sky.

It's all in the earth, there's nothing up there, right?

Or was there? If Cor had never tried to run, Eric would probably never have noticed it but there was something up there. Whatever it was moved like wind currents and was very very faint. Every time he tried to follow it, however, the currents would collapse and spread away like so much smoke.

Eric had to breathe softer, quieter and instead of tearing at the sky he snuck up into the eddies and flowing streamers. It was like sneaking into someone's house while they were still at home. One wrong move and they would wake up and it would all fall apart. Stealthily, he began tracing the barely glowing air currents until he found Cor, far away, almost undetectable. If he'd gotten any further Eric would have lost him for sure.

He grabbed at the trailing light and yanked hard, grinning in satisfaction as the shadow bird became a thrashing mess.

It took hours of concentration, by the end of which Eric had a pounding headache and needed sleep more than he had ever needed anything in his life. But Cor was back, muttering and kicking at the pebbles of the small river bank on which they'd camped down for the night.

"Don't do that again or I'll really have to hurt you, Cor. And don't try to kill me in my sleep. I'll know if you're planning something."

He tapped his forehead meaningfully. It was a bluff. He couldn't actually read Cor's mind but it would keep him guessing while Eric got some much needed rest. He slept immediately.

The next day, they continued on. Eric hiked along, mulling over a theory he was fleshing out. He wasn't sure about it yet and he knew he couldn't check it with Cor unless he did it in a roundabout way. Not only because they weren't exactly friends anymore but because Eric didn't think he could trust anything Cor had to say. He would try, though, because for once Eric thought he might have figured something out for himself and seen through lies and half-truths. For once he was going to be the one acting instead of reacting.

He was going to get his revenge.

"What's happened to me!"

She was shaking from the shock. She didn't feel blessed at all, she felt violated.

"You have been given a gift. It is a mark of favour that hasn't been seen in generations, not since the days of the buffalo."

"I don't want it! What's next, leopard-print skin? I look like the Bride of Frankenstein!" Aisling looked again in the mirror, but knowing full well she would just see the same thing. She fought back tears, "Why did she have to go and touch me?"

Martha stood up straight and Kokum tensed.

"Who? Who touched you?" her grandmother asked.

"The turtle. Um, Mother Earth, I guess. Wait a minute, I thought you knew about that, about my dreams."

"You dream of Mother Earth?"

"Well, yeah. I thought that's one of the things you wanted me to learn about, isn't it?"

Martha and Georgia exchanged a long, serious look.

"Aisling, how long have you been seeing her in your dreams?"

"I don't know, since a few days before Dad … well, before Dad died."

Martha was just shaking her head. "Amazing," she whispered.

"My dear," Kokum said, "you really are full of surprises. You're so much more than we ever could have hoped. Maybe we will have a chance after all."

"Kokum, please don't talk like that. I'm trying to keep up with everything, but please don't put that 'save the world' weight on me. I'm just Aisling. I'm just me. I'm no hero. Heroine? Whatever - you know what I mean."

Kokum simply reached out and touched the side of Aisling's hair, drawing the white tresses through her cracked, ancient fingers.

"We shall see."

"Hey! Nice look! Is that what all the noise is about?"

Jake was just crawling out of his tent, pulling his jacket on, the early morning sunlight breaking through the trees. He followed his nose, grabbing a few pieces of bacon before coming up to the small group.

"Look like you've seen a ghost, Matari. Uh, Ais? Why is everyone so worked up about your new hairstyle?" Jake looked around at everyone with confusion, "Is it against your culture or something to dye your hair?"

Aisling couldn't help but laugh, and with the sound, everyone relaxed and shared in the gentle release.

"What did I … ?"

She stood up and embraced Jake gratefully.

"Thank you."

"For what? Don't get me wrong, I'm glad you're happy, but - you know what? I'm just going to shut up and let you hug me."

"Smart boy." She gave him another squeeze. "Are you hungry? I made more than just bacon.

"Thanks. Maybe I'll have some of that charcoal. What do you call it? Toast?"

After breakfast they packed up what they could carry and broke camp. Jake said a sad farewell to his truck as the path they were following went deeper into the bush.

The day passed with very little talk as Matari set a quick pace. The women were breathing hard when they stopped for a rest, and Aisling found herself exhausted as well. She wasn't used to carrying so much weight on her back. It made her appreciate her ancestors and what they must have gone through as just a normal part of their lives.

We've gotten so weak, she thought. *I'm crying about my hair and I'm depressed about breaking every other nail. Some warrior.*

She examined her cracked fingernails and decided to trim them short that evening.

"Kokum, do you have nail trimmers?"

Her grandmother nodded, still catching her breath. Aisling couldn't imagine how hard all this walking must be on the woman's worn body. She looked at her Auntie, who just shook her head, guessing at Aisling's thoughts.

"We can't slow down, niece. We've been through worse. Besides, I could stand to lose a few pounds. It's been affecting my modelling career." She jiggled the fat on her belly with her hands.

Jake and Matari returned at that moment from scouting the area. Matari held up some wire.

"They stopped not far from here. They're catching small game with these snares. Does Eric have any training in bushcraft?"

"Well, he's gone camping a bit," Aisling said. "But no, nothing like that. We always packed our own food."

"His companion was very prepared to spend a long time out here. I think I know the general direction they'll be heading from here on. If what we guess is correct," he said, directing his comments to Kokum, "we can continue to track them, or we can take a risk and jump ahead. Try to cut them off."

Kokum nodded and looked at her daughter.

"How does it feel to you?"

Martha stood up and inhaled deeply, reaching up into the sky and letting her arms fall slowly to her sides.

"I sense danger on the path ahead, mother. But I get the feeling that if we stop following this trail something even worse lies in wait."

Kokum glanced up at Matari. He nodded his head, his great pile of soft, sun-bleached curls bobbing along, back and forth.

"Good enough for me. To be honest, I feel uneasy, as if we're being watched." He glanced about, his brow furrowed with concern. "If you're ready to keep hiking we're going to have to push hard to make up for lost time."

"Lost time..." Kokum said softly so only Aisling could hear. Then louder, "Yes, let's continue. I'm still strong but arthritis is catching up to me. I'll be okay," she patted her granddaughter's shoulder as she stood.

The sun had already set as they walked across a large, uneven meadow filled with dead, desiccated flowers and an annoyingly large amount of nettles, thistles, and spiky dandelion leaves.

But Aisling loved this time of day. The gloaming hour, her father had called it. All the colours were soft and muted and the world looked full of magic. She felt a pang of sorrow thinking of her father. She remembered the time he had stuck all those plastic, glow-in-the-dark stars to her bedroom ceiling. She had been so excited. Thinking about it made her feel closer to him.

As she walked, she watched the sky, looking for the evening's first star to appear, but it was still too light for any of them to make a shy appearance. She gazed across the field to the clump of trees a little ways off. There was something strange about it. Something not quite right. Then she noticed what it was. She turned to Jake who was walking a little behind her, the other three off to her right a few meters distant.

"Jake, do you see that?"

"What?"

"Over there, in the trees."

He gave a low whistle.

"That's a lot of birds."

"Yeah? That's what I was thinking. Like … too many birds."

Jake laughed. "You're not worried, are you?"

"I don't know. Maybe."

She angled their path to intersect with the others, each hurried step filling her with a deepening sense of dread.

"Matari, do you see those trees over there?"

He raised his head and quickly motioned for everyone to stop.

The older women paused in their quiet conversation, following the attention of the others. From the trees, like a black, shifting cloud, thousands of black birds took wing, calling out in their raucous, harsh voices. The sheer volume of their cries echoed all around them and the beating of their wings rushed across the field in a sharp, dry rustling and flapping, a hoarse whisper rising to a crescendo.

"Run!"

Matari led them back the way they came, back toward the deeper woods. Aisling stifled a scream of fright as she obeyed, taking her Kokum's arm in her own. She saw Jake do the same with Martha, but the large woman was practically dragging him along with her.

Aisling could feel her ankles being scraped raw by the sharp, thistly needles of the field but her fear was stronger than the pain. She could hear the birds approaching and she couldn't stop herself from sobbing. Her breath was raspy and harsh, her throat closing with fright.

She became aware of a screaming voice and thought it was her own, until she felt Kokum tugging at her, stopping her from running. Was her grandmother crazy? They had to get out of here. Martha's voice cut through the haze of panic she was in.

"Aisling, stop! Stop! Look up!"

She raised her eyes from the ground she had been watching with so much care, being cautious not to trip or step into a sudden dip.

Ahead of them, about fifteen meters away, was the tree line. She was so confused, why were they stopping? They had to get away.

As she watched the trees, her eyes started to pick out something she hadn't noticed. There was a misshapen clump just inside the shadows. It stood on two long, spindly legs that looked almost like trees themselves. It was enormous, at least twelve feet tall. Then the long arms moved slightly. Standing in the shadows - watching them - was a creature that Aisling knew couldn't be a man.

From what she could make out, it was more like a pile of bracken, grass, moss and mud balanced on two poles, head hunched down below the shoulders. There were twigs sticking out everywhere, giving the thing a dangerous look. She felt her vision fading, she was passing out though she tried to stop it. The sound of the birds was closer than before. It wouldn't be long now before they arrived with sharp beaks, and tearing filthy claws. She heard her Kokum's hiss.

"Walking Man! You have no business with us!"

And then the birds attacked.

Chapter 22 - Eric

The baby was crying in the wilderness and he was running, trying to find it. He looked behind trees, under fallen logs, in thick stands of dogwood and dried-up clumps of rushes and cattails.

He searched for hour after hour, over hills, across streams, and always the crying was just a little further ahead. When he stopped to rest he could hear the painful sounds, as if the child was nearby, just out of sight, abandoned and alone. When he stood up to follow it was as if someone picked up the baby and ran ahead, trying to move it out of reach.

Eric awoke in the tent with a start, sweating and disoriented. Eyes wild, he ran out, looking back and forth at the trees, the tall grass. He stopped and listened. Everything was quiet.

"Bad dream?"

Eric tensed up and then willed himself to relax. Cor was sitting up in the lower branches of an old oak tree, munching on some of the dried berries he was always collecting.

"Shut up."

"Well good morning to you, too, buddy. Want some?" he held out a handful of the little fruit.

Eric made no reply, he just walked away to be by himself. He heard Cor chuckling behind him and it filled him with anger.

Why does he have to keep pretending we're friends?

It was exhausting for Eric to have to hold on to his anger and mistrust all the time. He kept forgetting that Cor was his enemy and caught himself time and again on the verge of cracking a joke or sharing some new thought he had. And then he remembered that beak stabbing at him, trying to rip his life out from the roots.

He shuddered at the memory and from the deep chill of the air. It was definitely getting colder every day. Yesterday snow had fallen and hadn't melted, the whole world covered in a soft white powder. It had been blown about into drifts by the night breezes and was piled here and there in small clumps.

The sweat on his clothes gave him a chill, and he stalked back to the tent to put on dry things and his warm jacket.

"We're heading out," he said to Cor after he'd packed up the bags.

"Yessir, boss! Coming, sir!"

Again, Eric made no reply. The landscape was becoming more rugged, more hills to climb, more valleys to navigate. It was challenging just keeping a steady direction and as the morning passed they had to stop and follow a wide creek until they got to a bridge. That alone ate up hours.

Eric couldn't shake the chill of that morning or the sense of anxiety and dread with which he awoke. The low clouds of the day and the grey light were oppressive. It was like walking through a haze. He watched Cor's breath as it puffed into the cold air, blending with the greyness.

It had begun to feel like he and Cor were the only people in the world. Walking, walking, walking every day, all day was their only life. Step after monotonous step was wearing thin and Eric was on edge.

On impulse, he pulled the cold stone out of his pocket and felt some strength returning. Some calm.

He'd been giving the rock fresh blood every night, amazed at how much it could contain. He hadn't filled it up yet and he began to wonder if he actually could. Whatever it was he had learned, and whatever it was this rock did, he knew he shouldn't expect any of it to make sense or follow any rules.

I've got to stop feeding it, he told himself. *I think I'm going crazy.*

Suddenly, he heard the wailing of the baby again, clear and agonizing. He willed himself to ignore it and keep trudging along. It was getting louder, more insistent.

"Do you think we should check that out?" Cor asked.

Eric stumbled, almost falling.

"You can hear that?"

"Of course I can hear it. I'm half-blind not half-deaf."

Eric scanned the trees, trying to pinpoint the location of the pitiful sound.

"Over there," Cor pointed. Deeper into the pine trees, where grey began to give in to black. Eric peered into the shade. There was no underbrush, so the going would be relatively easy, but he hated to leave the wide trail. The cries became panicked, ragged, and Eric made up his mind. He slipped his pack off and stepped off the trail.

"You want me to tag along, or have you got this one?" Cor called.

"Stay there," Eric said. He actually really wanted Cor to come along so he wouldn't have to go alone but he didn't know what was ahead and he didn't trust Cor with what they might see. Eric knew that whatever it was that was out there, it was for him alone.

Inside the pines the wailing seemed to surround him. He wasn't certain of the direction, so he just kept heading directly away from the trail. Old Man's Beard hung from empty, forlorn branches stretching out like aged, brittle fingers, long since dead. His footsteps were muffled in the soft piles of fallen needles, and the forest floor was spongy and yielding. On occasion a root would be jutting out just above the surface and he paid attention to avoid tripping over them.

Just like in his dream, the cries seemed to be fading and he had to resist the urge to break out in chase. Instead, he stopped moving and stood very still. He closed his eyes and listened.

It was silent.

Frustrated, he started back and almost immediately the baby started again. Again Eric stopped and the crying continued, very loud and very close. Taking a tentative step behind himself, and then another, he followed the screams, letting his ears be his guide instead of his eyes. In his dream he had looked everywhere. Now, he would just listen.

As he stepped backward he closed his eyes. Now he was really getting close. The cries couldn't be more than a few meters away now. He shuffled slower through the needles, digging in slightly more with each step into the soft deep layer, the needles piling up behind his heels and up his legs. He was almost to his waist in needles and he was so close he could hear the intake of breath before a new scream began.

Eric kept shuffling along but it was getting more difficult the further he went. The needles were up to his shoulders now and the scent of the evergreens was strong, the sharp smell of turpentine was burning in his nose. His left heel snagged on a root and he was falling backward, into the needles, buried by them. He flailed about with his arms and landed on his back with a soft, whispering thud. He'd expected to be buried in needles, but instead he was lying on top of the soft forest floor.

He sat up and looked around. There was no baby and he was alone. Annoyed he stood up and brushed off his clothes, sweating from the effort. He felt warm and he noted that his breath wasn't even steaming. Birdsong filled the air.

Eric made his way back to the trail, giving up on his search and in a foul mood. He kept sweating so he took off his gloves and pulled off his jacket, bunching them under his arm. That's when it hit him. The air had turned warmer.

A chinook?

As he got nearer the trail a bee buzzed past him. Eric followed the progress of the insect with disbelieving eyes. He ran for the edge of the woods and burst out onto the path.

Cor was gone with all their gear and flowers were blooming under a clear blue sky and a hot, summer sun.

Chapter 23 - Aisling

"Take cover!" Matari yelled.

He took Kokum and Martha by the arms and pulled them into the trees, Aisling and Jake following behind. Aisling could feel warm blood running down the back of her neck even though she had her arms up, trying to protect herself from the pecking and scratching of the birds.

The flapping and screeching followed them, and while the ravens couldn't penetrate the cover in as many numbers, the attack still came. A bird cried out louder than the others, claws extended, coming right toward Aisling. Matari picked up a thick branch and knocked it out of the air.

"You okay?" he yelled over the din.

Aisling nodded and with one last, quick look, Matari turned. He began swinging his club back and forth and Jake, his own improvised bat in hand, followed suit.

Kokum and Auntie Martha were half hidden under a fallen tree, the long trunk providing some cover. And Aisling saw the huge thing Kokum had called Walking Man taking great, stiff legged strides toward them.

Slapping away a raven that was diving for her face, Aisling called out to her Kokum, pointing at the approaching giant but her grandmother couldn't hear her over the croaking, cawing screams. The creature slowly bent over, forming a mound. It was covered with hundreds of sharp, projecting twigs. Martha frantically motioned for Aisling to get down as she tackled the boys, knocking them to the ground. Wide-eyed, Aisling obeyed. As she lay down, she heard a sharp whistling sound all around her, and suddenly there were birds falling dead to the ground on all sides. Aisling looked up and saw the depleted flock wheel away, retreating into the falling darkness of the night.

She sat up and took stock of herself. Blood ran from various cuts and scrapes. Her left hand had a small chunk of flesh torn off on the side of her little finger and her ankles were torn from the run through the field. A thistle was caught in her skin and she plucked it out. The mound that was the Walking Man was just that, a mound. With no sticks or twigs poking out of it, it looked less frightening. The giant man rose back to standing position and Aisling saw that most of the dead ravens that littered the ground around them were pierced by the sharp sticks that had once covered him.

Like a porcupine.

Kokum was the first to speak as everyone rose, shock and fear on every face.

"What do you want, Walking Man? You should not be here."

A thin whispering sound emitted from the enormous figure that could be made out as words. It was like dry branches scraping together in the wind.

"Thisss is thankss?"

Kokum ignored the comment, continuing in an increasingly worried voice, "What if someone sees you? Go back to your own lands. If you are discovered, don't you know you will be destroyed? Man has no room for you anymore, I am sorry to say. But you know this is true. You have seen what happens."

"I havve no landsss. They are takinggg evvrrythingg. Therrre iss no placce for walllkingg. Theyy takke the foresstss, theyyy dirrrty the watersss. I amm dyinggg."

Jake was watching in open surprise. He looked to Aisling for an explanation but she was just as shocked. Matari walked over to the Walking Man, dwarfed by comparison. The young man bowed his head.

"Thank you," he said simply.

With a creak of wood and a squelch of moss, Walking Man returned the gesture with a slight bow.

"What are you?" Jake asked quietly.

"Sssomme calll mee *Wakaitcsssuuu*. I am nott a whatt but a whooo."

Kokum sat heavily on the tree trunk that she had been hiding under just moments before. There was blood on her face and she looked very old and very tired.

"*Wakaitcu*, Walking Man...this is one of the ancient spirits of the land. He lived here before any of our ancestors came to this place. His home is the forests."

"How come no one has ever heard of you?" asked Jake.

"I hhhave hiddenn mysselfff. My chilldrenn hhhave died, there arre fffew of uss who remainn."

"People have seen him, or ones like him," Martha spoke up, "but only glimpses. Ever hear of Bigfoot?"

"Seriously?"

"Seriously."

"Well, why hide?"

"Yourrr people will kill mee. Theyy alreadyy kill the foressts, theyy carve and dig and leavve emptinesss behind. We arre waitingg for a dayy whenn we can returrn."

Despite his lack of a recognizably human face, Walking Man managed to look sorrowful. His words themselves echoed with longing.

"Aren't there a lot of forests in the mountains? Can't you live there?"

"That's where they do live, Jake. But we keep going deeper and deeper into the mountains, exploring, excavating, even the animals are leaving, more and more of them wandering into towns and cities. Wakaitcu, and those like him are slowly being strangled to death."

"Which brings us back to my question," Kokum interjected, "Why are you here?"

"Therre iss sommeone who dreamms. Wee helpp."

"Yes, she is right here," Kokum nodded her head toward her granddaughter, "What do you want to help her with?"

Walking Man turned to regard Aisling. After a moment he pulled up one his legs from the ground and took a long step toward her, reaching out with his arms.

She backed up but Kokum motioned for her to stop so she stood still, trembling as long, bony fingers stretched toward her, gently grasping her by the sides of her head. Walking man's voice sounded inside her head. The rasping voice was replaced by clear, simple thoughts.

"You are not the one."

"What do you mean? Maybe you didn't notice, but I have a pretty stylin' fro because of my dreaming."

The twiggy fingers adjusted themselves on her head, "Interesting. Yes, you have spoken with the Mother and she has marked you as her own, but there are different kinds of dreams, young one. Darker dreamers. There is another."

"Another?"

"Eric!" she said aloud, "You're talking about Eric! Where is he? Have you seen him?"

Walking Man withdrew his hands and turned to Kokum.

"Thiss dreammerrr iss knownn to you?"

"It is why we are traveling, we are trying to find him. Why do you want to help him?"

"Therre iss a mmisstake. I do nott wannt to hellp him. I wwannt to desstroyy him!"

Chapter 24 - Eric

Not knowing what else to do, Eric walked back down to the river he and Cor had passed earlier in the day. The bridge wasn't there anymore. Instead a wide beaver dam stretched across the gap. Eric stood and looked at the wooden construction until finally he decided to take the risk and stepped onto the dam. It was uneven and he almost lost his footing at one point but it was sturdy. He made it across and continued back along the trail.

He didn't have a plan, but figured that he would go as far as their camp from the night before. Back to where he had first heard the crying of the baby.

There was no crying now.

As he approached the spot he saw no evidence of their stay. There was no fire pit, the ground was undisturbed.

Did I go backward in time?

"You look lost."

Eric was startled by the voice and looked around, then up in the trees in case Cor was up there. He saw no one. Did he just imagine it?

"Maybe that wasn't the right thing to say; let me try again. Hello, human boy. Are you lost?"

This time Eric followed the source of the speech and to his surprise saw a small red fox sitting in the shadows, its head cocked quizzically to one side.

Feeling foolish, Eric spoke, "Is that you talking?"

The fox looked behind itself, then left, then right.

"Do you see anyone else around here?"

Eric shook his head.

The fox stood up and padded softly into the clearing, its clever face fixed on Eric's.

"I've never seen a human in this place. How'd you get here anyway?"

"I don't really know. I was just walking in the trees a couple hours from here and fell down. When I got up … here I was. Thing is, I don't know where here is."

The fox sat down on her haunches.

"You're definitely lost. Being here is dangerous for you. Most people would've killed you on sight."

"People? I thought you said you'd never seen a human?"

Again, the fox just gazed at him, that quizzical expression on her face.

"Never mind. So how do I get back to where I'm supposed to be? And where is that baby I heard crying?"

A barking, yipping sound came from the red fox that Eric realized was laughter.

"Am I supposed to answer that? Humans are funnier than I've been led to believe."

"That's great but I wasn't making a joke. Seriously. Just this morning I was in this forest but it was wintertime and now here I am and my stuff is gone and I'm completely alone."

The fox sniffed, lifting its nose up and turning away its head.

"Well, if that's how you feel," and she turned to walk back into the forest.

"What did I say?"

"Nothing. Negating my presence is perfectly polite, quite obviously."

"I'm sorry, I didn't mean to offend you. I just meant that no one I knew was here with me. Cor is back in the real world."

At that the fox actually gasped.

"The what?"

"The - the real world?"

She rolled onto her back, her sinewy body swaying in laughter. Eric was growing annoyed with the fox and her condescension. He didn't like being laughed at, especially when he wasn't sure what he'd done that was so funny.

"You really are silly. Maybe I should have eaten you like I had planned."

Eric's irritation suddenly turned to anger.

"It wouldn't have been a good idea for you to try," he said quietly.

The fox rolled over again, front paws resting in front of her.

"Maybe not."

"Help me," Eric said. "I keep hearing a baby cry but when I look there's nothing there. And I need to get back home."

"Why should any of that matter to me?"

"Believe me," Eric said. "If you don't help I can make life very uncomfortable for you."

"Oh, I doubt that you, nasty little thing," the fox sniffed and like a flash of red fire disappeared into the woods.

You think I can't find you?

Eric closed his eyes to locate the veins of light. He concentrated, but they weren't there. Instead, everything was glowing white to his inner eye. There were no veins to be found. He pulled out his stone, to see if that would help but as soon as he grasped it, all the light simply faded, leaving behind utter darkness.

Eric opened his eyes to the summer forest. He put the rock away and started running after the fox on foot.

As he dodged trees and leaped over fallen branches and low bushes he caught flashes of red fire in the distance and increased his pace. Soon he was running faster than he had ever gone in his life. He was almost flying through the forest.

He crouched low and the ground sped by underfoot, his legs pushing him forward effortlessly, his hands balancing, finding purchase. His sense of smell had become more acute and he could hear every movement ahead of him, see the smallest detail. He grinned and his tongue lolled out from his mouth. He almost tripped but his tail balanced him and he jumped over a small stream, skidding to a stop on the opposite bank, panting from the sheer joy of the chase.

"Well, now. That *is* interesting."

The red fox was higher up on the bank, looking down at him. He tried to speak but all that came out of his throat was a complaining whine. He couldn't understand what was wrong. He knew he could talk, why wasn't it working? He tried again and this time the whine reached a higher pitch than before.

Frustrated, he sat down on his hind legs and bent over while one of his back paws scratched at his ear.

Paws?

He whirled around, trying to look at himself, but all he caught were glimpses of his tail. He tried again and again until the laughter from ahead brought him to a stop.

"Sweet Mother, you *are* just a pup!"

He directed a bark at the mocking fox, and attempted a low growl that ended up sounding more like he was clearing his throat.

She hopped down beside Eric and examined him more closely. Penetrating eyes twinkled with mischief.

"Well, you look normal and smell normal. If you are a person why were you pretending to be a human? You even had me fooled."

Afraid of what he might see, but needing to know, Eric rushed over to the stream. There in the undulating water his reflection stared up at him with the long, pointy nose and ears of a fox.

For the first time in his life, Eric howled.

Chapter 25 - Aisling

"You can't possibly be talking about Eric. He's just an innocent kid! What could he have done?"

"Itt iss what he willl doo," Walking Man replied, the ticking and scraping and whistling of his voice washing across them all.

"What he *will* do?" Jake asked, coming to stand beside Aisling. "What the heck does that mean?"

"I hhave been walkingg throughh other pathsss. I have seenn the darkness of his dreamsss. He mmeanss to go to that darknesss. He sseekss the Raven."

Kokum spoke, but her voice sounded small and defeated.

"Have you seen this, Walking Man? Truly?"

"It iss not farr off."

"Kokum? What does he mean? What paths? How can he know what Eric will do in the future?"

"In the Dreamtime," Matari spoke up.

"Yessss."

The darkness was descending on them, and the pain of Aisling's wounds started to throb and bite. She sat down where she was and hung her head.

I can't take any more of this. When will it end?

Auntie Martha had been silent until now.

"*Wakaitscu*, we're all injured. We need to tend to our cuts, we need to rest. But we will also need to build a fire. May we have your permission?"

A shudder ran through the tree-like creature, but he nodded.

"I wwill stayy awway fromm itt."

"Thank you."

Without a word, Matari stood and walked back out into the field they had run from not long before. Aisling forced herself to stand and went with him, wincing at the stabs of pain from her bloodied, torn ankles. In the darkness, they searched for the packs they had dropped in their run for safety.

"Matari, do you think it's true? Do you think Eric is dangerous?"

"I think it's important that we find him, Aisling. The wood spirit has been on different paths and believes what he's saying, but one thing I've learned about Dreamtime is that not everything is as it seems. Time is different there and you can't always trust what happens. Don't worry, I think there's hope yet. Here's my pack!"

She heard him unzip his bag. It was dark now and the stars she had been seeking to make a first appearance were out in full, no moon to dim their glory.

"Aha!" Matari turned on the flashlight he'd recovered from his bag. "This should make the rest easier to find."

Without thinking, Aisling reached out and took Matari's hand in her own and pulled him toward her. He lowered his flashlight and wrapped his arms around her shoulders. He was warm and his embrace was comforting in the cold night. She raised her head and there were tears streaming down her face. She didn't care. She pulled him down toward her and softly placed her lips on his. He allowed the kiss, but then straightened, his voice strange and thick.

"We'd better get back to the others."

Embarrassed, she helped him with the packs. She carried her own and pulled another along the ground behind her.

Why did I do that? What was I thinking?

When they returned with the bags, Jake got started on a fire and she watched him work with a twinge of guilt. When she heard Matari talking softly with Kokum she burned with shame again at her unexpected impulse. Was he telling Kokum about it right now? What would her grandmother think of her? What if Jake had seen?

She sat alone in her wretchedness, not even offering to help as her Auntie started preparing cloths and bandages from the First Aid kit.

"Drreammerrr..."

She started and looked up over her shoulder to see the Walking Man towering over her.

"Pleasse … accept this giffft."

He reached into his chest, pushing aside the moss and wood. After rummaging for a bit he withdrew his hand, bringing with it a small token. He held it out for Aisling, so she opened her hand and he dropped it into her waiting palm.

"What is it?" She held it up. In the dim light of the growing flames she saw that it was made of wood. A circle broken into quarters by a cross shape. "It looks like a Medicine Wheel. Or a Dream Catcher."

She glanced up for confirmation.

"I do nottt know thosse thingss. I give thiss fromm my heartt. Itt may be of helpp to youu."

"Why would you want to help me? You've already condemned my brother and Matari says he hasn't even done anything."

She omitted the "yet" that she had been thinking.

"Ifff he goess forrwarrd with hiss plann itt will meann all will die."

123

"Yeah, right. The end of the world. I've heard all about it. I don't want anything from someone who wants to kill my brother." She tossed the gift back at the giant hovering over her.

"Aisling!"

She looked guiltily to where her Kokum stood, anger and disbelief apparent in her grandmother's eyes.

"This is not how you were raised."

Aisling's eyes darted around and she saw that everyone had been watching her exchange with the Walking Man. Flustered she shot back.

"What? We're supposed to be friends with this monster? Am I the only one not crazy here? Jake," she said, "what do you think?"

"I, um … I don't think I know enough to say anything, Ais. Maybe we should just listen?"

Even though what he said made sense, Aisling shot him a look of pure disgust and walked away.

"Ais, wait! I mean, maybe we don't know the whole - "

"Forget it!" she shouted him down. "Why are you even here? Because you have a stupid crush on me or something?"

She saw his face contort between embarrassment and hurt and felt a stab of remorse, but instead of apologizing she walked out into the darkness.

She just needed to be alone. She needed time to think.

She walked far enough that she couldn't see the light of the fire or hear her Auntie's quiet murmur as she cleaned and dressed everyone's injuries. She was out in the field, her anger cooling and her shame returning.

Please don't let Matari come looking for me, she thought. She couldn't bear to see him right now. She didn't even know if she was attracted to him. She had just acted on impulse.

Pulling up the hood on her jacket, she lay down and gazed up into the endless Milky Way. There were so many stars, so many planets. What made anything here important anyway? What was it all about? What was it all for?

Her thoughts spiraled around in sadness and despair. She felt small and alone. In the midst of her thoughts, she almost missed the sound of wings flapping above her. It took her just a moment to register what was happening and she rolled away as quick as she could. The ground shook as the bird impacted on the spot where she had just lain. She looked up and saw a large black shape blacking out the stars. It was as big as a man and as she watched it extended its wings wider and wider, advancing toward her, its beak reflecting the dim light.

Too frightened to move she watched helplessly as the giant raven approached, the smell of death and rotting meat wafting toward her.

She tried to crawl away and heard a soft croak and a sudden rushing. Something clamped down hard on her leg and she screamed in fear in and blinding pain. She heard an enormous roar over her scream and suddenly her leg was free. There was a struggle in the darkness, and the bird shrieked in frustration and flew off into the night sky.

Aisling felt her leg. It was wet with blood. She tried to stand up but couldn't put any weight on her right leg. As she reached out to regain her balance her hand struck something warm and covered in fur. She was not alone.

Now she heard the low, slow breathing. She sensed the massive size of the beast that stood alongside her. It moved closer and bumped up against her body, almost knocking her over. She instinctively reached out with her other hand and found herself staying upright with both hands buried in thick fur.

The beast began moving slowly back toward camp. Frightened and not knowing what else to do, she limped along with it, allowing herself to be led.

As they approached the winking fire she looked at her companion and fell back with a small scream. She heard shouts come from direction of the flame and soon the sound of people crashing through the bushes toward her. It turned out to be Matari and Jake, running in from different directions. They bent to help Aisling before they even noticed the direction of her stare. Slowly, they raised their eyes in unison.

"Aisling? Are you all right?" her Kokum's voice called out.

"Stay back Kokum! Auntie, keep her away!"

"Like I could if I wanted to," Martha said as they came into view. She took in the scene at once and the humour on her face vanished.

From behind her the Walking Man came lumbering up and instead of freezing like the others had, he seemed to focus on Aisling's bloody leg and then hurtled himself toward the beast.

"No wait!" Aisling cried out. "It was helping me!"

But the two creatures were already tearing at each other, oblivious to her voice.

A single, piercing note cut through the violence, and Aisling clapped her hands to her ears. She looked toward the source of the sound and saw Kokum. Her mouth was open, her eyes shut tight, singing out the single, sky shattering sound.

It was enough to stop the fighting and Matari directed his flashlight toward the combatants. Walking Man looked more in shambles than before and there beside him stood a giant bear, Walking Man's arm still clamped in his fearsome jaws.

The bear opened his mouth, releasing the arm and Walking Man stood up, testing his limb, flexing it back and forth. Kokum walked up to the both of them. She was much shorter than the bear and had to look up at him. They regarded each other, the bear's heavy breathing blowing strands of hair back from her head. She reached out and embraced it. She was crying and praying and laughing all at once.

"Mother? Are you okay?" Martha asked warily.

Kokum turned away from the bear and stood as straight as she was able.

"Yes. I am."

She reached out again and ran her hand across the side of the mighty beast's muzzle.

"My son has returned. Aisling, say hello to your father."

Chapter 26 - Eric

Eric howled and the red fox joined in.

"Isn't this fun?" she asked, a smile in her voice.

They continued howling, and then the red fox stopped and watched Eric with a sparkle in her dark eye.

"How long should we keep this up for do you think?" she said.

Eric paused mid-howl, his head raised and his black lips pursed in a little "o." He had almost forgotten why he had begun in the first place, losing himself in the wildness, in the cleansing feeling of crying out into the sky. But he glanced at his companion and suddenly remembered himself.

Back hunched, he crawled under an overhang beside the stream bank and sulked.

The red fox eyed him suspiciously.

"What's wrong? Are you sick?"

"No, I'm dreaming. Leave me alone and let me wake up."

"Perhaps it will help if you recall that you were the one chasing me. I was perfectly happy to leave you alone," she said with a swish of her tail.

"Ha ha. You're so smart."

Without warning the red fox leapt at Eric, grabbing his throat in her mouth. She pulled him viciously out from under the overhang and rolled him onto his back, exposing his soft stomach. Instinct took over and Eric began to fight back, clawing at the fox, snapping at her muzzle with his own sharp fangs, but she was faster, stronger, and knew what she was doing beyond simple instinct and she soon had him pinned to the ground, a low, steady growl emanating from deep in her throat, slipping past curled lips and bloodied teeth.

"The same could *not* be said for you."

Eric wished he could use the stone and blast her off of him, punish her for humiliating him like this, for fighting him down.

"Get off me!" he shouted, "What did I do to you?"

Alone for one day and he was being bullied all over again.

"You little whelp!" she said, "You have threatened me and insulted me since our paths crossed. I am patient but do you think I would allow you to continue to debase me without consequence? I have honour! Something you would do well to learn."

"If we were in my world I would destroy you," he said as boldly as he could, despite the claws hovering over his abdomen.

"You are in mine and I could return your blood to the earth in a heartbeat. You are not a person. You have no honour, you have no strength. How is it that you have even lived this long?"

"I'm not a person? You're the animal here! I just look like one."

"Animal? You have gone too far, *gratling!*"

She swiped at his head, knocking it hard to the side. She was about to strike him again when her nose raised sharply, sniffing the air.

"Who's there?" she demanded. Eric saw she was distracted and tried to twist away from her hold on him. He was rewarded for his efforts by a quick nip on the snout and he held still. He rolled his eyes and saw a pair of human legs walking toward them. He tried to see higher but his face was being squished into the ground by the red fox.

"Standing Coyote," she whispered.

"Hello, Skia. What have you got there, little hunter? Dinner, maybe?"

The red fox, or Skia, as the man had called her, released her grip on Eric and he rolled over with a groan.

"Hey thanks, man," he said, shaking the dirt off his fur. "I really appreciate the … help …."

Standing Coyote grinned at him, but the smile was more alarming than reassuring, displaying an inordinate number of threatening teeth.

"No problem, Man."

The visitor was dressed in jeans and a plaid flannel shirt and he was lighting a pipe clenched in his mouth, being careful not to singe his whiskers. There would be nothing remarkable about him except for the fact that he had the head of a coyote.

His pipe lit, he ran his free hand over his forehead, smoothing out his fur. He paused to scratch behind one of his ears, eye closing in satisfaction. Finished, he opened his eyes, smiled again brusquely, and sat down cross-legged.

"Now then, where were we? Oh yes, thanks all around. That's a good place to start, don't you think? No matter the business at hand, it's good to follow the formalities."

He offered Eric a pull on his pipe but Eric shook his head.

Standing Coyote looked offended and glanced at Skia. She rolled her eyes, shaking her head at Eric.

"Not much for manners, eh?"

Hastily changing his tune, Eric stretched his neck towards the pipe, allowing Coyote to place the end in his mouth. Eric took a pull of the tobacco and started coughing, the acrid smoke burning his throat. He heard Skia's soft, mocking laughter. He instinctively began to growl and this just made the coughing worse.

"Are you okay?" Standing Coyote asked. "There, go drink some water." He indicated the little stream beside them. Eric complied and lowered his head to the stream, this time trying to ignore his own reflection. He lapped up several mouthfuls of the cold liquid and it filled him with a vital coolness he'd never experienced. Enjoying the sensation, he continued drinking.

"Ahem," said Skia, making a cartoon cough behind him. Eric glanced over his shoulder and saw the fox and the coyote-headed man waiting for him. Tail between his legs, he skulked back to rejoin them.

"What honour could be so great that our paths have crossed?" she asked Standing Coyote.

"Well, I was sent to find this one here," he said, indicating Eric.

"This one? As you can see for yourself there is nothing to recommend him. He is ill-mannered and I was deciding whether or not to kill him."

Eric shot Skia a startled glance.

Coyote chuckled ruefully.

"Then you would be doing a lot of people a great service," he said with a smile, and the smile grew so broad and toothsome that Eric had to check himself to make sure he didn't pee on the spot in a show of submission.

Skia noted his fear and huffed in disgust.

"I do not doubt it. He is so weak he could only end up as food. But surely not enough to feed as many you indicate?"

Again Coyote laughed.

"His death might serve one appetite, true, but no. This guy is a human and he's going to kill a lot of good people, maybe all the people. It's been seen, Skia. He's got to die."

"No time like the present," Skia said, rising.

"Wait!" Eric cried."Don't I get a say in this? I haven't done anything wrong!"

"That's really not the point, man," Standing Coyote said. "It's what you will do. You're going to see Him, after all."

"Him?" Eric's thoughts raced. "You mean Cor's father? How do you know about that? Please, I don't understand what's going on, you have to believe me."

Eric could hear the very real whine in his voice, and he was crouched very low to the ground, his belly dragging in the dust.

"Your future is shrouded in darkness and it spreads from you all over the place," said Coyote. "I'm talking everywhere. That's why you need to go, man."

He stuck his tongue out and drew his thumb across his throat in a pantomime of cutting someone's throat.

Skia chuckled.

"Shhh," Coyote said suddenly, his ears twitching and his eyes looking far off into the distance.

"Huh?" he said.

Skia looked expectantly towards Coyote.

He looked at Eric.

"You know something? You're one lucky dude."

Eric did not feel lucky.

"I hear voices, boy, and you know what this voice told me?"

"N-no."

"You've got a guardian angel and guess what she said."

Eric didn't make a sound, his breath stuck in his throat.

"She said that even though a lot of us see the problems you're going to cause, we can't see everything. If it were anyone else saying it but this guardian angel of yours, I'd ignore them and make sure your eyes closed forever."

Eric swallowed.

"Anyway, apparently you get to live." He paused again, his brows furrowing. "But you need watching, and since you've already become such fast friends, Skia here gets the job. That way, if anything goes too wrong, she can tear your throat out. Happily ever after."

"I look forward to it," Skia said.

"And kid, you should know something here. We're the good guys. Now move!"

Skia gave Eric a rough nudge in the shoulder with her muzzle, and Eric trotted off at a clip beside her. They hopped over the beaver dam, heading back to the deep stand of pine trees at the side of the trail, the place where Eric first entered this place.

Skia was talking the whole way and every word was a threat.

"If you try to run, I will kill you. If you try to hide, I will kill you. If you do anything I think is suspicious - "

"Let me guess. You'll kill me?"

She gave him a hard shove and he rolled head over tail.

"At least I know you can learn," she called out behind her. "Now get up!"

At last they came to the place where he had first stepped off the trail and together the two foxes slipped under the pines.

"I'm not sure exactly where - "

"Here," Skia said, leading him with her nose close to the ground. "Can you not smell the human stink?"

Eric realized he could and the realization made him gag. It was disgusting, like coming across an open sewer or a pig sty.

Skia noted his discomfort. "So at least you have some sense. Here is where the trail ends."

"Now what?"

"You're the one who came through. I thought you knew."

Eric shook his head. "I don't know. Maybe it has to be at a certain time of day?"

"You are stupid. I hope you know that."

Eric ignored the jab and settled himself down.

"What are you doing?"

"I'm waiting."

"Waiting? For what?"

"For you to be quiet. I'm sure I will grow old in the process."

Skia's head drew back in annoyance but she said nothing, lying down on the soft bed of pine needles on the forest floor.

After a while they began to doze.

It might have been minutes later, or seconds, but Eric's ears perked up.

The crying. Hearing it again sent a shiver through his body and he stood to shake it off. The sound was unmistakable.

"Where is it?" asked Skia, instantly awake.

"I'm not sure. Close."

She looked around, her head cocking from side to side.

"Down!" she said and began digging.

Eric listened, realizing she was right. The baby was buried under the needles. They had to help! He started digging beside her, widening the hole, making it deeper.

The cries were clearer now and they sped up their efforts. Together they tunneled downward, the screams almost surrounding them.

"It's so close!" Skia cried.

Eric was panting with the effort and could hear Skia's laboured breathing. They were almost there! Finally he could save that poor child. He thought he caught a glimpse of an arm, a flash of soft creamy skin, but it slipped deeper into the needles.

"Did you see that?" he shouted.

"Yes! Don't let it sink!"

They dove toward the infant.

Suddenly the ground exploded, filling their eyes with dirt, pine needles showering down around them. Falling back hard, Eric felt the wind knocked out of him.

He heard Skia groan and he rolled over. There was a girl, about his age, lying naked in the snow. She opened her almond-shaped eyes.

"So, you've turned human again," she said.

"Uhh..."

"Well, your brain hasn't improved. Why am I so cold?"

Skia pushed herself up on all fours, her long red hair falling into her face. Reaching up she pushed it back and gazed silently at her hand. She wiggled her fingers.

And she screamed.

Chapter 27 - Aisling

"Aisling, it's morning, and you need to eat. Here, put these on."

She awoke to the gentle touch of Auntie Martha.

Sandy-eyed, she felt like someone had beaten her up, which was pretty accurate if you counted dozens of birds and a nightmarish, oversized raven.

Her Auntie had left her a large bundle of clothes and had zipped the inner liner into Aisling's jacket. She gingerly slipped the clothing on, her eyes burning with tears as she tugged heavy socks up over the bandages covering her ravaged ankles and the deep cuts on her calfShe pulled on a clean pair of jeans, a t-shirt and sweater. Then she shrugged into her jacket and slipped on the boots that waited at the doorway to the tent. Taking a deep breath she unzipped the tent and climbed out into a world turned white with snow. The ground was a uniform, soft blank canvas, the sky only a shade more grey with a heavy cloud that was dropping huge, soft flakes through the thin, dry branches of the naked trees.

Only her Auntie and Grandmother were by the fire and she joined them, gratefully accepting a mug of steaming tea from her Auntie. She sat down with them, allowing her Kokum to pull her in under the blanket that covered her old shoulders, and so they sat, side by side with the small fire warming their faces and their toes.

"Where is everyone?" Aisling asked quietly. The cold, white morning seeming to demand reverence.

"They've gone ahead to make sure the road is safe. Your father and Walking Man will go further on, but Jake and Matari will wait for us just a ways away. I wanted to talk to you."

At the mention of her father, Aisling remembered the moment the previous night in which she had been reunited with him. Rather than being shocked or amazed that her father was alive and in the form of a bear, she had simply accepted it. What else could she do? She was so bone-tired, so hurt, so confused, that the easiest thing to do was to simply accept the hits that just kept coming.

"Hi, Dad," she had said, giving the monstrously large bear a quick wave of her hand. "Glad to see you're doing good."

And with that, she had gone back to the camp, crawled into her tent and slept.

Now, at her Kokum's words, she tensed. Whatever it was her grandmother wanted to say to her, it couldn't be good. She didn't want to be having this conversation but she was trapped. Not only by respect for her Kokum but by her own shame for her actions. She wanted to be able to excuse herself, tell herself that she was only fifteen and that it was okay that she acted immature. After all, she was still just a kid.

The problem was she didn't believe it herself. She was honest enough to admit that she knew better. She was being selfish while everyone around her was doing their best to help one another.

"Kokum, I'm sorry."

Kokum drank her tea, and Martha brought them some oatmeal for their breakfast and then slipped away to clean and pack up. When the last spoonful of the hot, bland porridge was eaten and Martha again appeared as if by magic to take away their dishes, Kokum stretched and smiled.

"We used to have so much fun on days like this when I was a small girl. Oh how we laughed! Sledding down the hills, making snowmen, throwing snowballs at our parents. My father used to pretend he didn't hear us sneaking up behind him even though we giggled the entire time. We'd shove snow down his jacket and he would roar and chase us around until we were too weak from laughing to stand. Those were the days. That's how it was."

She smiled her big crinkly smile and Aisling couldn't help but smile back.

"That's the way it should be but the world has changed around us, hasn't it?"

"It has, Kokum."

"Are you sad, my girl? It hasn't been easy for you and Eric and I wasn't there for you to help you smile. My travels took me away from you at the time you, perhaps, needed me most."

"Kokum..."

Aisling didn't know what to say. It was true. Her grandmother hadn't been there and life had been difficult. Maybe they had more things than Kokum did growing up, but life was also more complicated. The divorce, her mother's alcoholism, the pressure from friends to drink or smoke or pop a few pills simply to escape the neverending boredom. Aisling's mind went to darker places, to friends and relatives who took their own lives rather than have to live with the constant abuse or depression.

She shook her head and sat up straight.

"Kokum, worrying about the past doesn't help. I'm not in denial or anything. I know when things have sucked, but I just want to move on. I'm so tired of sadness. I want hope in my life. I was going to leave the Rez for good, you know. Not because it's all bad. It isn't. But I need to find out who I am."

She glanced at her grandmother to see how she would respond to that last part.

"Good girl," Kokum nodded. "Yes … good."

Aisling was surprised. She never told anyone that in case they made fun of her or got mad and called her an Apple. She could just imagine it. *Red on the outside, but white on the inside! What, you think you're better than us, college girl?*

"I'm proud of you, my love. You are a good woman."

Just hearing those words from her Kokum filled Aisling with a glowing warmth.

"I have wanted to talk to you all these days but..." she trailed off and Aisling nodded. It had been pretty wild from the moment Kokum had returned.

"Aisling, I wanted to be there for you all those years. You know I didn't go travelling for the fun of it, don't you?"

"Matari told me."

"Good."

There was a long pause.

"Kokum, is there something you want to say?"

"There is something I want to show. Watch."

Kokum reached down, sinking her hand into the snow. Murmuring a soft song, she closed her eyes in concentration. And up from between her fingers, up through the snow, a green tendril curled. Long feather leaves stretched up toward Kokum's soothing song. With her other hand she produced the gift Walking Man had tried to give to Aisling the evening before. She held it low to the growing plant and it grew around the circlet, weaving itself into the cross. Small, white flowers began to bloom, the soft floral scent rejuvenated Aisling, taking away the aches and pains of her cuts and bruises.

Kokum's song whispered into silence and she handed the gift to Aisling. She had wrapped a strip of hide thong around it, making a necklace.

"The plant is called *wapunewusk*. Yarrow. It's for healing and protection."

Aisling nodded and ducked her head, accepting the gesture and the gift, pulling the necklace on. With the circle of flowers hanging from her neck, the scent continued its good work. She even felt more alert.

"Now, you try."

"What?"

"Place your hand on the ground. Yes. Good. Now, can you repeat the song?"

Aisling knew she could. It was just like the games they used to play when she was a girl, but she never guessed there was any magic in it.

"Kokum, I can't. I don't have that kind of gift. I just … I just dream. And those don't really do anything except …." She indicated her white streaks.

"Just trust me, Aisling. Sing. It will help if you close your eyes. Find the Earthblood and draw it to you. Share your song. Share your energy with the light."

Aisling closed her eyes and immediately the soft, glowing network of veins appeared in her vision. There was a bright spot where Kokum had grown the flower.

Hesitantly, she began to sing. Nothing happened.

She opened one eye to peek at her Kokum, who whispered the song with her, nodding to the slow, steady rhythm.

Aisling closed her peeking eye and focused on the song. She began to feel a stirring inside her, a sense of happiness and anticipation. It swirled into a little ball and slowly grew. As she sang, she directed that little ball of light down into her hand, down into the ground. As she did so she could see the light gathering around her, pulsing toward the spot she touched. Encouraged, she kept singing, imagining springtime and sunshine, and the song of birds. She imagined that she found Eric, safe and happy and she held him close in her arms. A burst of joy spread out from her as the thought strengthened her and helped erase her doubts. The song grew and changed, she improvised and felt a surge of confidence. It became her song. Aisling's Song.

Kokum gasped and Aisling knew there must be a small tendril of green popping up from the snow. Smiling she finished singing and opened her eyes.

All around them, the forest had blossomed. There were flowers everywhere. Trees had grown leaves and new saplings had pushed themselves up out of the snow.

"Yes," she heard her Auntie say from behind them where she had been finishing up the packing. "I'd say she's ready."

Kokum was beaming.

"Yes, but now we have to talk about balance, I think," she said through her smile.

Aisling was still in shock.

"We - I - um .... We can do this?"

"You. You can do this," Martha said, coming up behind them. "Mother and I can't. In fact, I don't know anyone who could do all this. Hol-ay, girl."

She shook her head in wonder.

"Mother, let's try something else."

Kokum nodded.

"We can do this one as we walk," Martha said. "Come on."

"Wait, where's my pack?"

"Oh, your Jake insisted he take it for you. He had his on his back and yours on his front. Nice boy you got there."

Aisling flushed, but out of embarrassment for the way she'd treated Jake the night before, and for the kiss she had shared with Matari. Right now she didn't want to see either of them. She quickly changed the subject.

"What's the next trick?"

"I'll show you as we walk. We need to get moving. Daylight's burning. Come on Mother, let me help you."

Kokum stood and Aisling could practically hear the scraping of her grandmother's knee joints. *This cold weather must be excruciating for her, but she has never complained once.*

They left the small forest, taking to the open field, the tracks of their companions still visible under the falling layer of new snow. Aisling's attention was on her Auntie who was talking about birdsong and melodies, about how even the swaying grass had its own music.

Soon the blooming forest was left far behind them.

Over the rest of that winter a small patch of flowers grew in the middle of that space. The leaves and stalks intertwined, gaining strength and height. Where Aisling had touched her fingers to the ground two figures grew, made of those delicate, fragile flowers. They formed the shape of a young woman embracing a boy. Though the seasons would come and go, that small space in the wild world kept to its own laws and stayed forever fresh and forever in bloom.

Chapter 28 - Eric

"What did you do to me!"

The girl knocked Eric onto his back, baring her teeth like a wild animal.

"I didn't do anything! Get off of me!" He shoved her back and she rolled into a crouch, quickly surveying the world around her, her breath coming quick in small puffs of steam.

She sniffed the air. A look of consternation furrowed her brow and she tried again, inhaling, nostrils flaring.

"What is this?" she demanded. "All my senses are dulled! Do you mean to torture me by blinding me?"

"Skia, I didn't do anything. Look, I'm human, too. Did you turn me into a fox in your world?"

"Of course not! But I have no power."

"Neither did I. Not there anyway." Curious, he searched for the ribbons of light pulsing around them and forced one of them to his will. He held up his forefinger and a candle flame sprung up, illuminating the area around them.

Skia winced at the light.

"Why would you do that?"

"Uh, so we can see, of course."

"Well, it's stupid. Now I can't see anything beyond us, and anything that wants to eat us can see us even easier than before."

Eric scowled but blew out the little flame. In the darkness and the silence he could hear Skia's teeth chattering.

"You're freezing," he said. "Here."

He took off his jacket and handed it to her. She looked at it blankly.

He stepped closer and wrapped it around her shoulders. He felt suddenly awkward as the warm, summery scent of her hair filled his senses. He turned away, walking out of the forest. Skia followed close behind.

"How can you live in these weak bodies?" The chattering had stopped but her voice was still shaky and Eric could see her lips were very dark against her skin, which seemed to glow from within in the growing darkness.

"Well, for starters, we wear clothes. Once we get back to the path, I'll get some for you."

They emerged out of the wood to the trail and Eric could find no sign of Cor.

"I knew it!" Eric shouted. The first chance he had Cor had run off. Eric slumped down into the snow, filled with frustration. What was he going to do now? And what about Skia? She needed help soon, he knew, or she'd freeze to death.

Not that I should care. She almost killed me.

It occurred to Eric that almost everyone he had met lately wanted him dead.

It must be my charming personality.

"Eric, I can't feel my feet."

Eric glanced over and it hit home to him that she was barefoot in the snow. He rushed over just as she collapsed into his arms. He pulled her close to him.

"Am I dying?"

"No, of course not. Hold on."

He tried to block out the rising fear in his chest. How could he help her? Light a fire? Yes, but he would have to leave her to gather wood and he wasn't sure if he would come back to a frozen corpse.

Well, I can't light a stupid finger candle. That won't help.

He thought with longing of the summer air they had been breathing just an hour ago.

Warm air!

Slowly, and very carefully, he followed the same patterns in his mind that produced the small flame he conjured under the pines. Instead of thinking of a sudden wink of flame, he spread the idea out around him, including Skia in his thoughts. Then he pushed the air around them, slowly at first but then a little faster and a little faster. Not so much wind, although there was that, but even smaller movements. The little knowledge he had of molecules and atoms helped as he pictured the little particles bumping and crashing, making heat.

The wind whipping around them got warmer. But he was getting weaker so he slipped a few fingers into his pocket, just grazing the stone there with his fingertips. The air glowed around them and the snow beneath them melted. Sweat trickled down his forehead, not just from the concentration his efforts required, but because he was overheating, even though he was only wearing his shirt and hoodie. He opened his eyes and saw the flush of warmth on Skia's face.

So far so good, but I can't keep this up much longer. What am I supposed to do?

Her eyes fluttered opened and she opened her mouth in amazement. His strength spent, Eric let the wind go and sat back, exhausted. The cold immediately came rushing back to grasp them in its icy fingers.

Wearily he took off his boots and pulled them onto Skia's feet. She didn't struggle, something for which he was grateful as he didn't know how much strength he had left.

"I can't do anymore right now," he said.

"What can we do?" she asked, worry in her voice.

"We just have to keep warm. At least the ground has dried beneath us. Lie down here, I'll cover you as best I can."

Instead of following his suggestion, she scraped at the dry soil. Seeing what she was doing, Eric helped until they had a shallow depression dug. Skia curled up in it and Eric wrapped her in his arms, trying his best to cover her legs. He noted that despite the fact that she seemed so much more mature than he felt, she was actually close to his age.

They were both quiet and Eric could feel the cold sinking back into them. He was wondering if maybe they should try walking. His socks would get wet quickly but at least they would be burning up energy, creating some heat.

"Eric, thank you. I know you tried."

Instead of being reassured, her words pierced into him. He had tried. He tried to make Aisling proud of him by going to the school she suggested. He tried to make his Dad come home by being cheerful every time he came to visit so that maybe he'd want to come back and fix their family again. And now his Dad was dead. He tried to help his Mom, to love her, and all that happened was he'd ended up hurting her worse and to top it off, he had run away. He knew that everyone must be worried about him but he had gone too far and done too many things of which he was ashamed to ever go back home.

What good was his new power now? He was going to die in a pathetic little hole. He was going to freeze to death and because of him Skia was going to die, too.

"Some threat, huh? Aren't you glad you followed me here to make sure I didn't blow up the world or whatever it is that creepy Coyote thought I was going to do?"

She shook her head.

"No. But I know you have honour. I know you tried to save my life. If I'm to die, at least I will not have to be ashamed by the company I die in."

He bit back a bitter reply. There was nothing to be gained by bickering with his last breath. Instead he nodded and held her as she dug in closer for any last scraps of heat. She was so close he could feel her breath on his cheek and he looked down at her angular face, her sharp cheekbones. Her lips were wide but full. Her long lashes flicked upward as she met his gaze.

His breathing quickened and he didn't look away. How long they looked into each other's eyes he didn't know, but he knew that he never wanted to look away. Is this what being with a girl was like? Is this what love felt like?

"Am I interrupting anything?"

Eric twisted away from Skia and there was Cor. He was standing on the trail, one pack on his back, the other dragging behind him. He had a sardonic grin on his face.

"You didn't think I'd leave my little buddy, did you? I guess I didn't have to worry! It looks like you're in capable hands."

Chapter 29 - Aisling

When they'd come down the trail that first morning it snowed, Jake and Matari had been waiting for them. Aisling hadn't said a word. She had just collected her pack and continued on, the situation too awkward for her. She saw that Jake had tried to smile at her but she refused to look. She kept her head down and marched on as quickly as she could.

Please don't say anything, she sent out with her thoughts.

That night as she crawled into her sleeping bag she felt something underneath her pillow. Curious, she switched on her flashlight and dug around, revealing half a chocolate bar and a note.

Hi Aisling,

I don't know what I did to make you so angry with me, but I'm sorry, whatever it is. I only wanted to help you. I don't want to force you to talk with me but just know that if there's anything you need I'm here for you. I guess that probably doesn't count for much since there's nothing special about me but, well, like I said. I'm here.

Jake

ps. Sorry, I ate half the chocolate.

She bit into the chocolate and let it melt slowly in her mouth. The dark, rich sweetness filled her mouth and, strangely, she felt a sense of loss.

Jake was thoughtful and dependable, but she hated to admit that he was kind of forgettable. He was just there when you needed him and it was easy to take him for granted.

But Matari....

She felt a pang of guilt, eating the chocolate Jake had given her and thinking of someone else. Matari was older, but not too old. He was so confident and quiet. She'd never met anyone like him and she could tell he was mixed blood, which intrigued her even more. What had his life been like in Australia? How did he come to know how to live so easily in the wild and take care of himself? All she knew is that she felt calm and safe in his presence.

She glanced at Jake's note and folded it up, putting it aside with the candy. They weren't supposed to have food in their tents. Every night they wrapped it all up in bags, tied a rope to the end and hauled it up into the air away from where they slept.

It was so they wouldn't attract bears.

She listened to the loud snoring outside and gave a small snort of laughter. It was a little late to worry about dangerous animals coming around.

As she had with the two boys, Aisling had been avoiding the bear. She couldn't call it her father. It just didn't feel right. But she caught it watching her and she could swear at one point it winked at her. That it left her alone was telling enough. Her father always knew when she would be ready to talk and left her in peace until that time. The bear was doing the same thing.

Beyond the rumbling snore of the bear was the far-off sound of snapping twigs and the low moan of wood rubbing against wood. Walking Man was out there somewhere, patrolling the camp and watching for danger. Apparently, he didn't need to sleep, which allowed them all to get some much needed rest.

The next day she practiced as they walked. Aisling tried to keep everything Kokum and Martha told her in order in her head. Although she didn't admit it, sometimes the things they told her went straight into one ear and out the other. She found it more and more difficult to concentrate; her ankles were killing her with every step and she had a headache that wouldn't go away.

Kokum was teaching her how to draw light from the ground as she walked so that every time she wanted to do something she wouldn't have to find a vein, reach in and start building the energy. Instead, she would always have some in reserve.

"Why is that important, Kokum?"

"Make it melt!" shouted Matari unexpectedly as he threw a snowball in her direction.

She started building the power, gathering what heat there was from the air when the snowball hit her square in the chest.

"That's why!" Matari said over his shoulder, flashing a smile. As awkward as Aisling had felt since their kiss, he didn't seem the least bit bothered. This annoyed her a little, but she put it out of her mind.

"Okay, I get it," she said to her grandmother. "So what do I do?"

After that she tried to carry some light inside her, but it wasn't easy. She felt like a leaky bucket, the power spilling out from her whenever she stopped thinking about holding it. She could feel it seeping out, back into the earth. She tried explaining it to her Kokum.

"Yes, I understand," the old woman replied, "That happens when people get a lot older than me and they have to start wearing diapers."

She laughed at her own joke and Aisling had to join in.

"Well, I don't have any magic diapers, so what can I do?"

"There's nothing for it but to keep working. You will get it, don't worry."

"Isn't there a shortcut I can use? What about this? Can it help?" she pulled the talisman from under her jacket. The flowers were still fresh and growing.

Kokum lost her smile.

"Not that, no. It can't help. It has different ways to strengthen you but this is not one of them."

"So there is something?" Aisling pressed.

Kokum fell silent.

"A bloodstone would do it, but we don't talk about that." Martha said.

Jake was just coming back at that moment to bring them some fresh water.

"What's a bloodstone?" Aisling asked.

Martha looked to her mother.

"Very well," Kokum muttered.

Martha nodded. "Bloodstones are very rare. They don't come from this world, they came with Raven. They're fragments of the meteor that had surrounded him when he returned."

"What do they do?" Aisling asked.

"They're like magnifying glasses. Anything they touch becomes stronger. More emotions than anything else. The stronger the better."

"Do you have one?"

"Goodness no! I wouldn't touch one if my life depended on it."

"Why not? I thought you said they make you stronger."

"Let me put it this way. The last time anyone even saw one was back in the days of Louis Riel and the Red River battles. It fell from person to person and made them crazy. One man even claimed to have become Wendigo and he slaughtered his entire family. I can't imagine what it would do to someone who knew how to see Earthblood."

"But what if your thoughts are good? What if you know what you're getting into?"

"No one can imagine what they're getting into with something like that, Aisling. It doesn't draw power the way you do, borrowing and sharing the earth's light. It steals it. It tears it out, but it can't do that on its own. In order for it to work it has to be fed."

"Fed what?" Aisling asked, unsure that she wanted the answer.

"Blood. Fresh blood. It's bad medicine, Aisling. It's black arrows in the night. Just trust me when I say, listen to Kokum. Build your own strength."

Aisling nodded, deep in thought.

Jake handed her a water bottle. Still shy, she accepted it without a word. He waited for her to say something, but when it was apparent she was keeping to herself he left and headed back to the front of the line.

As evening approached, the group of them spread further and further apart on the trail. Martha was helping Kokum walk the last leg of the day's march and everyone else was so far ahead that Aisling couldn't see them. Her ankles were driving her crazy with itching.

I guess that means they're healing.

It was a thought that gave no relief. She wanted to tear her socks off and just scratch away but she knew if she did that she'd just open the scabs again.

The next thing she knew she was knocked down from behind by what could only be a train at full speed. Her chest was tight and she felt like she was suffocating. Rolling over, she saw the cougar. It was leaping toward her. She tried to dodge. One of its claws just grazing her arm. She winced in pain but didn't cry out, instead she closed her eyes and imagined a bubble around her, keeping her safe. She opened her eyes just as the cougar leapt for her again. This time it sort of slid past her but she was still knocked over again. That had taken all the reserve she had been practicing to hold. The large cat stood up and shook its head. Its eyes narrowed and it crouched low, ready to attack one more time. Aisling had nothing left and she was too filled with fear to concentrate. She kept trying to gather light and it kept slipping out of her grasp.

The cougar's muscles bunched, ready to jump - but then went slack. Blood spread across its head and it fell to the ground, lifeless.

That's when she heard the hard footfalls in the snow and turned in time to see Matari racing toward her. He came to a stop on his knees, sliding up to her and checking her for wounds.

"Just a scratch," she said shakily.

He looked at the wound.

"Lucky," he said.

He walked over to the cat and nudged it with his foot to make sure it wasn't going to suddenly spring to life like in some bad horror movie. He bent down and hefted a thin wooden tool, bent at an angle.

"Glad I'm a decent throw," he said, "Well, a lucky throw, with this boomerang. Not easy to aim in tight quarters like these woods."

She nodded dumbly. He held out his hand she took it, accepting the offered help. But she stumbled as she did so and he caught her up in his arms. For a moment, they held each other and looked into each other's eyes. But then Matari suddenly stiffened and she looked around.

Jake was standing on the trail taking in the scene. Without a word he turned his back and walked away.

"Jake, wait!" called Aisling. She disentangled herself from Matari, but after two steps her head started spinning. Everything in the world was blurry and the persistent headache she had been carrying with her roared into life, spreading shockwaves of pain through her skull.

She lost all sense of balance and watched as the entire world tipped over sideways. Her vision tunneled until all that was left was the barest light and the distant sound of her name being called over and over.

Retreating from the pain, she followed dark paths, long winding roads, making her way through deep and endless chambers within her being. Finally, after what felt like years of walking through darkness, she saw a light. Running toward it she watched as it grew and grew.

I must be dreaming! Maybe I can swim with Mother Earth again.

She was aware of a memory, of pain and snow, but it was unpleasant to think about, so she tried to block it from her mind. She stepped out of the darkness into light, hoping to be embraced by the soothing, loving light of her dreams once more.

All she found was fire. And more pain.

Chapter 30 - Eric

Wrapped in blankets, Eric felt warmth and life returning to him. He glanced over at Skia's sleeping face in the dim flickering of the fire. She was also wrapped up and he could see the blush of colour on her pale skin.

Cor handed him an aluminum mug of hot tea, steaming in the cold, wintry air.

"Here, drink this, it'll help."

Eric accepted the mug and took a small sip. It was scalding hot but he took a bigger swallow anyway, feeling the heat course down his chest into his gut, spreading warmth out from the core of his body. His fingers were still clumsy and he spilled some of the liquid, almost relishing the burning sensation because it wasn't cold. He was alive.

"So ...."

Eric returned Cor's questioning look with an impassive face. He didn't want to be grateful, he didn't want to feel like he owed Cor anything. But he did and he couldn't escape the fact. He owed his life to his enemy. Cor's one eyebrow raised with the unspoken question as he glanced at the young sleeping girl. The scar tissue on the other side of his face moved in an ugly, twisting, stretch - seeming to writhe in the dancing flame.

"We met in the woods," Eric finally conceded.

"Ah, I see."

Cor leaned back as if that answered everything. Eric realized that Cor probably didn't even care about the exact answer. He was just trying to get Eric to give something up no matter how trivial. It was a game and Cor had just scored a point. Eric sipped his tea and realized that it, too, was some kind of marker and he felt Cor was winning something here that Eric just couldn't figure out.

I owe him my life.

He hated the thought. He hated the burden and the twisted way it made him feel. This was a deeper magic, more compelling than the lightpower by which Eric could control Cor.

"Where were you?" Eric finally asked.

"Looking for you. You disappeared. I thought you'd gotten lost. What, you think I'm going to try to run away? No thanks, I've tried that, O mighty master. Hurts like hell."

He scratched at his empty eye socket.

"I am curious about one thing, though," he continued.

"What's that?"

"What took you so damned long? I was starting to worry I'd starve to death! Where the heck did you go? I thought I was good at following trails but yours just … vanished!"

"I was only gone a few hours, man. You can stop being so melodramatic."

Cor's one eye opened wide.

"A few hours? A few hours? You and me gotta get our timeframes together, buddy, because you've got yourself a real talent for underestimating. Pffft, a few hours. Can you believe this guy?" he turned his entreaty to the empty forest.

Eric's senses turned to high alert. Here was another situation where he could sense Cor about to score a big advantage, and he couldn't allow it. Mind racing, he realized he must have been gone a lot longer than he thought. The adrenaline rushing through his veins at the challenge and sense of danger sped his thoughts and brought him a new mental clarity.

A few hundred hours, maybe? I've been gone days? Weeks? Is it possible? Does time work different in that other place?

Carefully he pushed the shock of the realization down until his breathing calmed and he felt more in control of himself. He chuckled.

"Well, you know how it is. I guess I just lost track of time."

"And clothes too." He glanced meaningfully at the sleeping Skia and cracked a wry, lecherous grin.

Eric's pretense vanished and he barked out, "You leave her out of it. Don't even dare say anything about her!"

"Whoa, whoa! Settle down, little buddy. Hit a sore spot there, did I?"

Eric knew he had lost points again and that, if it kept going, it would never stop between him and the boy he once looked up to.

"Just be quiet about it," he muttered, and he heard how childish he sounded. He knew how easily Cor could manipulate him and push his buttons. An uncomfortable feeling started to slip inside him, a knowledge that he didn't want to face.

Cor was smarter than he was. Cor could have probably already figured out a way to escape him. If he'd really be gone for weeks, then Cor could have easily left and gotten as far away from this place as possible. But he didn't. He stayed. And he even saved Eric and Skia from freezing to death.

What game was he playing?

The uncomfortable feeling grew and Eric knew it for what it really was. A deep yawning chasm of fear and he felt he was about to fall in.

"Hey, don't worry, little man, you're the boss. I'll keep quiet about your girlfriend if you want."

There was a flurry of limbs and Cor was knocked sideways, almost landing in the fire. Red hair whipped back out of Skia's face and her eyes were black flashing jewels of obsidian in the dim flames.

"What's going on!" Cor demanded. His face was pressed sideways into the ground by Skia's knee. She ignored him and faced Eric.

"What are you doing with this … *kakachaya?*" she demanded.

"Hey…! Harsh!" Cor said into the snow.

She rasped a threatening sound at him.

"We should rip out his heart and throw it into this fire. Can you not smell his deceptions? The reek of it woke me."

Eric realized Skia's senses, though dulled from what she knew in the summer land, were still so sharp she could probably smell his own fear and he was ashamed.

"We can't kill him," he said.

"Yes we can, it's easy," she insisted. "I'll rip his throat out."

"No!" Eric said. "No, I need him alive."

"Alive? Why?"

"I'm taking him to my father," Cor mumbled.

She growled at Cor again and then said to Eric, "Are you insane enough to follow through with that plan? This is exactly why I was sent to travel with you. You *know* who he serves!"

"Shut up!" Cor snapped. Skia dug her knee harder into his jaw, never taking her eyes off Eric. Cor made pained sounds into the dirt.

"His father is the evil we fear most, the Devourer of the Light. He is taking you to your death, Eric. Don't you know that?"

Eric slowly nodded, then bowed his head so he wouldn't have to show his tears.

"Look what you're doing to him!" Cor shouted at Skia. "Why are you torturing him instead of helping him?"

Skia responded by twisting Cor's arm up behind his back. The sound he emitted was more screech than scream, and Eric looked up in time to see a black fog surround both Skia and Cor. As it coalesced, the giant Raven was there in place of the boy and he was free of his tormenter.

Skia crouched low. As Cor attacked, she leapt to the side, jammed her heel into the earth, pivoted almost instantaneously and landed hard on the great bird's back, gripping his wings, trying to pin them down, ripping feathers out of Cor's skin. He tried beating his wings harder and the sharp edges of his feathers cut into Skia's hands, across her bare skin.

Eric scrambled back in fright. He fumbled for his stone and with his second eyes he located and tore up veins of light, siphoning the energy fast and ruthlessly filling the stone with power but it wasn't enough. He pulled out his pocket knife and cut into his palm, blood gushing out and over the stone only to be absorbed as fast as it flowed. He held the stone, allowing his own living blood to keep feeding it until he began to feel a steady, pulsating strength.

"Enough!" he boomed, his voice amplified by the magic he was blending, his own life force with the life in the ground.

The two fighters ignored him, intent on destroying each other.

"I said enough!" and he sent a blast of rage at the sky, lighting the world around them with an eerie red glow, the snow at their feet evaporating into mist.

Cor and Skia stopped in surprise and Eric brought the light down to surround the three of them and, pushing against the earth, pulled them out of the forest, racing on a red flame toward the mountains glowing a cool blue in the distance of the night, lit by a placid, pale moon.

Chapter 31 - Aisling

She had been in agony for an eternity. There was no beginning to it, no end, just the searing, destroying pain that had consumed her body, devouring all thought, memory and emotion.

She didn't know her name. She didn't recall a life. In fact, there was nothing but the crucible in which she burned.

And then it stopped.

All was darkness and cold. It would have been a relief if all her senses were not raw and quivering from the feverish heat she had just endured. But they were and so the sudden end to her suffering was nearly worse than the ordeal itself.

She lay in darkness.

Eons could have passed and she would not know it. Eventually her skin cooled, her mind started coming back to her in small fragments like bits of coloured cloth blowing by in the wind. That she could remember wind she took as a good sign. She formed her first question.

Who am I?

A voice spoke from out of the darkness.

"Your name is Aisling."

She let that sink in. It took a very long time. She turned the phrase over in her mind, trying to remember what the words meant.

Aisling...yes. There was something about it that connected with her. It *means me.*
The concept of Me was incredible to her. That she existed was a miracle that threw her into a stupor of wonder.

Who are you? She asked the darkness.

"I'm a friend. I've come to help you."

This made her happy, more memories started coming back. She wanted more. She started reaching, straining for the fragments that were tantalizingly close, like small butterflies in the darkness that she could almost reach out and touch.

"Not too fast," the voice said. "Let them come to you slowly."

She nodded and let the pieces wash over her, fitting into the pattern of her that she was discovering as each fragment stitched itself into place. She felt substance returning to her, a sense of self and identity until at last, she was back. She was whole and knew everything.

"Matari," she said.

She heard a breath of relief.

"Yes, Aisling. Welcome back. You can open your eyes now."

Aisling did as she was instructed, propping herself up off the hard ground as she did so. Matari was sitting across from her, weariness lining his face and making him look much older than his young years. He was shirtless, his lean torso covered in dust, his lips dry and cracked. The sky stretched over them in a giant dome of deepest blue and the red desert spilled out to every horizon. Hard-packed dusty earth as far as the eye could see, with only a few twisted, stunted trees and bushes scattered about like an afterthought to break the unending desolation.

"Don't be alarmed," he said in response to her questioning look. "The worst is over. And yes, you are Dreaming."

"Dreaming. So … are you a part of my dream then?"

He smiled, his white teeth flashing as he nodded.

"Of course. Just as you are part of mine. But this is a real Dream, and you are really here and I am really here, and both of us are still back with your Grandmother and Auntie and Jake."
They were silent, listening to the wind scrape softly across the desert sands.

"I was hurt."

"Yes. You didn't tell us you were wounded. Anyone else would be dead by now, but you survived. You sent yourself out into the Dream."

"How did that save me?" She swallowed hard at the news that she had almost died.

"When in the Dream, our bodies slow down, almost stop."

"Like meditation."

"Yeah, that's it exactly."

"So why are we still here, why haven't I woken up?"

A thought occurred to her.

"I'm not okay, am I?"

Matari stood up, stretched his back. He looked into the distance, shielding his eyes against the sun.

"We should go that way," he finally said. He reached down to help Aisling to her feet. She stood and brushed off her clothes. They started walking.

"You didn't tell us about your wound," Matari said.

She thought back to that dark night, the giant raven that bit at her leg, the blood.

"I thought I was okay. It wasn't that deep and I washed it out."

"Yes, that would have been enough normally, especially since you Dream. The Dreaming helps your body heal, did you know that?"

She shook her head.

"Aisling, the thing that bit you was poisonous. It was no bird, even though it looked like one. It was the offspring of darkness. And some of it infected you. Right now your Kokum is building a sweat lodge and there is a fire burning to heat the rocks. While they're doing that I have to take you to see someone here who can heal you."
"Heal me here? In a dream?"

"Look at your leg."

In the Dream, she was wearing a linen button-up shirt, a brimmed hat, light socks and durable hiking boots. She was also wearing shorts and had a clear view of her calf. It was an open wound, wet with blood and pus. All she could think of was how there was no pain.

"The wound goes deep, but while you are here it moves slowly. We should have enough time."

She didn't have to ask for what. She knew he was talking about her life.

She tried to swallow but her throat was dry and tight.

"Do you have any water?" she asked Matari.

He pointed to the ground beside them.

Was he mocking her? She waited to see if some miraculous stream was going to bubble up from the ground. Nothing happened and she glared at him.

He looked puzzled and Aisling watched in disbelief as he crouched over, scooped some of the dust into his hands and brought it to his mouth, swallowing it easily, his lips covered in the dry, yellow dirt.

Her eyes filled with tears.

He's not really here, is he? I'm just in some kind of bad dream and I'm dying alone.

"Aisling, what's wrong?" There was worry in his voice.

"I can't drink dust. You're only my imagination and this is a nightmare."

Matari bit his lower lip and regarded her, a frown of concern creasing his brow.

"No, Aisling, it would be easier if none of this were happening, but it is. I am here, and we must hurry." He walked away, swiftly covering ground. The urgency in his voice made her wipe her eyes and hurry to catch up with him.

"Are you really here with me?" she asked, uncertain.

He turned quickly and pulled her to his body. He picked her up and was carrying her.

"There is no time to waste."

"Are you really here?" she asked again, almost in a whisper. She was feeling weaker with every moment.

He looked into her eyes and her upturned face and pressed his lips against hers, softly, carefully. The dust on his lips transformed into precious drops of clean water and she swallowed them gratefully.

"I am here," he said, and began to run.

Chapter 32 - Eric

The dawn's light was pink and rosy, a counterpoint in light to the rage Eric had been feeling. But now he was calm as the silent morning, his heart icy and alone.

He flexed his hand, examining the wound he had inflicted just hours ago. It was healed over, but more than that, the skin of his palm was greyish, hard and cold. He tested it with the knife and saw that it dimpled at the pressure but the knife didn't pierce. He would have to apply real pressure to cut himself again. He ran his fingers across the new skin and found it had a slightly different texture than his own. It also extended up around his knuckles and down his wrist a couple inches.

They had landed just outside of a town called Canmore. Walking along the tree line edging the highway so as not to be noticed, they made town early enough that no shops were open. Eric tried the handle of one supply store and it crumpled under his grip. He drew back his hand in wonder and flexed it.

I'm so strong!

He tried with his other hand but that one still just had the soft, weak grip of a kid. Was he twelve now or thirteen? He suspected that his birthday had come and gone while he was in Skia's summer world.

He punched his right hand into the door of the shop and it went right through the heavy wood.

"Come on," he told his two companions. "We can go inside."

They followed him and found Skia some clothes, heavy jeans and work boots, a flannel shirt, a heavy jacket. They replenished their packs. Cor was leaving when Eric called him over.

"I'm not a thief," he said. "Pay for what we're taking."

"Umm, so it's just okay to take *my* money, then?"

Eric simply held Cor's gaze until the other relented and pulled a stack of bills out of his pocket. It was more than enough to cover the goods and damage to the door.

"Now what?" Cor asked as they made their way along the highway. There were more cars on the road and people were out, walking their dogs, cross-country skiing, jogging.

Eric felt like he was an alien in a strange world. All these things seemed so … normal.

"Now we go for breakfast. I don't know about you guys but I'm starved."

Skia said nothing but followed along. She hadn't said a word since Eric had displayed the power he wielded. Eric could understand. He was just going with it right now, finally feeling like he had the upper hand with Cor. On the ragged edge of his mind, however, he was still scared out of his wits at what he had been able to do.

All that blood.

He pictured it gushing out of the deep gash he had dug into his hand.

All that power.

And it had paid off, hadn't it? Not only was he able to take control of the situation, he had gained some kind of super strength and super skin as well. He would worry about it later. Or maybe he wouldn't. When was he going to stop being such a suck and stop worrying about everything he didn't understand? He was still getting lessons from Cor, he realized. Cor wasn't freaking out or acting any differently than before. He just rolled with the punches, didn't he?

As if on cue, the older boy said, "How about the Husky's Diner over there? I could really go for some steak and eggs."

For the first time Skia came out of her silence.

"That's hideous."

"What, you think I'm a cannibal because I eat eggs?" Cor asked, "I'm as much a carnivore as you. Maybe more. You're a human now but from the way you fought last night let me guess. A wolf? No, no, not friendly enough. A coyote?"

Skia took a swipe at Cor's eyes and he jumped back.

"Okay, too early for small talk, I get it. Hey just hold up. I don't want to make little children cry when they look at my pretty face."

He closed his eyes and concentrated. A shadow passed over his face and when it was gone, so too was the scarring.

"You healed yourself?" asked Eric, dumbfounded.

"I wish. Just a bit of … makeup, I guess you would say." He winked and walked on.

The bell on the door jingled as they pushed their way in to the diner. A pretty waitress with auburn hair, pale eyes, and a petite nose glanced over.

"Just seat yourselves," she called over her shoulder as she cleared a table of dishes and gave it a quick swipe with a damp rag.

They slid into a booth and she dropped off their menus.

"What can I get you to drink?"

Despising himself, Eric ordered something only because he remembered the first night Cor and he had started out on the road together. A drink that Cor had thought was cool.

"Coffee, please."

He thought he saw a small smirk on Cor's face but couldn't tell as the older boy flashed his winning smile at the waitress.

"Rachel," he said reading her name tag, "I'd like to order you to give me your phone number, but instead I'd absolutely love a large orange juice and some Earl Grey tea."

"You got it," she said, smiling back at the charming boy. It took her a second to shake off the spell and she appeared annoyed at having to break away from Cor to talk to Skia. "And for you, miss?"

"Me what?"

"What do you want to drink?"

A look of confusion passed over Skia's face, "What else would I drink? Clean water, please."

Rachel gave a huff and glanced at Cor who rolled his eyes good-naturedly. They shared a quick smile and she went off to grab their drinks.

"What was that about?" Eric asked.

"What was what about?" Cor said innocently.

"Were you flirting with her?"

"Uh, yeah, of course. I haven't seen an attractive girl in ages! What, jealous?"

Eric's cheeks reddened.

"No! Don't be stupid!"

"Ah, I'm just hassling you, man. Besides, that one over there seems to be crushing on you hardcore."

Eric looked across the diner to a family just getting up from their meal. A girl with deep brown eyes smiled shyly at him. His red cheeks turned even darker.

"Are these normal mating rituals or are you two socially inept?" Skia asked with acid in her voice. "You do realize I exist, yes?"

"Uh oh, now I think *she's* jealous," Cor whispered loudly in a dramatic aside.

Eric couldn't help but laugh.

And then he sobered. He did it again! Cor could make himself so likeable, could appear to be such a good friend. It was wearing Eric down. Instead of thinking about it he just opened his menu and buried his nose in it.

He looked askance at Skia beside him. She was holding her menu upside down and he realized she couldn't read. He explained everything on the menu to her and despite her look of skepticism she agreed to try the pancakes, eggs and sausage. Being close to her - helping her - made him feel awkward and happy at the same time. His hands were trembling slightly and he clenched them into fists. Chagrined, he hid the spoon he'd bent out shape with his new, strong hand.

When the food arrived and Skia started eating with her fingers he just sighed and let her enjoy herself. And enjoy herself she did.

"This is wonderful!" she exclaimed as she shoved another piece of syrupy pancake into her mouth. "Maybe you humans aren't completely stupid after all."

Eric was doubtful as he took another sip of the bitter coffee he had ordered out of pride.

When they were finished, Cor went to pay the waitress and Eric saw that she wrote her number down on a slip of paper and handed it to Cor with the change. He tucked a twenty dollar bill into her apron and as he turned to walk away she grabbed his arm and gave him a quick kiss.

"Call me!" she said as they left the restaurant. Cor smiled and gave her a small wave. As they rounded the corner he crumpled up the slip of paper and tossed it aside.

"Well, I feel like a new man! Where to next, Cochise?"

"You tell me. You always said we had to get to the mountains. Well, here we are."

"Can I object again to this course of action?" Skia asked.

"Sure, why not?" Cor murmured as he put his arm around Eric's shoulder and steered him away from the girl.

"Right you are, Eric, my brother. Now we just have to get in a little further. There's a mountain up ahead called Tunnel Mountain and getting there will take us where we need to go a lot faster than walking, or flying for that matter."

"Okay, well, let's go. I don't want to spend too much longer here. I'm worried about the police recognizing us."

"Well, we've got this red-headed spitfire here to help throw off the scent, so to speak. So cool your jets. Not far to go now."

"You still have money?"

"More than I'll ever need. I'll be right back, I'm going to go hit that ATM over there."

"Good. Skia, you ever ridden a Greyhound?"

"Don't be absurd."

"Oh! I mean a bus … look, forget it. But I think this is something you might like."

"As much as you like doe-eyed girls who probably can't even catch a mouse?"

"What? You mean that girl from the restaurant?"

"Oh, you remember. It's enlightening to learn all males here treat females like inferiors. I'm certain 'that girl' you initiated courting with had a name."

Eric was thrown for a loop.

"Uh. What?"

"It makes sense. You are of a kind."

"I wasn't courting anyone! I - what? No?"

"Was *that* supposed to make sense? If so, you'll have trouble with your lady friend."

"Skia ...."

She raised an eyebrow.

"I'm sorry. I don't know how all this stuff is supposed to work."

She softened and gave his cheek a gentle pat.

"That's all right, dear. Just try to keep up." She leaned in and gave him a quick lick on the cheek with the tip of her tongue and left to talk to Cor. Eric watched her go, feeling the damp spot on his cheek and a flush of warmth sweep over him.

"So what are you doing?" she asked Cor suspiciously as he entered his PIN into the machine.

"Playing the lotto," Cor muttered.

Eric touched his cheek where Skia's tongue had licked him. She had smelled of warm, dry grass and strawberries when she had been so close to him.

As if a drop of water had fallen from his temporarily melted heart and spread ripples on a calm liquid surface, small waves of awareness hit Eric with a pleasing, tiny swell.

He was falling in love.

Chapter 33 - Aisling

"There!" Matari panted, relief audible in his voice.

Aisling turned her face away from Matari's chest to gaze out into the shimmering heat. A small round hut was barely visible along the horizon. It looked as if it were made of wood and blankets.

Skins?

As they neared she could see a fire was burning a few paces away from the hut. There were rocks in the flames, heating in the coals.

"A sweat lodge?" she asked. "How?"

"I called ahead before you awoke. With my bullroarer." He indicated the string and wood slung over his shoulder. The wood was shaped like a seed a little longer than Aisling's hand. She had a vague memory of Matari swinging it around his head. It was a relief to know the buzzing, wailing sound was real and not a part of her feverish dreaming.

"Your Gran said we need to sweat you in both worlds," he explained as he set her down carefully. They had reached the hut just in time to see a man emerge from a small door covered with a loose flap of animal hide.

Aisling wanted cool air but she knew it was far hotter inside the hut than even the desert air.

"Ah, you're here. Good. Help me, Matari," the old man said, handing the young man a pitchfork. Matari seemed at a loss.

"The stones! The stones. Pick one up and bring it inside."

Matari obeyed, digging into the ashes of the fire pit. He balanced a rock the size of a man's head on the tongs of the pitchfork and carefully took it to the hut. As he walked by Aisling could feel the dry heat emanating from it.

"Into the pit," the man said. Aisling saw the rock pit inside glowing with a pink hue.

"So Aisling, we have to get you inside, but first, drink this please."

The man was old. How old she couldn't say but he was shrivelled and wrinkled, lean and thin. But he had vitality to him and, as he wore nothing but a cloth around his waist to cover himself, she noted that his muscles rippled as he moved. His afro was mostly white with specks of black in it. His creased face was lined with good humour, but right now he looked concerned.

At her hesitation he said, "Forgive me. My name is Inkata. I am a friend of your *Mamaay*, your grandmother. I spent many years with your grandfather, your *Mosum*, as you say, when we were young men, a looong time ago. I was wandering, drawn to your land. I was adopted by your family. I served as an *Oskapêwis*, learning so much of the powerful Cree culture. In many ways, although we have never met I feel that you are as dear to me as my own granddaughter." He looked at her leg, but his face remained calm, "Now please, drink this. We have only a short time left."

"I - I can't. It's dust."

Matari was digging for another stone but Inkata whistled him over.

"We have to begin. Now." He flicked an anxious glance at Aisling.

"Yes, sir."

They carried Aisling into the sweat lodge. Inside it was blacker than the darkest night save for the stones glowing like they'd just come up from the molten depths of the earth. There was the familiar scent of smudge in the air and of the medicines, the herbs and plants of the sweat.

Inkata sat at the spot directly opposite the door, only the stone pit between him and the entrance. Aisling lay at his right. She could hear Matari settle down across from her on Inkata's left. The air was heavy in her lungs and she had already begun to sweat profusely.

The old man cleared his throat and began speaking in a language Aisling didn't recognize, but the cadence was familiar. He was praying. After a time he stopped. Then he said in English, "These ways are not the ways of my own people, but I call on the Creator to help us, to help me be strong, to bring my prayers and the prayers of your *Mamaay* together, to bridge the space between this world and the other. Then your *Mamaay* will lead us."

She heard water sloshing in a bucket and the next moment listened as the dipper poured its contents onto the rocks. The resulting steam hit her face like a slap, the already terrible heat became almost unbearable and she felt her heart begin to beat faster as her body began to panic. She turned inward and focused on her breathing, on her limbs and her core. She breathed in the herbs and the unexpected moisture.

Then Inkata began to sing. Matari was keeping the rhythm of the song with a rattle and Aisling's heart drummed in time. Or so she thought. The sound of rattles grew louder and with it came singing. The words wafted in and out of hearing but suddenly grew clear. Cree words. Sung by her Grandmother and her Auntie. Aisling couldn't believe it. It was as though they were there in the sweat lodge with them.

The song came to an end and there was silence.

"If it's too hot my love, let Mother Earth help cool you."

"Kokum?"

"Yes. We are here, but not here, my dear. I am so happy to hear your voice. Now, hush and let yourself be healed. Any hurts, any pains, in your body, in your heart, in your thoughts, in your spirit. Let them go. We Elders will take them in for you, we will carry your burdens. Only let yourself be healed."

A new song began.

Aisling placed her palm on the ground beside her and felt the cooling strength of the earth take away some of the heat in her body, just as she felt the throbbing pain in her leg begin to fade and the worries she felt lift from her brow and heart. Her chest relaxed and her blood began pumping in cadence to the music. More steam, more heat, more music. She fell into a reverie.

She saw a comet streaking across the winter sky, heading towards her. As it descended she saw it wasn't a comet at all but Eric. He looked older. It was his eyes, the tight set of his jaw and the grimness of his mouth. He had company. An older boy with jet black hair and a young woman who looked almost as serious as her brother.

He's alive!

That he was flying didn't strike her as unusual, not after all she had seen. All that mattered was Eric was alive. He was in the mountains and he was alive.

The vision faded and a new one arose. Out of the darkness a great bear approached.

"Father," she said.

The bear ambled up beside her and sat down on his haunches. He had a smoke in his paw and took a drag.

As he blew a few smoke rings he glanced down at her, managing a rueful expression.

"I always thought it was these that'd kill me."

She smiled up at him. For the first time she wasn't afraid or awkward next to the beast.

"What are we going to do, hey, my girl?"

"I was kind of hoping you'd tell me, Dad."

"Right. I was never good about any of this stuff. You think it was easy trying to ignore it all? Trying to keep you and Eric out of Kokum's insanity? We thought it was all just an old woman's crazy dreams, your Mom and me. Neither of us wanted to be different."

"But you were, and so are we. Why didn't you even try to help me and Eric with these … gifts?"

"We thought we were. Here's a news flash: parents don't know what the hell they're doing."

Aisling considered his statement. She'd never really given it that much thought but some of her cousins were already parents at sixteen.

"I guess they don't give out manuals," she said.

"Well, no. But to be honest I wish they did. Maybe if they had Dr. Phil when we were growing up …."

She smiled again.

"Dad? Why are you a bear?"

"To protect you, my girl. That was my thing. I could turn into a bear. It scared your Auntie Martha pretty good first time it happened! I was really angry at her for something, I can't even remember what, and the next thing I know instead of shouting at her I was roaring! Good thing your Kokum was there to calm everything down. After that I was always worried that if I got angry I'd change again."

"You wouldn't like me when I'm angry," Aisling intoned.

"Yup, a regular Bruce Banner over here. Talented and good-looking to boot."

"Ha! Not even!"

"Hey! I can't help my weight" He hefted his drooping midsection with his paws.

"But seriously, Aisling. I knew I was dead when I saw those explosions heading toward me at the plant. Next thing I know I'm racing through the woods on all fours. Only thing is ...." he paused and his bear face hung low.

"What?"

"I don't think I changed in time. I think I lost something important in that explosion, a part of me burned away or something. I can feel myself fading. I don't know how long I've got but at night when the Northern Lights are dancing I can hear the song, Aisling. I can feel the love and the urge to join them."

"You're dying?"

"I am already dead. I'm just grateful that I get to spend a little more time with you."

Aisling felt her eyes fill with tears.

"I've had time to think about it," her father said. "And you can stop crying any time. You already mourned for me, didn't you?"

"Yes," she said, wiping her tears. "But now I'll have to do it all over again."

"Tss! Be happy, girl! Be thankful for the time we've got. It's a rare gift, isn't it?"

She nodded and hugged the big smelly creature beside her.

"I love you, Dad."

"Love you, too. Now there's another reason I'm here."

"Okay?"

"When you wake up things are going to be a little different for you. Just remember that life is a gift, right? And don't get scared, everything's just fine."

"But -"

"Nope. Just a yessir, please.

"Yes, sir."

"That's my girl. Always up for humouring her old man. See you on the other side."

He ambled off into the darkness, leaving the smell of wet fur behind.

The songs had stopped and the air was cool in her lungs. She opened her eyes. She was in a tent and Martha and Kokum were with her. The tent was glowing from the sunlight outside.

"Am I awake?"

"Yes," Martha said. "How do you feel?"

Aisling realized she had absolutely no aches or pains; she felt healthy, happy and calm. She said as much.

Kokum spoke. "It was close my dear. We can't stay much longer but you'll return from here soon enough. You need to stay in both worlds to allow the healing to complete itself."

Aisling pulled aside her blankets to look at her calf. There was no more wound. In fact there was no more calf.

In place of her leg from the knee down was a living prosthetic in the shape of her foot and lower leg which entwined perfectly with her flesh. It was a tree branch, complete with a few small, green leaves.

Chapter 34 - Eric

When they bought their tickets he still felt the warm glow of happiness growing within him.

"The Three Wolves!" Skia had said in surprise before they boarded the bus. Eric looked to the mountain range she was pointing at. Three massive peaks jutted up into the sky like the ragged remainder of a giant jawbone.

"Oh, you mean the Three Sisters," a woman said helpfully.

"Sisters? Well, maybe, I guess," Skia said.

"They do look like wolves, though, if you think of it that way," the woman replied. She smiled kindly and got on board.

As they passed different peaks and valleys Eric wondered at how they were named. He heard a man telling his son that the upcoming mountain was once named Squaw's Tit, but no one called it that for obvious reasons. Cor almost choked on his drink when he heard that one.

The trees whipped by quickly and more than once they passed a smear of blood across the road where an unlucky driver and beast had met – with disastrous results. Once they saw an elk carcass still on the side of the road, a murder of crows picking at the body. These visions came and went in a flash.

Faster than he thought possible they were pulling up to their stop. They had arrived. After weeks of travel they were in the townsite of Banff National Park. They waited for their bags to unload and then hiked over to Banff Avenue, the main street. There were hundreds of people strolling the avenue, popping into the various stores and malls, cafes and restaurants.

Skia's eyes darted about.

"So many people!" she gasped. "How do they all eat without running out of food?"

Cor smiled condescendingly. "They ship it in, Madame Curie. Listen, while we're in, you know, a people place - would you mind shutting your jaw and trying to act like you fit in? The idea is to not attract attention and I don't want people noticing you drooling in shock like a backwards savage."

Eric expected Skia to fight back and he tensed himself for her attack, but it never came. Instead, she looked cowed and maybe even a little frightened. Her ears pulled back and she hunched over, making herself appear smaller. He looked away, uncomfortable.

"Better," Cor said. "Now come on, we've got to find someone who looks like a sucker."

They passed by art galleries and every time Eric noticed Skia's eyes widen at the beautiful images. He didn't blame her. His artistic heart responded to the work and he felt that wild thing inside of him begin to wake at the inspiration and beauty of it all. He saw her face go from amazed to horrified as they passed a fur shop. There were beautiful coats and hats on display, one of them made of rich, deep fox fur. He took her hand in his and squeezed it.

"Come on, try not to think about it. Things are different here, animals can't talk or think in this place."

"I do."

"Yeah, but you're a human here."

She yanked her hand out of his, but then looked apologetic.

"I'm sorry, Eric. I'm overwhelmed."

And with that simple statement his heart went out to her. From the little time they had spent together he understood what that admission had cost her, how lost she must really be feeling.

"It's okay. Come on we better keep up. Looks like Cor found his sucker."

They hurried over to where Cor was in conversation with a man in his twenties, bearded and thin.

"Look," he was saying, "I'll give you the cash right now so you won't be out a cent. What, you want my brother and cousin here to freeze to death just because my parent's flight got delayed? My Dad put a load of cash into my bank account and now I just need an adult with a credit card to help us out. We can't check in without one, you know?"

"Sure you can, kid. Just hit the Hostel and leave a cash deposit, no biggie."

"Look at my cousin. You really think she'll be okay in a hostel? She has no social skills, is kind of dumb, to be honest, and really, her family would go nuts if they heard she was slumming it on her vacation."

"I dunno, man."

"Here," Cor said and he pulled out a wad of twenty dollar bills. "That's two grand, you can count it. And there's another two grand after we check in."

"Four thousand bucks to check you into the Banff Springs for one night?"

"Fine, walk away," Cor said looking over the man's shoulder. "I'm sure someone else could use the money."

"Now hold on. I never said I wouldn't do it, it's just … this is crazy."

"Well then, let's go." Cor flagged down a minivan cab and they piled in. He gave the destination and off they went. As they drove they passed over a bridge spanning a frozen river.

"Time was, you could sleep under this bridge," Cor said to Eric. "Up on the struts just under the roadway. A good way to keep dry in wet weather."

The man looked sharply at Cor.

"What?" Cor asked.

"Huh? Nothing. Just wondering when you would have stayed under a bridge and now you've got all this money."

"Practice," Cor said. "Just in case. I was a Boy Scout, you know. Be Prepared. That's our motto."

The man gave half a snort of laughter and let it pass. They drove up a slight slope of a road and the trees opened up before them revealing what Eric could only describe as an enormous castle.

The van drove past the grounds, under a walkway and around to the lobby entryway. After the cabbie was paid up they went inside. Eric and Skia hung back while Cor went with the bearded man to the front desk and made the arrangements.

"Pretty nice place, huh?" Eric said looking around at the beautiful marble stairs, the woodwork carved into ornate designs.

"I don't know," Skia said, still subdued.

"Of course it's nice. That's why we got the executive suite," Cor smiled as he rejoined them.

"You rich kids," the man said. "You're all weirdos."

Cor paid him no attention beyond passing him an envelope into which the man gave a furtive glance and satisfied, patted Cor on the shoulder.

"You be good now, kids," he said and left the hotel.

"Did he really believe your story?" Eric asked as they made their way to the elevators.

"Of course not, but that was the point. He needed something to attach to so his mind wouldn't start asking a lot of inconvenient questions like was this legal? He wanted the money and I could have pretty much said anything and he would've half convinced himself he believed it."

"Oh. So he was just greedy?"

"Aren't we all, Uhhr? Aren't we all?"

The elevator doors opened and they rode to the top floor.

Cor pulled out a key card and inserted it into the door at the end of the hallway.

"Don't worry, I got us one with a view," he said as he opened the door wide for them. "Settle in and relax. Tomorrow we go to meet my father."

Chapter 35 - Aisling

As she recovered, she spent many hours each day in the Dreaming with Matari. Being with him made her feel less lost and certainly less alone.

When she emerged from the sweat lodge, the landscape had changed. Instead of the dry barren wasteland the place had appeared to be while in her feverish state, she now saw a paradise of rolling fields of grass, little streams and rivers, beautiful flowers and great, thick-trunked trees providing shade from the warm sun in the midday heat. Under the cool shade of undulating, flickering leaves they feasted on fruits right from the branches. They also ate the delicious, fresh vegetables and even flowers from the abundance that grew all around them.

The evenings were soft and gentle, and the hint of humidity and salt water from some not too distant sea wafted on the air from the darkness beyond.

Matari and Aisling walked, hand-in-hand, under unfamiliar stars. Her new leg felt strong, but much more sensitive than before. Not in any painful way, but more attuned to the grass that caressed it, the air that whispered along her bark-like skin. She had expected it to be rough and said so to Matari.

He knelt down and ran his hand across the back of her calf. She shivered at the sensation.

"It's smooth," he said, his voice almost cracking even though he whispered. "And warm."

She knelt down beside him in the tall grass and looked into his eyes. They were close enough that she could feel his breath on her face and she knew he could feel hers as well. They stayed like that for some time, breathing each other, gazing into eyes filled with thoughts to which neither could give voice. The darkness of the night made everything so simple, so honest. So true. Their hands found each other and their fingers intertwined, strengthening the connection that caused their hearts to beat so loudly, their breathing to come in such a rush.

In the night an animal howled, far off and lonely.

"That's how I feel," Matari said.

The spell that held them began to unwind, loosening its hold on Aisling.

"Lonely? Here with me?"

"I'm never lonely when I'm with you, Aisling! But I already feel your absence. I already miss you."

"But I'm right here."

"Tomorrow I won't be. Inkata needs me to help him return to his own lands. He's weakened after the sweat and asked me to assist him. How could I say no?"

Easy, Aisling thought, *just say no and come back with me. Stay with me*!

Instead she said aloud, "It's the right thing to do."

She meant it. She was grateful. In fact, she didn't know how to ever repay the debt. She had been preparing Inkata's meals, fetching him water, squeezing juice from the fruits for him to drink. She knew she would always owe him her life.

"I leave in the morning."

"Yeah. Okay, so walk with me, show me the way back. Let's get these adventures done so we can do something normal like go to the movies or hang out with elves or whatever."

Matari's smile was easily visible in the darkness.

"That's a plan and a half then, isn't it? Fair enough then, girl. Let's go."

He led her back to her tent and they both lay down on the blankets.

"Just close your eyes, match my breathing, and we're on our way."

"It sounds so simple."

"Nothing simpler. Now breathe."

She listened and followed his breaths. Nothing happened. She tried being patient, tried clearing her mind. It wasn't working.

"It's not working," she said.

Matari didn't reply. Was he sleeping?

She pushed herself up on one elbow to look at him but he was gone. Then she felt the chill in the air. She sat up on her knees and saw the two mounds in the darkness that she knew were her Auntie and Kokum. There was a little snoring.

Carefully, she made her way out of the tent, slipping into her boots and jacket laid out as if she were expected today, which of course, she was. Her footsteps crunched in the snow, breaking through the brittle top layer into the powdery stuff underneath. *It must have been warmer today*, she thought absently.

She came to a fallen tree and sat down on the long, dead trunk. She pulled up her pant leg to examine her new calf, then pulled off her boot and sock. It seemed the same here in what she considered the real world. A living limb, all right. But it still looked like it was grown from a tree.

What else are you going to change about me?

She closed her eyes and there was the light again, the bloodlines she had missed more than she had known. It was only seeing them now that made her realize just how much. She coaxed the pulsing light toward her, letting it fill her. A thought occurred to her and she decided to follow it. Breathing slowly and deliberately she built a picture in her mind of Mother Earth - her beautiful Turtle form - glowing with light. Maybe if she followed the paths of light deep enough she would find her again.

The light grew increasingly brighter but there was no turtle. Instead she saw a great flowing vein. It was so large she couldn't see to the other side of it. It flowed like a river and sitting on the darkened banks was a woman. It was impossible to tell her age. One moment she seemed old and wise, the next a child. Then she was a woman in the prime of her strength and energy. She kept shifting but, then again, never really changing at all.

"Hello," Aisling said. "Is it You?"

"I should hope so! Who else would it be? But then, I have a feeling it's not really me you're looking for."

"Oh. So you're not ...."

"No. I am a daughter, like you. Well, not exactly like you. I was born human but now I've become something else."

"What are you?"

"I suppose I'm like a shepherd, but I think you'd call me a buffalo herder to be more accurate. When I make an appearance, which is rare these days for obvious reasons, I am known as White Buffalo Calf Woman. A lofty title, no?"

"I'm - well, I'm just Aisling."

"Just? A little more than just, I think." The woman glanced at Aisling's hair, her leg. "You've been through a lot, I see."

"Kind of, I guess."

"And power? You have power I assume?"

"Sort of. I can sing and make things grow, if that counts."

"Well, of course that counts, dear girl! My goodness, yes. Is that the price you've paid, then, for your power?" She indicated Aisling's leg.

"Price? No this was a wound. My Kokum helped heal me."

"I see. It was certainly a noble sacrifice on her part, then."

"What do you mean?" Aisling suddenly felt a pit in her stomach. A fear and a burden she wasn't sure she wanted to know about.

"Oh dear. Young woman, what have you been taught?"

"Not much. I just started learning."

"So old to learn! Well, never mind that. Having the kind of power you do comes at a cost."

"You're telling me." Aisling rolled her eyes.

Without warning, she was surrounded by lightning and fire. It shocked her body and singed her skin. Fearful, she looked at the White Buffalo Calf Woman.

"Do not dare mock the gifts you have been given, young woman!"

And the lightning stopped as quick as it began.

"I'm sorry," Aisling said, rubbing her arm.

The woman softened quickly.

"Don't mind me," she said, but with no apology in her voice, "It's a quirk of mine. I do not suffer fools gladly. But enough of that. I feel you should know your power is not a toy."

"I never thought that it was," Aisling said, trying not to be afraid of this volatile woman. "But what did you mean about having a price? What price?"

"It affects everyone differently. Each according to what they have been given. For me, the price was to lose some of my patience, to become more like the lightning I control. I forget what it was like to be a woman, to be human. By accepting this responsibility I forfeited the chance at an ordinary life and I mourned it for centuries, but now I can't even seem to recall why I cared. For you, I think you will lose yourself in your growing things. That's why I thought you had already begun to change."

"My Kokum can calm people, help them relax and feel safe."

"Ah, a beautiful gift. But one that has endangered everything. It has made her far too complacent."

"You know my Kokum?"

"I know of her. I rarely stray far from these rivers anymore. I mostly watch the world through the eyes of the remaining buffalo, piecing together what I can. I know you wouldn't know it from my temper, but I am so glad to have a visitor."

"Yes, well I ...."

"Yes, I understand. You had better be getting back. You do know you are trailing far behind your brother, though, don't you?"

"You know where Eric is?"

"It takes no great skill. He and his friends are very close to my Gateway. And Aisling, you should know I have to let everyone pass who finds it."

"Where is it? How can I find it?"

"Sleeping Buffalo. A mountain."

Aisling snapped awake. Her mind reeled at the unexpected shift from dream to concrete reality. Why had she woken? She listened to the predawn silence.

Something was out there in the darkness and the cold. Something was watching her. Something was waiting.

Chapter 36 - Eric

They could have stared at the view forever. The valley stretched out before them, the mountains reaching up toward the clear, clean sky. The trees reached up along the mountain shoulders as high as they could before the altitude and the thinning of the air allowed them no higher. They were a dark green, almost black, those pines, with a light dusting of snow on them like so much powdered sugar sprinkled on a fairyland gingerbread forest. A river cut through the valley, cold and swift, and rising out of it somewhat unexpectedly, a giant hill in the broad plain between ranges, was Tunnel Mountain.

There were buildings arrayed on the lower face of it. Eric had asked around and they had been told it was the Banff Centre for the Arts, an international centre of study. Artists visited from around the world to study, share, create and perform. They were encouraged to go see it.

"Oh we'll see it, all right," Cor said acidly. "That's exactly where we're going."

He was getting ready to go down to the dining room to have dinner with a pretty girl he'd met in the hotel lobby.

"Hey, a guy's gotta date, right? After tonight I'm not sure how much free time I'll have to enjoy the … simple things."

He drew the camouflaging shadow around him, hiding his hideous scarring, smoothing out the imperfections in his skin.

"How do I look?" he asked as he adjusted his collar in the mirror.

"Stupid," Eric said.

"Excellent," Cor smirked. "I'd say wish me luck, but when you're this good-looking, you just don't need it. Am I right?" He directed his question to Skia. She simply snarled.

"Ah, I do love good predictable idiots," he said. "Oh, if you're hungry just order down, order anything you want. In fact, order like it's your last supper."

And he left the room.

They had done just that. They ordered everything and anything that looked good and Eric explained to Skia what each food was they were eating. She was amazed at the concepts of reading and writing and so he started to teach her the alphabet as they munched on a plate of French Fries drizzled with gravy.

He printed out her name for her. Fascinated she tried to duplicate the symbols, scrawling with the pen underneath his letters.

"That means me?"

"Sort of, yeah." He smiled.

"Hmmm..." and she tried again, forcing herself to memorize the pattern. Her tongue stuck out of the side of her mouth in concentration. When she was done she sat back, a proud look on her face.

"Show me your name," she ordered. Obligingly, he did so and she watched in fascination as Eric's name took form.

She studied it, gauging the difficulty of reproducing the letters and soon she had copied them as best she could.

"And now," she asked, suddenly shy. "What would be the name of our first daughter?"

Eric's heart flipped over in his chest.

Just be cool, man. Be cool like Cor.

He cleared his throat, and faking a calm smile said, "Aria."

It was the first thing that came to mind and he couldn't help looking toward Skia for approval.

"It's perfect," she said. "Now, are you going to kiss me or not?"

At the look on his face she laughed in merriment.

"Just a kiss, silly. We're not making a daughter tonight or any other night for many, *many* years to come. But a kiss? I think a kiss is alright."

She sat beside him on the couch, regarding him with humour and some slight impatience.

His swallow was audible.

He leaned toward her, fire in his veins.

His forehead bumped the bridge of her nose and she winced in pain, but before he could apologize she turned her head, mischief in her eyes, and gave his lip a soft bite, then an even softer kiss on his mouth.

She drew back, a wide smile on her face and said, "So teach me to write something new."

Eric returned her smile - if somewhat awkwardly - and dutifully picked up the pen and traced out some more letters. His hand shook a little, feeling as light as the butterflies in his stomach.

The next morning they looked out the large picture window into the wilderness and the violent beauty it represented, waiting for Cor to return to lead them into the unknown.

"Hello, hello, my little love birds! Watched the sunrise, did you? Oh too sweet. It's a good thing I can't actually get cavities or my teeth would be falling out."

"If you don't watch your tongue I can still help your teeth out of your mouth," Skia growled.

"Not even you can ruin my mood right now, you fanged atrocity. Now, who's ready for some fun?"

"Let's just get going," Eric said.

"Are you sure you're just thirteen? Because you act like a sour old man, you know that? You should be happy. I've done every little thing you've asked me."

"And what'll happen when I meet your father, Cor?"

"Oh, he'll probably kill you."

"So you can see why I should be overjoyed."

"Hmmph. You're a real buzzkill, Eric. We're on the greatest adventure of your life and all you can do is sulk about getting killed. Believe me, there are worse things, but hey, don't let me darken your day. Just let me know when you're good to go."

"I'm ready now."

"Well then saddle up cowboys and carnivores. I'm excited. Are you excited?"

An hour later they were walking the main road through the Banff Centre. There were a variety of buildings, some older, some very modern. The open grounds undulated up the mountain side. Paved walkways snaked between buildings. The people who passed them were either lost in thought or smiled a cheery hello.

"Imagine," Eric said to Skia, "all people do here is learn about art, work on their skills, spend weeks at a time just … creating stuff!"

"Is that what you would like to do?" she asked him, her eyes intent on his face.

"Yeah, it would be awesome," he breathed. "But I never dreamed I could do anything like what they do here."

"Why not?"

He shrugged his shoulders.

"Well, I'm from the Rez. I just can't imagine going anywhere, really."

"That's silly. You know when you talk about art your face lights up? It actually glows with the fire you have inside you. I think it's what you are meant to do."

Eric grew silent and they walked like that for a time. Eric had expected a wisecrack from Cor, but the older boy said nothing.

They heard the sound of singing and they all stopped. It was difficult to pinpoint where it was coming from but it was a choir of voices. It was a melancholy song, but full of emotion and power. They couldn't make out the words but it held all of them with its beauty. It stopped abruptly and then moments later started again from the beginning.

"Huh. A rehearsal. Not bad, either. Mäntyjärvi, if I'm not mistaken. Too bad we can't stay for a performance," Cor said as they continued walking.

They passed by various sculptures and Eric saw even more art as he peered into the windows of the buildings as they passed. One long, blue building was framed almost entirely in glass.

Eventually they passed out of the campus grounds and Cor cut off the path into the trees. The snow was deep under the woods, but it soon tapered down until they could slough through it with a little effort.

After an hour of trudging they broke out of the trees into a wide meadow. A jumble of stones lay in the middle of the clearing, reaching up a couple dozen feet.

"Well, here we are. The Gateway."

"Where exactly does it lead?" Eric asked.

"A few places, actually, but we're taking only one path. We'll have to hold hands to make sure we don't lose each other, not that something like that would be a total disaster," he said looking directly at Skia.

She walked past him, ignoring the barb but knocking him aside with her shoulder.

"I'm always so misunderstood," he said plaintively.

"There is no gateway here," she said suspiciously. "I see no passage at all."

"What?" Eric said. "Hey, what are you trying to pull here, Cor?"

"Patience, patience, my little sleuths. What, you think they just leave Gateways hanging open for any fool to see? Stand back and bow in awe of you-know-who."

Cor turned to the flat, smooth face of the monolithic slab in front of them. He raised his hands and bellowed, "Open sesame!"

Nothing happened.

"Just kidding," he said. "Hold hands, kiddies, and come with me."

Skia held tightly to Eric. He was careful to grasp as lightly as possible so as not to crush her bones by accident. He still hadn't gotten completely used to his increased strength.

Cor examined the rock face intently and finally whispered a small "aha!"

He stepped forward and vanished. A second later his arm appeared out of solid stone and grabbed Eric by the front of his jacket and dragged him and Skia into the wall.

The clearing stood empty and silent.

Chapter 37 - Aisling

She had just enough warning to leap out of the way before it hit.

The large black bird that had assaulted her once before was here again, intent on finishing what it started.

Her breath steamed out in a quick fog, crystallizing in the faint glow of the snow and the moon. She had no weapons, no knowledge of how to defend herself. She backed up a step, then another. The raven raised itself up and she gasped at the size of it. Its eyes were on level with her own and its head kept cocking back and forth, calculating the distance between them. Off in the forest an owl shrieked, then was silent.

The raven lunged and Aisling just managed to push its beak aside before it would have torn into her throat. It screamed in frustration, a croaking, broken sound and knocked her down with a twist of its head. Wings spread out for balance, the raven hopped closer to get its claws within striking range. Impossibly quick talons shot toward her and Aisling cried out as they tore a jagged strip along her upper left arm. It was about to slash at her again when it looked up and, flapping hard, almost made it off the ground in retreat before the great bear came rushing from the trees, roaring in fury.

A swat of its mighty arm sent the raven backward, sprawling and rolling in the snow. Walking Man ran up beside her and leaned down, offering her his arm.

"I'm okay! Just help my Dad!"

Walking Man turned to the fighting just as the raven flapped up into the branches of a tree, taking itself beyond reach of the giant bear. Frustrated, the beast began knocking at the trunk, ramming it with his shoulder.

Walking Man approached.

"Ssstannd baaackk, my friiiennd," he said in that voice that was less speech than it was a grinding and rubbing of wood, the suggestion of wind through dense bramble.

The bear stepped back a few paces and Aisling watched Walking Man do something to his arm, sliding a length of wood like a spear into his wrist. He looked up, aimed, and the spear shot out, fast and true, passing through one of the raven's wings. An undulating cloud formed around it and when it dispersed, Aisling began to cry.

Sitting in the tree, grasping his bleeding arm was Jake. Sweet, boring Jake for whom she had tried to develop feelings, who had helped her so much along the way.

"Why?" she cried out.

He looked out at her, the first gray of dawn allowing them to see each other's faces.

"It's my task."

Then he pulled out a canister and streamed liquid out of it onto the watching Walking Man and bear below.

He pulled out a silver object and it took Aisling a moment to understand what was happening.

"Run!" she cried out. "Run! He's going to burn you!"

As she said it, the lighter fell from the trees, the flame touched Walking Man and spread quickly, fed by the combustible fluid Jake had just sprayed on them. It danced along his limbs and jumped to her father's fur. It was so fast. Walking Man shrieked out in terrible agony, shaking and swaying to a pain she couldn't begin to imagine. Her father's fur was completely engulfed and the smell of burning hair was everywhere.

Above it all was the sound of cruel laughter.

Walking Man's legs split and crumbled and he fell onto his side. Whatever force that was holding him together weakened and pieces of him were falling apart, feeding the flames.

Her father had tried to roll out the fire and had mostly succeeded but he was a wet, burned and bloody ruin, whimpering in pain. He looked at her with eyes filled with apology.

"No!" she shouted, tears flowing freely. "No!"

Her throat was tight with shock and grief and she rushed to her father, holding his head in her lap. Walking Man was dead beside them, smoke still curling up from glowing embers.

"Father, no. I thought we would have just a little more time. Just a little more -"

She was interrupted by Jake's mocking voice

"Just a little more tiiimee..." he sneered, "They're dead, Aisling. Your protectors are dead. And soon, you'll wish you were, too."

"But Jake, I don't understand," she said through her pain. "Why would you do this?"

"Who cares? I did it, it's done, and so are you. You were supposed to fall in love with me, but that idiot Matari got in the way. So now I'll just have to force you to come with me. I'm just glad I don't have to act like a pathetic, lovesick boy anymore."

He began transforming again, the cloud billowing around him, pulling in.

Her father gently licked her hand, and then his breathing stopped in a shuddering sigh and he was no more.

Aisling took a deep breath and released it.

"Stop, Jake. If you're going to hurt me at least do it like a man, don't hide behind a mask."

He smirked from up above her.

"I'll do whatever I damn well please. You remember way back when Matari screamed out in pain? Back when we first started after your brother? Remember when it was just he and I by the stream in the woods?"

"Yes. He said he deflected some kind of trap."

"Wrong. I shot a dart into him. A special kind of dart. If I die, he dies, so you should be glad I'm still breathing. So yeah, I'll face you like a man and there's nothing you can do. In fact, I can do pretty much anything I want to you and you'd have to let me, wouldn't you? Or else your precious Matari drops dead."

"I don't believe you."

"Want to risk it?"

She made no reply.

He climbed to the ground and rested against the trunk, calming his breath.

"Now, come here."

She obeyed.

"Kiss me. Not on the cheek, right here. On my mouth."

There, in the smoldering ruins of the dead, she leaned forward and kissed him on the lips. She had to control the sickness that washed over her.

"Yeah, this is good. This is working out even better than I planned. Aisling, tell me you love me."

He reached out and grabbed her by the chin, twisting her head up to look him in the eyes.

"I said, tell me you love me, slave."

Silent tears cut through the soot on her cheeks. She closed her eyes and tried to calm herself, to escape into the comfort of the pulsing energies that surrounded her. She let the light flow into her, through her, she let it become a part of her. She was still so afraid. Then Aisling looked Jake in the eyes. She took a deep breath and opened her mouth.

"What's that?" he sneered. "I can't hear you."

She took a deeper breath and again opened her mouth. Again there was no sound.

"Look, you little bitch, I gave you an order! Say you love me!"

Aisling tried to breathe. She was filled with the light of the earth, she could feel it warming her, lending her strength. She glanced at the death around her. She looked once more at Jake and opened her mouth.

And she began to sing.

"If I want a song, I'll tell you to sing me a - hey! What's the idea?"

Jake looked at his wrists which were held by strong, leafy vines, as were his ankles.

He laughed.

"Really? Plants? That's your way of fighting back? Ohh, I'm going to enjoy watching you suffer. Maybe I'll even torture you for a few days just to enjoy it more."

Aisling ignored him and kept singing. A sad, mournful song, but full of warm memories and love. More vines grew up around Jake, wrapping him, holding him, pulling him closer to the tree.

He started to look alarmed and began to transform, to become the raven, but the vines just grasped tighter and Aisling's song blew the dark mist away.

The tree itself opened with a sudden, sharp crack and Jake was pushed into its heart, even as the outer layers of bark and bole reshaped around him.

"You'll kill him if I die! I swear he'll die!"

"I believe you," Aisling said at last. "And that's why you'll never die. You're going to live forever, here in this tree. Don't worry, you'll be well taken care of."

She resumed her song, and the bark covered Jake's face, his eyes, his mouth, leaving only a woody, mournful frown, and from indents where his eyes had been dripped a thick, amber sap as a reminder that he would be trapped inside for as long as the tree lived.

Aisling finished her song with a blessing of strength and long life for the tree. It would outlast this forest, and the one after that.

She dropped to her knees and rested.

After a time she stumbled back to camp, back to where her Auntie and Kokum still slept. The rising sun made the way easy, and she would soon return with them to say her goodbyes and bury her dead.

Chapter 38 - Eric

They were surrounded by towering pieces of jagged stone and rubble. And wind. A roaring, tearing, ripping wind that blew dust into their eyes and stole their breath.

"What is this?" Eric shouted.

"It's a trap! He's betrayed us already," Skia cried against the buffeting din.

Cor stepped carefully over the rubble to crouch down against the shelter of one of the huge boulders. They were as though a giant had been using them for building blocks and then knocked them all down in a fit of rage. Cor motioned for them to join him.

"Calm down! You're like a couple of old ladies! We just jumped hundreds of kilometres. We're in the ruins of Turtle Mountain. Follow me! I'll show you where we have to go next."

He turned and climbed up the rocks and they followed suit. As they clambered on top of one of the great blocks they were able to see far into a valley that stretched to their right and out into the open plains. A few hundred meters away a highway snaked by, dotted with traffic. It cut right through the rubble-strewn plain on the valley floor.

Eric looked behind him and could see where the face of the mountain must have slipped away and he shuddered at the thought of all that mass bearing down at once.

"Impressive, isn't it?" Cor asked proudly. "My father did this!"

He spread his arms wide in a proprietary fashion, beaming with delight.

Eric's stomach dropped. He felt shaky with the fear of what awaited him.

I always knew I was going to my death. Why get nerves now?

"So where must we travel now?" Skia asked.

Cor pointed and they followed the direction of his outstretched arm. In the distance was a mountain peak with a mound-shaped top. It didn't seem like it would take them long to get there, a half day's walk at the most, maybe less if they caught a ride.

"What is it?" Eric asked.

Cor smirked.

"Well, we're standing on the ruins of Turtle Mountain, my friend. The peak you see over there is the place I was created. That, dear Uhhr, we call Crowsnest."

He led them down the rocky terrain to the highway, whistling the whole time. Eric only heard snatches of it against the pounding, merciless wind.

"This is a bad place," Skia said into his ear. "It feels wrong somehow. It's not a good place to stay."

"Can you see the towns in the distance? They seem to be okay."

She looked doubtful but nodded her head.

Once they reached the road they kept on the shoulder of the highway. Eric's nerves were on edge from the constant beating of the wind.

"This sucks, Cor! We need shelter or something!"

"Patience, Padawan! There's a place up ahead. I can call us a cab from there."

"A cab?"

"Sure, they run from town to town in this valley."

Eventually they made their way up a side road from the highway. There was an Interpretive Centre at the top.

"They teach about this?" Eric asked doubtfully.

"Oh, not the real story," Cor said as they pushed their way into the doors. "But sure, why not? Can you think of anything bigger that would've happened here than a whole town being crushed by a mountain?"

It sickened Eric to think of all the people who would have been instantly killed in a torrent of sound and weight, never knowing what was happening in the few moments before their death. It stayed with him even as they were humming along the highway in the promised taxi a half hour later. He had started out planning to fight against Cor's father, to stand up for himself, even if it meant his death. But, now, seeing the ruin of the valley he was more determined to find out what this was all about. And more frightened.

"Welcome to Hell's Tailpipe!" The driver said gleefully as the winds buffeted the vehicle from side to side, "Where can I take you fine young'uns?"

"Just as close as possible to Crowsnest there, if you please," Cor instructed.

"Ah! Sightseeing! Well, it's none of my business but you should be careful. This valley has stories, let me tell you."

"So we've heard," Skia replied, slipping her hand into Eric's.

An hour later they were hiking up a trail leading from a campground at the base of the mountain. The footing was treacherous and only got worse. Shifting skree - flat, sharp pieces of shale - slipped under their boots, threatening to turn into a rock slide and take them down with it. It was made all the worse by the snow and ice and unforgiving wind.

They made their way into a deep chasm and started to make a steep ascent. They found a chain that someone had bolted into the solid rock of the mountain that helped with their climb. Eric was at the rear of their little party. He slipped and caught his knee on a jutting piece of shale. It tore through his pant leg and he felt the warm gush of blood that spilled from the cut. Gingerly, he peeled back the bloody fabric. He was torn open, revealing his knee cap amidst gore and gristle.

Grimacing, he pulled out his stone and pressed it to the gash. It sucked up the blood quietly and efficiently. The cut began closing of its own accord and before he knew it, Eric was back on his feet. The skin of his knee was the same as on his strong hand and his leg did feel more powerful. All the weariness and cold was gone. He felt strong and warm and hurried to catch up with the others.

"You're bleeding!" Skia gasped when she saw the tattered shreds of his torn pants.

"No, no I'm fine, I promise. See?" Eric spread open the tear to reveal a whole, intact knee unmarred by any wound.

"How?"

"Don't worry about it. Let's just keep going."

After hours of struggle, they made it to the snowy peak of the mountain.

They looked around at the beauty of the world displayed for them below. To one side of them was a row of jagged, razor-like peaks.

"The Seven Sisters," Cor volunteered. "Trust me, you don't want to know the real story about those." He wore a sickly, unconvincing grin. Whatever the story was, Eric agreed that he probably didn't want to know.

"Well, now that we're here ...." Cor took a deep breath. "Yeah. Now that we're here. I can't believe I'm saying this but, Eric, you can run. Run away. Get out of here, hide, and keep low. Stay out of cities, don't fly or take the train, just go. Stay under the radar. You can live."

"What?"

"It's another trick!" Skia said, "Don't trust him! Don't believe him!"

Yet Eric could see the sincerity in Cor's eyes. They almost seemed to be pleading with him.

"You've fooled me one too many times, Cor. I don't know what this trick is. You're going to push me down the mountain as soon as my back's turned to you? Forget it. I'm never trusting you again. Let's get on with this."

Cor nodded, his eyes downcast. When he raised them he was looking off into the distance.

"Sure thing, Uhhr. You got me. I was just playing another one of my games."

He turned and walked a little further on.

"Well, come on. The entrance is right over here. But you'll have to open it."

"How?"

"You're the brains of this operation, aren't you?"

"You mean, you don't even know how to get in?" Skia asked.

"I can't get in. My key was supposed to be either the smell of his carcass or his corruption. I tried both. Look, don't ask me to explain because I can't, but if I don't do what I'm told the way doesn't open for me."

If Skia made a reply Eric didn't notice. The stone was throbbing in his grip, leading him onward and suddenly it grew hot. He kept holding onto it, untouched by the growing waves of heat. The snow beneath him melted and he was sinking out of sight. After a dozen or so feet he stood on solid rock. The stone cooled as rapidly as it had heated and the melted walls solidified into ice.

"Nice one!" Cor called down and a moment later he dropped into the hole, landing softly. Skia jumped down after Cor, using him to break her fall.

He would have retaliated but the rock surface beneath them turned to sand and they were sucked down, into the mountain itself.

Chapter 39 - Aisling

By the time she got back to camp Aisling was seething with anger. She needed to scream and rage and strike out against this darkness that had been overshadowing her entire life and the lives of everyone she loved. It was like a disease that had no cure and it had been taking its toll on every new generation, only to be passed down to the next one after that.

It all had to stop and she was going to be the one to stop it.

She passed by the impromptu sweat lodge they'd erected while she was sick. It still smelled of medicines and cleanliness. That soothed the fire in her chest somewhat.

The tent with her Auntie and Kokum was still zippered shut and she could hear the slight snoring from both of them. She couldn't believe they were still sleeping after something so momentous had occurred. Something so tragic. She had a sudden insight into humanity at that moment. Half the world slept while her life crumbled around her. They slept and didn't care. After all, why should they? Was she sitting up at nights worried about someone else's misfortune? Someone that she never met?

Strangely though, these thoughts calmed her. People had their burdens and they shouldered them. Life went on. Not forever for anyone, but it did go on. And she meant to be a part of it. It was time for her to stand up and fight to save the world.

But first, breakfast.

She started the fire and began to prepare tea and eggs. As they were heating she went down to a trickling creek and filled the water canteens. When she returned to the fire her Auntie was awake, removing the boiling kettle from the hot, flat stone and pouring cups of tea.

When she saw Aisling she dropped the kettle mid pour. It made a crashing, clanging sound in the quiet morning.

"Aisling! When did you get back?"

"Very early this morning. Is Kokum up?"

"Not yet, but what's wrong with your arm? It's bleeding. Come here. Why, you're covered in blood and soot. What happened!"

"They're dead, Auntie. Father, Walking Man … and Jake."

"Oh my God."

Martha sat down heavily, her hands wringing.

"How? When?"

"Not long ago. I'll take you to them. I'll need help with - with Dad."

Martha looked afraid.

"Don't worry. The danger's passed. I - I took care of it."

Martha shook off the shock of the news and went to their pile of packs and pulled out her first aid kit.

"I'll mend you up while you tell me what happened."

By the time Aisling had finished her tale, the stitching was complete.

"You're amassing quite the collection of battle scars, aren't you?"

Aisling turned. Her Kokum was standing a few feet away, tears in her eyes.

"I heard you tell Martha everything," she said.

Aisling rose and gave her Kokum a hug. It felt different. She stepped back and saw that one of her grandmother's sleeves was empty.

"Your arm?"

"A small price to pay in exchange for a leg, don't you think?" Kokum said.

"What do you mean?"

Martha spoke up, "We had to save your leg, Aisling. I didn't know what the cost would be but Mom did. She sacrificed her arm so you could walk."

"Sacrificed? But what - ?"

Aisling's head was spinning.

All this loss. All this bloody loss.

She pulled herself together, her face grim.

"Kokum, oh Kokum. I would never ask -"

"I know, my love. Don't worry yourself. I promise you, there was no pain, and I'm feeling my years anyhow. Better I lose this old arm than you lose your leg."

"But why an arm? I don't understand."

"You think I should have given up one of my legs? I haven't given up chasing men yet!"

Despite all the shocks of the day, or perhaps because of them, Aisling laughed. The laugh managed to release the intense anxiety she had been carrying inside, easing its vise-like grip on her heart.

"None of the magic is free, is it?" she asked quietly. "There's always something to lose."

"That's right," said Martha. "But just remember it works that way for everyone. Everyone."

Aisling nodded, understanding. If there was a price, then Raven would have to pay it too. At first she had thought that Jake was the Raven her grandmother had told her about, but Martha had quickly crushed that hope.

"Raven is far more powerful than what you describe, but he has many spies. I can't believe we were taken in so easily. Looking back it makes no sense that there would be no warning signs."

"But there were," Kokum said. "Clear your mind and you will see them. He must have been able to hide from us, wrapping our doubts in shadow, hiding them from ourselves."

Aisling shuddered at the thought. Then again, how was it different from what her Kokum could do? Or Auntie Martha?

Is it intent? Does that justify manipulating people? Make it good or evil?

She looked at her tired grandmother, how wearily she chewed her food. Aisling knew the old woman only ever tried to help others, and that her Auntie would never harm a soul. She had her answer.

After breakfast, they broke camp and left behind all the things they wouldn't be needing. Then Aisling led them to the scene of the carnage.

Kokum said nothing but began the sad work of gathering, cleaning, preparing the remains. Georgia and Aisling worked along beside her.

Hours of sweat, labour and tears passed but eventually it was finished. Kokum and Aisling sang a song of farewell and Martha said her own goodbyes to her brother and to Walking Man. All the while, the mournful face in the tree watched and cried its yellowish sap.

They left the place and after walking along a game trail, they left the forest. The land rolled gently downward toward a large lake, its shoreline dotted with clumps of trees.

"Since we know where Eric is we can move much faster," Kokum said.

"Good," said Aisling. "To be honest, I really hate camping. And my cell phone's been dead this whole time."

"What?" Martha cried. "No Facebook?"

They all laughed again. It was their way. Strangers might never understand, but they needed their humour. They needed to feel that joy was still possible.

"Let's get down to that lake first. We can boil water and scrub ourselves clean."

They did, and once they were dry and warm they ate a late lunch. The sun was already nearing the horizon. The days were getting much shorter.

"Now, Aisling. You must take us. Take us to Eric."

"But how? I don't exactly know where he is."

"What did White Buffalo Calf Woman say?"

"Something about a Sleeping Buffalo, about gates or something."

"Yes. I know where she is talking about."

"So what do you want me to do? I can find a farm or a highway or something. I can come back with someone to drive us?"

Kokum's eyes glinted with humour, "There is no need for that, Aisling. You will take us through your dreams."

"But what about our bodies? Are we just going to leave them sleeping beside the lake?"

"This will be a different state of Dreaming, Aisling. In this one we'll bring our bodies with us. You've only ever gone halfway there but I'll help you go deeper. Didn't you notice Matari wasn't in the camp? He'd gone fully into this other place to help Inkata home."

Aisling nodded dumbly. She hadn't even thought about that.

"Okay. How do I learn to do this?"

"First you must understand that even I don't know everything. There are different levels of Dreaming, different worlds, you could say. Some we can go to, some we can only see when we sleep. But there is a world like our own where there is a … consensus. Where things are stable and make a certain amount of sense. That's where we need to go."

"So, are we in a dream world now?"

"I don't know, Aisling. It feels real enough to me."

Aisling was silent for a minute. Dream or not, it was still her life, and they still had to help Eric.

"Tell me more," she urged.

After more instruction Aisling said she was ready to try. They set out blankets, laid down and closed their eyes to the world.

And opened them again. They were in the same place but it was warm. Aisling was sweating profusely under all her winter gear.

"Don't take it off, we'll only be here for a short time," Kokum said. "Look at me, and I'll send you the image as I promised."

Aisling looked into her grandmother's eyes and was shocked to find it was true! They had told her that in this dreamplace she would have the power to see into their thoughts if they allowed it and what Aisling saw was incredibly vivid.

Mountains. What looked like a castle on one mountain, and a college or convention centre on the facing slope.

"There," Kokum said, and Aisling knew she meant the collection of various buildings on the smaller mountain.

"Look closer," Kokum instructed.

Aisling entered into the vision and found herself soaring over the buildings and out again into the valley. She swept around and saw that the mountain, from a certain angle, did indeed look like a sleeping buffalo.

"They call this Tunnel Mountain," Kokum said in her ear, "after a railroad issue."

She chuckled.

"This is the place White Buffalo Calf Woman brought the last great herd of free, wild buffalo before the white man could slaughter the last of them. They entered her Gateway and were saved. When the time is right, they say the mountain will shake and people will know: the time for the buffalo's return is at hand. Now come, land over there."

Aisling's mind was directed toward a small stand of stones in a small clearing. She flapped her wings and approached. She was enjoying the sensation of flying and swept past the buildings in exultation. She caught a glimpse of her reflection in the windows and screamed out.

"Kokum!"

"I'm here, dear. Just get to the meadow. Don't stop, just get to the meadow."

Aisling landed somewhat clumsily, unused to negotiating distances in such a new and unfamiliar way.

The rocks looked much larger once she was standing beside them.

"Now, sweet girl, the same way I let you into my vision of this place, let us into yours."

Aisling felt something strange happening to her perceptions, but she didn't fight it. She had the sensation of something passing out of her eyes from some place behind her retinas. She blinked a few times and standing beside her were her Kokum and her Auntie.

"Yes," her Kokum said before she could ask. "You're a raven. A beautiful, amazing, raven. Look close, though your feathers appear white, you carry all the colours of the rainbow."

"And we're foxes!" Martha said happily. She was dashing around through the snow, chasing her tail. "I almost forgot how great this feels!"

Kokum half limped toward Aisling as best she could with one of her front legs missing, and she gave her granddaughter a nuzzle on her lowered head.

"Right now we are wearing our totem forms but no one could see if they looked. We're like spirits here. Your father had the unique ability to bring his totem form out into our world with him, but most of us can't do that."

"Well, why are you two foxes if he was bear? And why am I a - a raven? Am I evil?"

"Of course not. Not all ravens are evil, is that what you thought? Never mind, dear girl. Your mother is a raven, too, Aisling. Just as my dear Henry, your *mosum*, was a Bear. The blood mixes and we never know who will be what, but so far we haven't had any horse-fishes or anything like that."

"But why are mother and I - why are we ravens?"

Aisling couldn't shake the feeling that there was something deeply disturbing about this.

"I wouldn't read that much into it," Martha called. She was whipping back and forth across the clearing in a display of energy and happiness.

"She's right, dear. You're still you, as you always will be."

"Yeah, don't be a specist!"

"Will you stop!" Aisling cried out, a smile crooking up her beak.
"Where's my Auntie and who is this insanely energetic person who has replaced her?"

Martha trotted up, her tongue hanging out of her mouth.

"Sorry, but I do carry a little extra weight as a human. It's nice to feel light as a feather!"

Aisling cawed in laughter and then snapped her beak shut. This was all going to take some getting used to. But it would have to be while they were on the move. Kokum was already directing them to follow her.

"When we pass through this Gateway I'll take us the final step into the other world. I warn you, it will seem very much different than what you've known. Stay as close as you can," she said as they walked into the rocks.

"We could be heading into danger."

They emerged into chaos.

Chapter 40 - Eric

They were in a vast, dark emptiness. The sound of water dripping in the far off distance was magnified into thousands of little whispers by the echoing chamber. Small siftings of sand blended with hiss of their heavy, frightened breathing. The cold of the winter was replaced by a suffocating warmth, heavy and still.

Eric stepped forward and snapped the small flame at his fingertips into existence.

"Eric!" Skia shouted.

"Stand still, buddy, don't move," Cor said at the same time.

"What is it?" Eric asked, alerted by the urgency in their voice.

He raised his hand so the flame was no longer in his eyes and saw that he was standing at the very edge of a deep, endless precipice, emptying downward into darkness and death. The stench of rot and decay came wafting up toward him on a small, hot breeze.

He took a shaky step backward but the rock crumbled. He slipped and was falling, the sand underfoot a devilish, dry lubricant beneath his boot.

A strong hand grabbed his wrist and pulled him back, his legs scrambling in retreat from the edge.

He turned to thank Skia but found himself eye to eye with Cor.

"Watch that first step," Cor said wryly. "It's a doozy"

Eric nodded and raised his arm again so they could look out into the enormous cave. The heat was oppressive and they shed their coats.

"Might as well leave most of our stuff here, too," he said. "But first things first, we have to find a way down. Cor?"

"I've always just kind of flown down. I guess I could try to carry you, but it would have to be one at a time."

"Yeah, I don't think so. We're not separating and anyway, what's to stop you from dropping us?"

"Nothing, I guess. Why don't you just, you know, flame us down with your power?"

Eric didn't want to admit that he didn't really have that much control over it, that most of what he'd done so far on that large of a scale had been by instinct, not design. He just shook his head.

"I kind of figured as much. There must be a way for others to get down. I've seen people here before. People not like me."

They began searching the edge.

"Here," said Skia. "I found it."

A stairway was carved into the side of the cliff leading deep into the shadows below. It was steep and only extended two or three feet away from the wall itself, but the steps were regular. There was no railing, however, and one stumble would mean falling for who knew how long until you just didn't fall anymore. Eric had an idea what the rotting stench was that drifted up from the deep. He tried not to think about it as he rummaged through his pack for small essentials like water and a bit of food.

When he was ready Eric made eye contact with the others, nodded, and led the way.

At first it wasn't too bad, the going was easy if treacherous, but it was the monotony that almost killed them. The hypnotic necessity of putting one foot in front of the other again and again and again. It wasn't long before Eric was praying for some kind of variation to the evenly cut stairs, something to give his mind something to latch onto, but the descent was as regular as a metronome. He caught himself at one point veering toward the edge of the steps. The wall had curved ever so slightly but he hadn't noticed. His ankle bent as his foot slipped off the edge of the stair. He fell forward and just managed to stop his momentum. Shakily, he righted himself, and stood, assuring his companions that he was okay although he was sweating and breathing hard. He pressed his body against the wall, allowing his heart to slow, waiting for the chilling fright to clear.

How long have I been walking without being aware? It's like I was sleeping!

He shook his head and tried to concentrate, to count, to sing loudly in his head, to review his plans. Anything that would keep him alert. He kept walking, kept the damnable pace.

It was no use, he kept falling into that same stupor until a sudden scream jolted him out of his sopor.

"Skia!" He cried as she disappeared into the darkness, her flaming red hair streaming behind her.

He heard the impact and scurried down the steps to where she had landed.

She pushed herself up with a groan, blood smearing the side of her head, her hair matted and tangled.

"I'm okay, just a little bruised." She touched her head gingerly. "And a little cut, but I'm okay, honest," she said in reply to his look of concern.

"Looks like you found the floor," Cor said, grinning. "Thank goodness, I was worried Eric would think I pushed you."

"Did you?" Eric asked.

Cor just folded his arms and leaned back against the rock wall.

"No, it was stupid," Skia said. "I just kind of fell asleep and then I was falling. How can you people make a thing like this?" she asked with an irritated wave of her hand. She stood and brushed herself off. Eric tore some fabric from his shirt to clean the blood off her face. He noted with relief that the cut wasn't as bad as it had seemed.

"Are those bones?" Eric asked, glancing past Skia into the darkness.

"Eric, trust me," Cor said. "You really don't want to go that way."

"Why not?" he took a few steps into shadows, holding his flame up over his head. He thought he could almost spot movement at the edge of the firelight.

"Listen!" Skia whispered. There was a shuffling, scuttling sound deep in the darkness.

"Eric …." Cor's voice was breathless but urgent.

The shuffling whisper was getting nearer, and there seemed to be more than one thing making the sound. The shifting, scratching, slithering noises increased exponentially. Eric was pulled toward it by a morbid curiosity, a sick need to know what was in that darkness.

"Eric!" Skia shouted, and there was fear in her voice. "Please!"

A hand grabbed his shoulder and he jumped in surprise. He spun around and Skia's eyes were begging him and he saw the tears of fear she was holding at bay.

"Eric, if you go that way we all die," Cor said quietly. Eric thought he could almost hear a sense of relief in the older boy's voice.

"Right. Come on."

Eric took Skia's hand and raced in the other direction, away from the whispers. As he ran he could feel something grasping at his soul, like rough claws pulling at a woolen sweater. Despite the heat, a cold shudder passed through him.

Cor caught up to them.

"It's okay," he panted. "We're safe."

He glared at Eric.

"What possessed you to walk that way? There are worse things than a quick death and that was one of them."

"What was it?"

"You don't want to know. If these are your last hours, this is one image I'll spare you. Let's just say I've woken up screaming just at the memory of glimpsing that horror. Now come on, this way. We're not too far."

They followed him, keeping up with his urgent pace.

"It's so hot!" Skia said.

"It gets better once we make our way to the smaller caverns," Cor assured her. "I know where we are. We head along the wall here until things narrow out and then boom, we're there."

Sure enough they saw the opposite wall flicker into sight from the light of Eric's flame. As they walked it appeared to get closer as the cavern contracted to more comprehensible proportions. At last they came to a tunnel that had the distinct glow of light shining from the far end.

"What's ahead?" Eric asked in a whisper. "Is it safe?"

"A-a-a hallllwwaayyy ...." Cor whispered sarcastically, with an exaggeratedly wicked laugh. "No need to be dramatic," he added, in his normal voice. "It's just a series of hallways. Quite the anticlimax to the cavern here, I know."

They followed Cor toward the glow. It ended up being light seepage around the seams of a door.

"Do we need a key?"

Cor scoffed at the question and opened the door.

The light was blinding and they all shielded their eyes for a moment until they adjusted to the sudden brilliance after the long hours in the cave. Eric saw that, indeed, it was just a regular hallway - and it was air-conditioned.

"It looks like a hospital or something."

"Oh, I assure you, it's nothing like a hospital," Cor replied. "But I do know what you mean. Antiseptic. Lifeless. Or as I like to call it, home."

Eric drank the rest of his water and replaced the bottle in the small daypack that he'd brought with him. Skia did the same.

"Where next, Cor?"

Cor looked hesitant.

"Don't hold out on me now," Eric warned.

"Yeah right, whatever. Come on."

They kept walking. Around corners, down stairs, passing numbered doors and empty rooms. Eventually they came to larger chamber with a red door at the end of it.

"There it is," Cor said.

That's all he had to say. Eric felt the fear he had been trying to push down come screaming up to the surface. He couldn't seem to control it. He clenched his stone and pushed his fear into it, pushed everything into it until he was in control of himself once more.

He walked boldly to the simple, plain door. He reached out for the ornate, golden handle.

"Wait," Skia said suddenly. "Wait, Eric. Please."

Eric turned to her. He observed her dispassionately. Everything was cold now. Slow. Empty.

"What about the prophecy? What about the darkness?"

"I don't care about that."

Skia glanced uncomfortably at Cor who was taking in this last conversation.

"Eric, what about us?"

A twinge of remorse and regret winnowed through his barriers. He would have run away with her at that moment if the stone hadn't fallen from his hand cracking loudly against the floor.

He bent to pick it up and when he straightened his heart had cooled once more.

Good. This is where I need to be. Strong. Sure. No doubts.

He turned his back on the pleading Skia.

And opened the door.

Chapter 41 - Aisling

"What's going on?" Aisling shouted against the violence of the wind. Her feathers were blown askew by the buffeting of gales. A spray of water, stone and fire were flying around them in a mad display of elements.

"It's a battle!" Kokum shouted back.

Aisling shaded her eyes with her wing and saw that there were figures everywhere, their shadows stretching out in the slanted light of sunset. There were animals of every kind, all in confused, patternless motion. She saw a man make an impossible leap towards them and when he landed she was shocked to see he had the head of a toad as large as a man's head. The giant eyes bulged outward, heavy lids blinking as he checked them out.

"Georgia!" he croaked. "What are you doing here?"

"We're here to find my grandson. What in the world is happening, Laughing Toad?"

"He's here! On the Other Side but he's here!"

"Wait! Where?" Aisling interrupted. "Where's Eric, where is he?"

Her voice was filled with desperation and she was blinking back the tears of relief that threatened to flood from her.

"In the mountain!"

That's when she heard the call going out, "To the Mountain! To the Mountain!" It was the rallying cry of these creatures as they made their way across the valley.

She watched, horrified, as a group of rabbits were dive-bombed by crows and the speed at which the talons and beaks shredded the rabbits into a bloody pulp.

"Why is this happening?" she screamed.

"We have to stop him!" Laughing Toad yelled against the noise of the chaos. "He's about to start the tide of darkness that will cover all the worlds!"

"Take us to him!" Kokum demanded.

Laughing Toad's chest swelled to three times its normal size and he released a massive bellow that rang down the valley, louder even than all the violence and commotion.

"My people are coming," he said.

Aisling saw so much fighting she didn't know where to look. She closed her eyes and gasped. Her inner eyes revealed an overwhelming display of colour and light, streams of power flowing rapidly. Sparks of glowing life would grow dark and she knew combatants out there had died. The Earthblood was flowing out of the mountain on which they stood but it was flowing the wrong way. Not down and out of the valley, but up toward what appeared to be a spinning whirlpool, sucked into darkness.

When she opened her eyes she saw a strange, round-topped mountain at the centre of that spinning, black vortex.

"There!" she said, pointing.

"Yes," Laughing Toad said then stepped back, his eyes widening in fear. "Who are you?"

"Don't be afraid. This is my granddaughter. This is Aisling. She is a Dreamer."

Laughing Toad looked Aisling up and down, his great eyes blinking as he took in the information.

"My apologies," he said and dropped to one knee. "You are both terrible and beautiful, sweet one."

Aisling didn't know what to say and so stood speechless. A burst of fire struck the rocks nearby and the stones disappeared into a sharp spray of debris.

Laughing Toad knocked Aisling and Kokum down and covered them with his own body.

Martha came bounding back toward them. In all the confusion Aisling hadn't even noticed she had been gone.

As Aisling and Kokum disentangled from each other, Martha told Kokum what she had learned.

"They've been gathering for days. It wasn't until they figured out where Eric was going that they were sure this was the place Raven has been hiding. Of course, it makes perfect sense. He already toppled Turtle Mountain in our world. If he can topple it here he will have made a wound so severe he could call on the full force of the Power."

"Power?" Aisling asked

"The Earthblood! If Raven can get it in both worlds he can start drawing from at least two levels of reality. Mother Earth won't be able to close the cut. She won't be able to heal."

"The last time I was in the dream world I couldn't even see the Earthblood. I thought it wasn't here?"

"You couldn't see it because of your sickness. The infection was evil and it was affecting you, blinding you. Raven can't find Earthblood either, but they think he will force Eric to show him where it is."

"And that's what all this is? Is this the last battle?"

Laughing Toad snorted, "This is only the first battle, Light Finder." He looked far away into the valley. "Only the first."

The sound of screams and shouted orders filled the air. The ground was rocked by percussive explosions of power and the dead were littering the battlefield.

Two more toad men bounded to a stop just a few meters below them on the mountainside.

"Come, we will carry you. We haven't time to lose!"

Kokum and Martha leaped up into the arms of the men.

"But I can fly!" Aisling protested.

Laughing Toad pointed upward just as a blue heron was struck by an arrow and plummeted to the ground.

"Come on!" he shouted, and Aisling jumped into his outstretched arms.

"We have prepared the way. We will take you directly!"

They leaped off into the midst of the fighting, the screaming, the uncounted dead. Aisling saw horrors that would haunt her for the rest of her life and Laughing Toad's words echoed in her heart.

This is only the first battle, Light Finder. Only the first.

They were carried safely through it all and finally came to a stop at the base of the strange mountain she had seen from a distance. There were people waiting for them there. One in particular frightened Aisling but she didn't know why. Perhaps it was because, despite the fact it was man with the head of a coyote, he seemed so human. He was dressed in cowboy boots and jeans and a plaid shirt. A pipe was clenched in his jaws.

"Georgia, at last. How did it come to this?"

"We were unprepared, Standing Coyote. But the time for regrets are passed. Now we just have to salvage what we can."

"Salvage? I'm not sure I like the sound of that."

"I have no better way of putting it. I had a vision a few days ago. It was of Caroline, she was speaking to me. She shared with me. After all these years she finally shared with me. Now I know why she tried to escape from this life, from this world. It's going to get much, much worse, I'm afraid."

Aisling couldn't believe it. They were talking about her mother. As confusing as everything was at the beginning of their travels she had assumed it would all come to make sense eventually. But now things were just getting more and more convoluted. There was so much happening and she felt that the enormity of it all was just starting to be revealed.

"Well, as you say, Truth Singer, there is no time for regret. Come, we have been tunneling since we first suspected this was the place. We have broken through, they say. I'm sorry we have to move so quickly. It's been so long."

All the time he was speaking Walking Coyote had been glancing at Aisling. She saw the surprise in his eyes and then the fear. He turned abruptly and led them up the trail.

Why is everyone so afraid of me? So afraid of Eric? Don't they know we're just a couple of kids?

As they walked toward the wall of the mountain she caught up with Martha.

"Martha, why is everyone so afraid of me? And why did Laughing Toad call me Light Finder? What does it mean?"

Aisling could see Martha considering her response, even behind her bright fox eyes.

"You're early," she said at last. "Everyone knew the troubles were coming, that war was on the horizon, but no one believed it would be in our lifetime. Correction: no one *wanted* to believe it. Including me. As to why they're frightened, it's the raven totem you wear as your skin. Only the most powerful Tricksters have ever worn the raven totem. I have to admit, my heart skips a beat just looking at you myself!"

"But I'm no Trickster! I'm the worst liar I know!"

"Yes, I know. You're something else entirely. You're the other kind. You're the giver, the revealer, the wisdom bearer. You're a bridge, I think."

"Wisdom? Hello, Auntie, it's me! Aisling."

"Give it time."

"How much time do you think we have?"

"I believe we have enough. Look at me. Look into my eyes. I can hear the hysteria in the back of your voice. Let me help you."

Aisling understood and allowed her Auntie's calming influence to wash over her like a cleansing water. She took a deep breath and released it, feeling the tension in her brow ease.

"Better?" Martha said.

"Yes, a little. Do you mind if I ask one more question?"

"Not at all, what is it?"

"Well, it's the Light Finder thing."

"Ah, yes. Well, as you heard, Raven can't see the blood of the Mother. And as we've told you, most of us can't and those who are able can just sense it, like the memory of a touch. You're different, Aisling."

"And Eric?"

"We don't know, but just the threat that he might have the ability has been enough to start this war. If you had been left unprotected, unattended, this battle might be even worse. Can you imagine it?"

Aisling had a sudden, chilling insight.

"Some of the people here want to kill me, don't they? They're as scared of me as they are of Eric."

"See?" Martha said and laughed without humour. "Wisdom."

"How do we know who to trust?"

"We don't. I've gone over everything so many times in my head that I suspect everyone, then I chide myself for being silly. I suspected Jake was no good, but told myself it was just me being overprotective, that he was just a teenage boy who was interested in you. And of course he was but in a different way. He was supposed to build trust with you, draw you away, isolate you. I see that now. It's what they did with Eric." Her eyes brimmed with tears. "I've made myself sick over my failures, but we can't get anything done if we're paralyzed by fear and indecision. And so at this point we have no choice but to trust who we must, Aisling. So far these are all old friends, it's the newer generation who are frightened. And why shouldn't they be?"

"Because I never asked for any of this!"

"And yet it's yours. You have already shown more power than we've ever seen. And everyone here knows it. There are eyes and ears everywhere, my dear. Nothing stays secret for long."

"And now we have to stop Eric from doing something terrible? Was Walking Man right? Does he have to die? Do I?"

"Don't even say a thing like that," Kokum said, limping back down the trail they had been following. "Hurry now, they're all waiting for us."

Martha ran ahead and Kokum turned to Aisling as she approached, her three-legged gait awkward and painful.

"Aisling, try not to be afraid. Just have faith that you are walking your path."

"*My path?* It feels like anything but my path."

"Then it's time you make it yours, isn't it?"

It was a simple question but it lingered in her thoughts as they met up with Standing Coyote, Laughing Toad and Auntie Martha. They were waiting in front of a dark tunnel.

"Are you sure you need to go alone?" Standing Coyote asked Kokum.

"Positive. Besides, you're needed here. Keep fighting and we'll have a chance that it will offer the distraction we need."

"A lot of deaths for a distraction."

Kokum's shoulders sagged, but then she pulled herself upright as best she could, standing strong on her three legs.

"We weren't meant for such burdens, my friend. But then, who is?"

Without another word she walked into the tunnel. Martha followed but as Aisling brought up the rear Standing Coyote stepped in front of her.

"I had a chance to kill your brother not that long ago, girl. I should have taken it."

Make it your own path.

"Well, unless you're going to try with me, then step aside before you find out what a Light Finder can do."

"And what can you do? Anger, hatred and fear accelerates the use of the power, but it also does deep damage to the person using it. I can already sense you've been instructed in the gentler way."

225

"Then I suppose I can gently bury you six feet under the ground right here," Aisling replied with mock sweetness.

Standing Coyote stiffened, his eyes narrowing as he stepped aside.

She entered into the darkness.

Chapter 42 - Eric

There was a man seated behind a wooden desk. Surrounding him was a large empty cavern. Eric couldn't tell how it was illuminated as there were no light fixtures, but it was bright enough that it hurt his eyes. The man looked up and a warm smile spread across his face.

"Ah, Eric! At last you've come! Why, I'm so glad you're here, I've so wanted to meet you for the longest time."

Eric couldn't tell where the man might have come from. He didn't look like any sort of person he'd seen before. Either a mixture of every race in the world, or not belonging to any group at all. It made the man seem somehow innocuous, like he could stand in any group and be the first person forgotten. Unremarkable.

The man stood up slowly and his dark eyes twinkled in welcome. He wore corduroy pants and a light-grey dress shirt under a sweater vest. His shoes were a pair of comfortable loafers.

Eric stood in stunned silence. This was not at all what he'd expected. Fire breathing dragons? A nest of ravens ready to claw him to pieces? Sure, but not this.

"Uh, hi."

The man let out a genuine but kindly laugh.

"Yes, not so impressive, am I?" he said shrugging his shoulders. "But who is this you've brought? A beautiful young woman, I must say. My lady."

He nodded his head and gave a small wave. Skia made no response. The man pulled a comically sad face but then turned his attention to Cor.

"And my loving son, my beamish boy! My that is a nasty scar, dear Cor. Tangling with a Jabberwocky?"

"Father," Cor said formally.

"Oh, he's always so stiff and cold with me. Never really warmed to his old man," he said in a mock aside to Eric, "I suppose it's because he always refused his *discipline.*"

The friendliness gone in a heartbeat, the man reached out and smacked Cor across the face.

Cor cried out and fell to his knees.

"Oh stand up, you snivelling worm. I can't stand weakness, you know that."

Cor stood and dropped his hands to his side. His scarred face didn't show the redness of a slap, but instead three gouges, deep and bloody.

"Yes, father," he said.

"Better. You disappoint me. I told you to kill this boy or bring him ready to assist me, and yet you arrive a failure. Please don't be offended, dear Eric. It was only business, you understand."

"He was stronger than me."

"Shut up, boy, I'm speaking to Eric." He smiled to Eric with deep sincerity and affection.

"Why did you want me dead?" Eric asked.

"Oh, it was only to provoke your grandmother into bringing your sister to me. This worked out just as well, though. As we speak, they're on their way here to save you. They think they're being quite clever about it."

Eric was astonished by the news but kept his poker face.

"I- I didn't know they were trying to find me."

The man's face twitched in annoyance.

"Yes, well. The power of love, you know.

Eric couldn't believe it. He never suspected anyone would come so far to try to help him. He was a fool for thinking he was on his own, that no one cared. But things had gone too far for him to turn back. Just knowing he had led his own family into danger was proof enough for him that he had to stop things now.

"Why do you want my sister?"

"She can do something for me. She can see a certain kind of ... *light*."

As the man said the word light, his human face faded for a moment and Eric saw something terrifying. An emptiness. A hunger. He knew that hunger. He had felt it himself. The first time he had ever used his power it had almost drained him. After that he had learned to borrow from the power that flowed in the ground. The Power.

"I can see that light," he said.

The desperate emptiness flickered again on the man's face.

"The light. It runs in the ground, a little in the air, too, right? I never checked the water, but I bet it's there."

"Yessss...." The word was a harsh whisper.

"So you don't need my sister at all. You already have me."

"Eric, no!" Skia said fearfully.

"What are you suggesting?" The man licked his lips.

"I'll find the light for you, just let everyone go. Including Cor."

Eric heard Cor gasp but didn't dare break eye contact with the man. His pupils had dilated until there were only two black pools swirling in hunger.

Skia tugged on Eric's arm. "No," she said, "How can you do this? This is exactly what they warned you would become. Oh please, Eric, please, no."

The man flicked his finger and Skia went flying backwards. Eric reached out with his power and slowed her down so that she only gently collided with the wall and slid easily to her feet.

"Don't do that again," Eric said, "or there's no deal."

The man smirked.

"Forgive me, Eric. I can be … impulsive."

There was a shimmering in the air behind the man, on the far side of the desk that was the only furniture in the large cavern. To his shock, Eric saw his Kokum and Auntie Martha materialize out of thin air. His grandmother surveyed the situation and stepped forward.

"Raven! Leave that boy be!" His Kokum's voice snapped across the room.

The man kept his eyes on Eric. "You hurt my feelings, Georgia. Not even a hello?"

"Don't dare use my name, monster. We have never met before."

"No? Are you certain? What about those long nights of self doubt as you travelled the world? What about the sluggishness that infected your will, blinding you to the time I would make my final move? Oh we have met many times, old woman, but you choose to deny it for your own comfort."

Kokum laughed.

"I'm not surprised you'd try to take credit for my own weaknesses, Raven. But we both know you don't have that much power."

"Oh, don't I?" he snarled and he spun around, flinging darkness from his long, bony fingers. It was a seething mass of shadows filled with mournful, lonely wails and Eric could feel fear billowing from it as it undulated around his family.

Then a sound broke through the screeching. It was a song. It rose in volume, overpowering the cries of misery. The dark cloud tore apart and his Kokum and Aisling stood together, holding hands, singing something so sweet it almost broke his heart. And then the darkness was gone.

"Impressive. Your bloodlines have grown stronger, I see."

"More than you know, old Raven, sitting here like a spider. You have been busy casting your webs, manipulating governments, playing corporations like pawns. Oh yes, you've put mankind to work for you, led humanity to foul his own home with the power of greed and fear. But it has made you blind to the individual, to the community. But then, you never could understand that in the first place, could you? That's what you fear, the bonds of love. The ability of our species to overcome our instincts and act with the good of our children and grandchildren as our guide."

As she spoke, Eric, couldn't help but feel she was teaching him, instructing him as she used to when he was small.

"Not that blind, Georgia. I've almost destroyed humanity's love of the earth, of your living Mother," the word twisted in his mouth, "and in turn I've given them comfort, luxuries, 4K televisions. Now all men worship at my altar. The altar of money, the altar of apathy. I hardly need to lift a finger anymore. Your race is running on autopilot and soon I will feast. I have no fear of humans. Humans are becoming more my children than hers."

"If that were true we wouldn't be here, you craven liar. You do fear us. You fear the truth of our song. We are rising. One by one."

The man spat on the ground.

"Dear me, old crone. Save me from your speeches. This is all moot anyway. Your young grandson, the future of your oh-so great nation, has become my willing partner."

Eric heard Aisling gasp. She looked past Raven to her brother standing on the opposite side of the room.

"Eric!" She called and ran toward him.

"No, Aisling!" Martha moved faster than her weight would suggest she was capable of. She stepped in front of Aisling just as Raven gave a flick of his wrist. Martha was thrown back hard against the wall and fell to the ground, an unmoving heap. Aisling froze in shock.

There was a momentarily blinding flash of light and then the light in the room darkened to a brooding red.

The man curled in on himself, his shoulders bulging outward, stretching and straining. His clothing ripped off his back revealing his pale skin, riddled with blue veins. Something was writhing under that skin, straining against it until two large black wings ripped free, covered in gore. A beak pushed through the flesh of his face, leaving it in tatters, gobbets of skin dropping to his feet. He reached down and tore off his human legs with his beak. Spindly claws curled out from the ruined flesh. His long, bony, human arms shrivelled up and fell off, revealing the Raven. It was more smoke and darkness than solid creature, and as it moved it left its own shadowy afterimage behind.

Although he could see Raven right in front of him, Eric's eyes registered something closer to a mirage or a hologram than an actual thing. His head ached and spasms of pain shot through his skull.

"I've had enough of this little family reunion," Raven said in a broken voice and stepped toward Aisling. "If you want some killing done, it's so much better to do it yourself."

"Stop!" Eric shouted. "Stop! I won't help you if you hurt her!"

Raven paused and craned his neck around, fixing Eric with one dark eye.

"Then come, boy. Join me!"

"Eric, you don't have to do this!" Kokum called.

Everything happened within the space of mere seconds. There was no time for Eric to choose anything else.

He went to Raven, stone in hand, willing his power to be joined with this monster. If he could just get him to connect, Eric knew he could use the stone to draw the creature in, to trap him inside. Just like the snares Cor had taught him to set.

"Yesss!!!" The Raven cawed in triumph, "YESSSS! Return my stone to me! I can feel you have used it wisely, it is so full of fear and blood." A shudder ran through the spectral thing that was Raven.

"NO!"

Eric saw a flash of red in front of him.

"NOO!" Skia cried again. She put herself between Eric and Raven and she was wincing in pain at the emptiness that stretched between them. She leapt at Eric, the knife in her hand glinting in the dim, red twilight of the cavern. Her eyes filled with tears.

"I love you, Eric," she whispered. "I always will."

She stabbed upward into his chest and reached inside his body.

Through the pain, Eric saw her hand emerge with something large and wet, still beating.

232

My heart. She pulled out my heart. She's killed me!

Eric fell to the ground. He caught flashes, images. Skia raced past Raven. She ran to where the women in his family crouched against the waves of blackness pulsating from Raven. Or was it coming from himself? He couldn't tell.

His vision faded and dimmed and he focused on his hand. It was grasping the stone.

The stone.

As if of its own accord he watched as his hand brought the stone closer to himself. Inch by inch, his arm dragged the rock closer to his body. He was slipping out of consciousness. He gathered the last of his will and urged his hand into the wet, bloody ruin of his chest.

When he withdrew his hand the stone was left behind, buried inside him.

Nothing happened.

Fool. What did you think would happen?

As if in response, the cut Skia had made fused shut. A small wave of strength surged through him, clearing his head. He cast about, searching for veins of light. They were everywhere! Fuelled by betrayal he wrenched at the light and was satisfied to feel it recoil, as if in pain. He pulled harder and squeezed it, as cruelly as he could, pulling it into himself, laughing at the feeling of life returning to him.

He rolled onto his knees, reborn.

Eric stood, wrapped in an angry, flickering flame.

Chapter 43 - Aisling

It was her nightmare.

In less than a minute everything had come undone. Her Auntie lay dying, Kokum doing everything she could to save her daughter, and Eric, poor Eric. Stabbed by this strange, wild girl who was running toward them, surely intent on killing them all. Raven followed behind.

She braced herself, ready to defend herself from this wild creature, but the girl leaped past Aisling, turned and crouched low, fear and sorrow etched on her young face.

Raven advanced. His piercing, empty eyes focused on her, a starving, predatory look that left her limbs useless with fear. She felt all her courage drain away, leaving her hopeless. Frozen.

The flicker of fire caught Aisling's attention and she saw something that should have been impossible. Eric alive, standing, wreathed in fire.

"Raven, we are not finished!"

She was taken aback by the authority in her brother's voice. And so was Raven.

Eric spread his arms wide and at the same time Raven attacked. Instead of avoiding it, Eric embraced the monster, pulling him in toward himself. Raven's claws came up and shredded Eric's face, scratching out his eyes, flaying open his chest, ripping the skin from his bones.

Eric laughed. A bubbling, burbling laugh that sprayed blood into the air. Horrified, Aisling watched, unable to turn away. But her brother was healing. The torn skin and muscle reattaching, the cuts closing on their own.

Her Kokum made a fearful sound.

"A bloodstone? Only a bloodstone could do this!"

For the first time in her life Aisling saw her grandmother afraid. She remembered their warning of the bloodstone, how scared they had been at the mere mention of the thing.

"Go, Aisling! Run! Hide. Take what cover you can!"

"Kokum!"

"I said go now, while you can!" She reached out and touched Aisling on the cheek. "Oh, I love you, but I have to act now or there will be nowhere for you to hide. You *must* take up my work, girl. And do a better job of it than I have. Now go!"

Aisling's world fell apart. She tried to protest but her throat was so tight there were no words to speak.

"Go!"

Kokum walked past her into the growing maelstrom of fire surrounding the battling Raven and her brother.

But no, there was no Raven. Only Eric and a whirlwind of shadow. Her brother grew larger and larger, laughing all the while but with no love in the sound. He looked straight at Aisling and his eyes were gone. Only twin pools of hunger existed in those empty sockets.

A simple song broke through the sound of flame, through the thunder and Eric's cruel laughter. An old, tired song, but true. It was the song Kokum used to sing to Eric when he was a baby. Aisling remembered Eric with his bad colic and the only thing that had helped was this song that Kokum shared only with her grandson, her *nôsisim*. As a girl she would watch his sad little face calm into sleep. Oh, how she loved him.

And Kokum sang it now. As she sang she began to fade, to break apart into the wind, and she turned into a pure energy that Aisling could see Eric pulling into himself. She watched as her Kokum's energy flowed into Eric, sucked into the maelstrom, into the stone where his heart used to be. And the force was so strong that he began pulling everything in the cavern into himself. Aisling closed her eyes and saw the Earthblood streaming into him, changing as it neared him into an angry, sullen red.

But Kokum's energy was a pure light against the corruption that surrounded Eric. The bloodstone began to fill with Kokum's life, the life she sacrificed to save her grandson.

A fissure appeared on the surface of the stone and Eric's laughter stopped. The fissure began to spread and with a deafening crack the stone broke, power flooding through Eric's eyes, mouth, nose, ears.

He looked around frantically and through a willpower she knew she could never match Aisling watched as, by sheer force of will, he pulled the power deeper into himself and wrapped it around the bloodstone.

It remained broken but the energy he stole from the earth kept it bound.

But he needed more. Much more. She could sense it. And she could sense he was pulling it from everything around him. She could feel her own life slipping away from her.

Desperately, Aisling looked for a flow of Earthblood Eric hadn't already tapped. It was there, but so deep in the earth she could barely see it, much less connect with it.

I have to try, or we're all dead.

Reaching down she stretched her awareness through the earth's crust. Deeper she delved. Deeper. And to her surprise she made contact. It was different than what she had known. It was stronger, brighter. She said a quick prayer of gratitude and allowed the vibrant light to flow into her. She allowed more than she thought possible to surround her and her Auntie and the strange girl with the red hair. She relaxed and strengthened the shell that now protected them. The girl still held Eric's heart but Aisling was too overwhelmed to notice. Martha regained consciousness and was shouting.

"You have to let go! Come on!"

Aisling was about to protest that she wasn't holding on to anything when she glanced down at her leg. It was buried in the stone beneath her. She sensed how she had taken root and was tapping into the earth blood with her new leg. She imagined it retracting into her body and she shuddered as it did exactly as she had wished.

"We have to escape from here. Now! Aisling can you take us?"

"I don't know how, Auntie," Aisling said desperately. The ceiling was crumbling, collapsing around them. The floor was shaking with suppressed violence.

The girl with the red hair reached out and touched Aisling's amulet.

Aisling put her hand over the girl's and Martha did the same. Aisling pictured the cave they had entered from the tunnel in the mountain. The cave in the summer land. She dreamed it while they were still awake and the room that was rapidly turning to rubble faded from view.

They were in darkness and quiet. A gentle glow rose from the gloom and Aisling looked about. It was coming from her own body. Aisling's feathers began to glow, giving off a clean, clear light.

Her Auntie sat up on her haunches and padded toward Aisling and sniffed her, cocking her head from side to side, taking in the glowing light emanating from her niece.

"Well, that's something new."

They were safe.

The girl with the red hair was gone. In her place was a stunning red fox with a thick, bushy tail. Beside her lay another fox, brown and grey, waking as if from a long sleep.

"Is it you?" the red fox asked.

"Who? What?" the brown one asked.

"Is it you?" she asked, more urgently.

"Yeah, of course, who else would it be?"

Aisling interrupted.

"Who is this? What's going on?"

At the sound of her voice, the brown fox turned.

"Aisling?"

"Yes?"
He leaped at her. She was about to defend herself when she realized he was licking her.

"I can't believe it's you! Oh, Aisling, I've been so scared, so messed up. I'm so sorry, so sorry."

"Is it, is this … are you …?"

"Aisling," Martha said, "it's Eric. I don't know how, but it's your brother."

"Eric? This fox is Eric?"

"It's me Aisling. It's me."

She held back the tears of relief. They did it. They found him. They saved him. But he sounded so sad.

"What's wrong," she asked. "Why are you so sorry?"

But Eric was already talking to Martha.

"I can't change anything that happened, I can never take it back, can I?" the brown fox asked.

"No, Eric, you can't," Martha said.

He was quiet for a long time. They all were. Aisling was trying to put the pieces together but they kept falling apart, just as she was falling apart. Then Eric asked the one question she couldn't bear to hear because there was so much that was unknown in the asking.

"So what do we do now?"

Make it your own path.

"Well," Aisling said with more resolve than she felt, "we leave this cave, for starters."

"And then?"

"And then we see what's left of the world."

"And if there's nothing?"

"Then we start over. We start over and make something new."

Chapter 44 - Eric

It had been two weeks since he had awakened without the pain. They had told him everything that had happened. The last thing he remembered was Skia carving out his heart.

Not the fondest of memories.

But he understood now why she had done it.

It was the only way she could fulfill her duty. She killed the Eric who would have spread darkness through the world and saved the heart of the person she loved.

There was only one catch. He could never travel through the worlds again. This summer land was the only place he could live. Not that he minded. He liked being a fox, even though he seemed to insult everyone he met. He had a lot to learn, but Skia was helping him. For the first week she never left his side. She kept nuzzling him to make sure he was real. Not that he minded.

He was happy to have Auntie Martha stay and help out, too. She taught him the tricks to hunting that "only an old fox would know" and the protocols of relating to others in this world.

When he was alone, he cried over the death of Kokum.

They had held a ceremony in her honour. Hundreds had attended, but it was still too hard for him to accept that she was really gone. Sometimes it was almost as if he could hear her singing.

He and Aisling spent long days together. He told her about his adventures and she flapped her wings in amazement. He told of his humiliations and crimes and she stroked him gently, comforting him.

"You'll have to find a way to make up for the wrongs you did, Eric."

"I know, but how?"

"Live well. Help others. The danger isn't over yet, you know. There are whisperings and reports from all over the world. Something still lurks in the shadows."

"But we have peace, don't we?"

"For now, my brother, for now."

"Then that's enough. I'll live well, Aisling, I promise."

"I know you will, Eric."

"When do you leave?"

"Tomorrow. In the other world, our old world, Crowsnest Mountain has collapsed in on itself. There are a lot of questions but for those who understand it's a rallying cry. Kokum asked me to take over her work and that's what I intend on doing. I'm going to help other people understand what they can do so they can help to heal the Earth."

Eric felt a sadness overwhelm him. Aisling had told him how Kokum had sacrificed herself to save him, to save them all. That he would never know her beyond his old, faded memories, that she had died for him....

He was suddenly very lonely.

"Will you visit?"

"All the time."

"Matari, too?"

"I don't know, you'll have to ask him."

Matari had returned. In this world, his form was that of a Wedge-Tailed Eagle. It fit his free, easygoing personality and he would soar on his own for hours. But he never let Aisling out of his sight for long.

"Never again, mate," he winked at Eric.

Eric and Matari got along well, and Eric could tell Aisling was glad. Matari knew a lot and had an easy confidence Eric admired. He tried not to admit it to himself but he missed Cor, and Matari was a welcome replacement for that friendship. If friendship was what he and Cor had. His memory was hazy. He couldn't remember what had happened to Cor in all the chaos exploding around them in that nightmare of a cave. He didn't even know if the boy was still alive. Something told him Cor of all people would have found a way to escape, to survive. It bothered him that he might never know.

Eric shook his snout. Some things were painful to remember.

They said their goodbyes and Eric settled in for the night beside Martha and Skia.

His sleep was, as always, fraught with dreams he didn't remember upon awakening.

Chapter 45

His heart hurt.

His heart hurt, but it was his own.

He was buried, he knew, and his heart was broken but he was gathering his strength. His body was crushed beyond form, but the stone that his heart had become would heal him. He recalled that much, but not much more. He hurt. He didn't know who he was.

And he hungered.

END BOOK 1
of the Light Finder Saga

Biography

At the age of three years old, Aaron Paquette was terrified and enchanted by his Mother's impersonation of Gollum while reading the Hobbit. It was then that he knew he wanted to tell stories. As an artist, his work has gone around the world. As a speaker he is in great demand for his powerful messages. And as a writer, well, Lightfinder is his first novel and he sincerely hopes you enjoy it!

Aaron lives in Edmonton, Alberta with his wife and children.
